Andrew Linfield is a family doctor working in a group practice. For some years he has written widely for British and American medical magazines. He and his wife met when they were at school and married when he was a medical student. They have two children. He did, at one time, work as a bus conductor.

ANDREW LINFIELD

Getting into Practice

Fontana/Collins

First published by Fontana Paperbacks 1989

Copyright © Andrew Linfield 1989

Printed and bound in Great Britain by
William Collins Sons & Co, Ltd, Glasgow

To my wife and children

AUTHOR'S NOTE

The patients looked after by Harry Brinckley and Neville James are entirely fictional. But the diseases and complaints from which they suffer are not. Indeed, in some cases, millions of people in real life will have experienced similar problems.

PROLOGUE

Summer 1984

'. . . And I should have told you before, Doctor. I just didn't feel able to. I . . .' She sat in front of me holding the paper tissue to her face. The tears had come at last. I leant forward but said nothing. The provocative silence. I knew she was about to disclose, at long last, the secretly guarded cause of her depression. She cleared her throat and wiped her eyes. 'You see, I . . .'

There was a ringing from the phone at my elbow. Blast! I ignored it. 'Yes?'

'Well, ever since . . .'

The phone rang again, insistently. I smiled weakly.

'I'm terribly sorry. Excuse me for just a minute. Yes?' I rasped down the phone. 'What is it?'

The receptionist was most apologetic. 'I'm terribly sorry to disturb you, Doctor James, but it's Mrs Hawkins. She says it's her husband. He wants to see you as soon as possible.'

'I'll speak to her. Put her through.'

'No. I can't, Doctor. She was in a call box and she just hung up. You know what she's like.'

I did. Damn! Damn! Damn! Annie Hawkins hated phones. Wouldn't have one in the house and it could be urgent. Alf had had two coronaries in the last three years.

'Could you get one of the other doctors to call, Sally?'

'I'm sorry but they're all out on visits.'

9

I groaned with frustration and sighed. 'All right. Put him down as a visit for me. I'll go in a minute.'

I turned once again to the sad-faced lady but it was too late. She had composed herself. The shutters were back down again. Perhaps forever.

'I'm terribly sorry I was so silly,' she said, and before I could reply she had hurried out of the door clutching her prescription for antidepressants.

I arrived at the Hawkins's bungalow with a squeal of brakes. Hurrying out of the car, I hopped over the small picket fence and tore my trousers on a rose bush.

Annie Hawkins was waiting at the front door. Smiling. 'Hallo, Doctor.'

'Hallo, Mrs Hawkins.' I was halfway up the stairs before she stopped me.

'He's in the kitchen.'

The kitchen? Collapsed? She didn't look upset at all. Alf was sitting at the table. He smiled and stood when he saw me. 'I've got something for you,' he said, and with a great flourish produced from behind his back the reason for my hurried presence.

'You know what that is?' he beamed.

'It's a cucumber, Alf.'

'It is indeed, Doc. The first of the season – and it's for you.'

I accepted the gift as gracefully as possible. 'That's very kind of you, Alf.'

Annie Hawkins came into the kitchen grinning from ear to ear and bobbing her head with pleasure. 'He hasn't grown any for years, Doctor,' she said, 'but he's started this summer again. "I'll let Doctor James have the first one," he said. He couldn't wait to give it to you.'

What could one say? I thought I'd better make sure there was nothing else. 'Are you both keeping well?'

'Oh, very well, thank you.'

10

'And you don't need any prescriptions or anything?'

'No. We're all right for pills.'

That was it then. It was the cucumber. Their intention had solely been to please me.

As I was going out through the front door, Alf took my arm. 'You don't remember, Doc, do you?'

'What?'

'When I gave you the first cucumber I ever grew. You told me to take up a hobby. I still had the newsagent's then. It was your first year here in Amblesham — with Doctor Brinckley.'

Now that I came to think of it I did remember. Though it was twenty-three years before.

Chapter 1

The first day I went to Harry Brinckley's house he was busy teaching Albert to talk. He held the book in front of his pupil's nose and said slowly and with much emphasis, 'Book, Albert, BOOK!'

The large golden labrador gazed at him and yawned. Harry waved me into a chair.

'Book, Albert, BOOK!'

Harry turned to me for a moment. 'Doctor James. Harry Brinckley. How do you do?'

He returned his attention to the dog whose expression was one of mournful long-suffering.

'He could do it, of course. It's just a matter of time.'

I realized that he was addressing me. 'I'm sorry?'

'Talk. He's quite intelligent enough. I'm sure the only reason nobody has succeeded in teaching a dog to talk is that they haven't tried long enough. But I give you fifteen minutes every day, don't I, Albert?' He leant towards his student. 'Nose, Albert, nose.'

The dog whined softly and licked his master's moustachioed face.

'That's a good boy, Albert. That's enough for today.' He slapped the old dog's shoulder and Albert panted with pleasure.

There was a rattling at the living-room door. Harry stood up and strode towards it. To my surprise he was very tall. About six foot three. He opened the door and in came the friendly lady who had ushered me in a few minutes before. She was carrying a large plate of sandwiches which she placed on the table beside me.

'This is Doctor Neville James, Mary,' said Harry from behind a cloud of blue smoke. 'Mary is my housekeeper.'

I tried to get to my feet but caught my knee under the table. Mary caught the tray before it tipped on to the floor.

'We've already met.' She smiled.

'Of course,' said Harry Brinckley. He picked up the plate of sandwiches. 'Do you like geese?' he asked.

I said that I'd prefer the cheese and tomato.

'No. Not the sandwiches. They're chicken – aren't they, Mary? The geese are in the garden.'

I turned. Through the window two rather moth-eaten geese glared at us with some venom.

'You never need a lawnmower when you've got geese,' said Harry. 'Splendid creatures. They keep the grass short, you know. And frighten away intruders. Better than a Doberman. Certainly better than you, eh, Albert?'

He poked the slumbering dog with his foot. 'Well, you'd better tell me about yourself. The hospital secretary wrote in his letter that you wanted to be a GP.'

'Well, sir . . . er, Doctor Brinckley.'

'Harry.'

'Well, Harry, I . . .'

Where did I begin? I had never wanted to be anything else but a doctor – a family doctor – for as long as I could remember. Perhaps it was because when I was a child they had the biggest cars – the *only* ones in the war – or perhaps because people liked them or feared them. Or perhaps it was because they had special private places where other people couldn't go. Dark rooms that smelt of cough medicine and methylated spirits.

Grammar school. Medical school. Married as a student to Beth, my girlfriend from school days. Qualification, our first baby, my first house job.

'ENT, wasn't it, Neville?'

'Yes, Doctor – Harry.'

'Splendid. Best training for general practice. It's all ears and snotty noses, you know. That and skins, of course. Skins are good.'

I went on to describe how my hospital experiences had only confirmed my feelings that general practice was where I wanted to be. I explained how I felt that it was *true* medicine. It gave the chance to know the *whole* person, to get involved not only in the health of one's patients but in their hopes, their aspirations, their fears, their . . .

'I don't suppose you know anybody with an old stirrup pump going spare, do you, old chap?' Harry was drumming his fingers on the arm of his chair, sucking on his pipe in an attempt to bring the embers back to life. He took the pipe out of his mouth, looked into the bowl with some disappointment and tapped it out on the hearth. 'You know. A stirrup pump. Like they used to put out incendiary bombs. In the war.'

'I'm terribly sorry. I don't.'

'Hhhhhmmmm.' He scratched his chin. 'I didn't think you would. But you never know.'

It transpired that he needed a stirrup pump to clean out the more inaccessible parts of an ancient cabin cruiser that he had been refurbishing over the previous five years. Suddenly he slapped the front of his thighs and stood.

'Well. I'd better show you around!'

Outside, on the front drive, stood what appeared to be a derelict vehicle. Abandoned by person or persons unknown. Harry patted the bonnet lovingly.

'This, my boy, is a real car, you know, a Riley one and a half.'

He carefully undid the string which held the door closed and we got in. My first reaction was to stand up. The front seat had collapsed to such a degree that I was unable to see out through the windscreen. Harry, with his tall gangling frame, was better placed. He pumped the choke a few times, pressed the starter, and with a loud clatter and an overwhelming whiff of petrol, the engine burst into life.

Harry took out a large brass lighter and attempted to light his pipe. I winced, expecting us to go up in a ball of flame. He grasped the enormous steering wheel, let out the handbrake, and, in a cloud of smoke and flying gravel, we were off.

'Had the cylinders chrome lined, you know. The engine will last another hundred thou' at least.'

I was sure it would have done, but nothing else about this groaning contraption would still have been with it. I soon noticed Harry's disconcerting habit of using the handbrake to slow down at corners. The footbrake pedal flapped up and down in a way that suggested it was only of cosmetic value. Gradually, I eased myself up in the seat and was able to see, for the first time, out of the window.

We were on the outskirts of the small town where Harry had his practice – Amblesham. My previous experience of Sussex had been limited to daytrips to Brighton. This was something entirely different. Whitewashed cottages, houses clad in half flint or tile hung, functional solid-looking houses built in the twenties, and a small Georgian manor. We drove into a yellow brick, red-roofed council estate. Children scattered from the path of the snarling Riley. Out through the other end, up a wooded lane, and we were on the top of a small rise. Harry stopped the car. Below, with its church steeple and haphazard collection of streets, the small town stretched out in front of us. Everywhere else, fields. Fields of young wheat, barley, mustard and lucerne. And beyond the fields – and surprisingly close – the South Downs.

There are days, I now realize, when the Downs can be particularly undistinguished. There are other days when they can be uniquely beautiful. Soft, smooth green hills

16

framed against a sky of brilliant blue. A sky, itself, made even more magnificent by the white, cotton-wool clouds scudding in from the Channel. It was such a day.

'Beautiful!' I said.

'Yes, it certainly is,' said Harry. 'Mind you, I only use top-quality petrol and change the plugs every thousand miles.'

We got out of the car and sat on a stump of grass. Harry pointed out what he regarded as his town's salient points. The High Street. Grange Street where the other Amblesham medical practice was situated. Some of the dozen or more pubs.

'Not bad for a population of nine thousand. The Kings Arms there, next door The Duck and Donkey and, opposite, The Ram.' He pointed with his empty pipe. 'That space over there is the market. Every Thursday, market day. The fire station there and the police station. The church – lovely spire. Medieval. Some style or other, I'm not really sure. But the vicar's a good bloke – damn good batsman. Do you play cricket?'

'Yes – but I haven't done since . . .'

'You should. Oh yes, over there and over there –' he made a sweeping gesture taking in the clusters of houses and estates to the north of the town – 'that's where most of the people live.'

He filled the bowl of his pipe again and pointed the brass lighter into it.

'Some work locally,' he sucked. There was a wet noise from the bowl but no smoke. 'Damn!' He never did master that pipe, I was to find later. At last the tobacco caught. 'Some work locally in one of the two factories. That one down there, with the green roof, that makes woven mats. And that one over there – see, near the playing fields, on the right – that makes sports equipment. Cricket bats, hockey sticks, that kind of thing. But a large number work in or

17

around Westhaven. Nice place. Have you been there?'

I had to admit that I hadn't but I knew of it as one of the prettier south coast towns.

'Some go across to Hailsham – that's not very far, a slightly bigger place – some go to Eastbourne, Lewes . . . even as far as Brighton. Ordinary kind of folk. Nice, though. Quite a lot of gentry, still, in the old houses. And farmers, of course, and a lot of farmworkers, but not as many as there used to be. Mechanization.'

It was very quiet except for the hum of insects and the muted whine of a distant power saw.

Harry had moved to Amblesham, he told me, at the end of the war. He had been engaged to marry a Westhaven girl. Unhappily she had died of a subarachnoid haemorrhage just after he had started his practice. Back into old memories, he was silent for a moment.

'You were in the army, were you, Harry?'

'Good Lord, no! Navy – on destroyers mostly. When I wasn't doctoring I used to like pottering around down in the engine room. Couldn't keep away from railway engines when I was a kid. I loved steam,' he grinned, 'the sound, the feel, the smell . . . the grease!'

He sucked on the soggy tobacco and shook his head with pleasure. The cabin cruiser, he told me, was kept in a barn behind the house but it had not, as yet, seen the water. He had acquired some costly and elaborate engineering machinery which he had taught himself to use, making bits and pieces for both engine and structure.

'Saves you money in the long run,' he said. 'And I like playing about with engines. They're much the same as people, really. Sometimes they go like a bomb. Sometimes they're quirky and temperamental.'

He looked at his watch. 'Ah well! We'd better be going . . . I've a couple of visits to do.'

We both stood and I looked down once again. Amblesham. Not a segment of something bigger but a community complete in itself. There would be a lot of people interested in this job.

Harry drove back down through the council estate and stopped outside a house with a small front garden. There was a children's paddling pool filled with floating toys. As soon as Harry rang the bell, the sound of barking and a dog hurling itself at the other side of the door could be heard.

'Down, Rex, down!' shouted a muffled voice. 'Just a minute, Doctor. I'll put him in the kitchen.'

Moments later a rather flustered, red-haired young woman opened the door.

'Sorry, Doctor.'

'Hallo, Molly. This is Doctor James.'

'Hallo, Doctor.'

Harry made for the stairs. 'Vincent, is it?'

'Yes – again,' she said in a resigned manner.

The wallpaper of the small bedroom was missing in patches, torn off by violent games, I assumed. What was left depicted racing cars and aeroplanes. There was no patient to be seen.

'Don't be silly, Vincent.' Molly addressed the large lump under the bedclothes on one of the two beds in the room.

There was a rustling and a freckled face appeared above the sheets.

'Hallo, Vincent,' said Harry. 'Vincent is nearly four, aren't you, Vincent?'

Vincent grizzled and disappeared back under the covers.

'What's the trouble, Molly?'

'He's burning hot, Doctor, he's been sick a lot and he says he's got the tummy ache.'

Harry turned to me. 'There you are, Neville. You tell me. What is the commonest cause of abdominal pain, a high fever and vomiting in a small child?'

19

I looked at Harry questioningly.

'Go ahead,' he said.

I turned to Vincent whose eyes were visible again.

'Do you hurt anywhere else, Vincent?'

He shook his head.

'No cough?'

'No, Doctor,' said his mother.

'No diarrhoea?'

'No.'

I turned to Harry. 'Well . . . I suppose . . . appendicitis.'

Molly suddenly looked worried.

'Or a kidney infection . . . or . . .'

Harry smiled. 'You tell him, Molly.'

'I expect it's his tonsils again, Doctor. Lorraine had it last week. She's waiting to have hers out.'

Harry got Vincent to open his mouth. The tonsils were large, very red and covered in yellow spots.

'Acute tonsillitis,' said Harry. 'It is, nearly every time.'

So much for six months' ear, nose and throat, I thought. By way of apology, I protested.

'He didn't *complain* of a sore throat!'

Harry smiled. 'They very often don't, children of this age. You don't see this kind of thing in hospital. It's too ordinary.'

He was quite right, of course. We rarely saw ordinary things.

Harry wrote a prescription for Penicillin V syrup and we were just leaving when Molly drew her breath sharply. 'Oh, Doctor. I nearly forgot. The lady at the surgery rang. Could you call her? Something about a visit.'

'Chest pain,' said Harry as we drove up the farm track. 'Could be anything. Ron Godden's a very fit chap, usually. Only thirty-five. Very important man on two scores. He's my accountant and our cricket team's wicketkeeper.'

The man in bed was obviously in pain. He tried to

20

sit up but flopped back on the pillow. His wife anxiously touched his arm. Harry sat on the bed beside him.

'Hallo, Ron.'

The man winced. 'Hallo, Harry.'

Harry leant forward and took Ron's pulse.

'What happened, Sylvia?'

'Well, Doctor, he was getting some heavy boxes off the top of the wardrobe when he suddenly got this terrible pain in his back and across the front of his chest. And he couldn't catch his breath.'

'Reaching up, you say?' said Harry.

'Yes.'

Harry pursed his lips.

'And the pain went right across your chest, Ron?'

Ron nodded.

Coronary thrombosis, I thought.

'Is the pain worse when you try and take a deep breath?'

'Yes.'

No. Not a coronary. Pleurisy. Or a pulmonary embolism.

'And you feel the pain in your back as well, between your shoulders?'

Ron winced his agreement.

No. Not pleurisy . . . a dissecting aneurysm of the aorta.

'Short of breath, you say?'

I'd got it! A pneumothorax!

'Well, Neville. There you are. Was it Osler who said, "Listen to the patient – he's telling you the diagnosis"? What do you think?'

'Pneumothorax!' Harry said nothing. 'Dissecting aneurysm? Pleurisy? Coronary thrombosis?'

'Let's have a look,' Harry said.

He listened to the heart and lungs and took Ron's blood pressure.

'Nothing there.'

He sat Ron up in bed and pressed on the spine in between the shoulder blades. Ron suddenly yelped.

'That's where it's coming from. Sylvia, could you get me a kitchen stool?'

Harry eased Ron out of bed and got him sitting on the stool. He moved behind him. Picking up a small cushion, he placed it up against Ron's back. Then, like an all-in wrestler, he put his arms under Ron's armpits, brought his hands up and behind Ron's neck until the fingers locked into each other. Lifting his leg, he put his knee into the cushion and gave a sudden jerk. There was a loud crunching noise from the spine.

'Christ!' shouted Ron . . . and suddenly smiled.

He raised his arms and moved them in a large circle, sniffing in a generous breath.

'Oh! That's better. Thanks, Harry.'

I looked at Harry with questioning amazement.

'Thoracic disc or whatever,' he said. 'Something snarled up in the thoracic spine, anyway. That's where the pain was coming from. If you'd have gone to an osteopath, Ron, he'd have charged you a fiver for that. As it is, you can put a new grip on my cricket bat for me.'

Ron grinned and enjoyed the unrestricted movement that he usually took for granted.

'Only one more, Neville,' said Harry, as we got back on to the main road again. 'I know what you're thinking. You didn't learn about that in medical school.'

He was right. Manipulation was almost a dirty word. Neither had I impressed with my powers as a diagnostician.

The final call was in the town itself. A terraced, Victorian house beside the fire station.

'There's not much change in him, Doctor, but the pain is better than it was.'

The middle-aged daughter led us into the front room. The old man lay on the couch in his pyjamas and dressing

22

gown. He was reading a newspaper. He turned as he heard us enter. Bright eyes shining out of a gaunt face. Like a memory of Belsen, the cachexia of terminal cancer.

'What's that you're looking at, Tom?' said Harry, bending over to look at the paper. It was a picture of the latest Hollywood starlet. Legs up to her armpits. 'How about that, then, Tom,' said Harry with a wink.

'God bless you, Doc,' said the old man, 'but I'd rather have a steak and kidney pudding.'

Harry introduced me. He started to examine Tom.

'How are you keeping?'

'Much better, thank you, Doctor. Getting stronger all the time. That new medicine is wonderful.' He pointed to the large medicine bottle half full of a colourless liquid labelled 'Mist Brompt', Brompton mixture. A concoction of morphine, cocaine, chloroform water and brandy. For the relief of severe pain.

'I knew that the hospital was wrong, Doctor. They said I had all kinds of things. First an ulcer, then a growth. That might be so. But I know what's causing me the worst part of my trouble.'

Harry felt Tom's abdomen, painfully distended against his skeletal-like frame. He stood aside for me to palpate it.

The mass in the upper part of the abdomen. The huge liver. It was all there. A very advanced cancer of the stomach. Tom looked up at me.

'A gastric stomach. That's what's doing it. A gastric stomach. I've had one ever since I was a kid. And acid indigestion. That's the trouble. Wouldn't you agree, Doctor?'

I looked down into his eyes. Eyes that begged a glimmer of reassurance. I didn't know what to say.

'Well. Yes, Mr ... Tom. I have to agree with you. I'm sure you do have a gastric stomach . . . . . . And acid indigestion.'

Tom smiled and turned to Harry. 'I knew I was right. There you are, Doctor Brinckley.' Then, turning to me again, 'Are you staying here for long, Doctor?'

Harry answered before I could. 'Of course he is, Tom. He's going to work with me.'

I sat in Harry's surgery — in the patient's chair. I still couldn't believe it.

'You'll be able to start in two months, won't you? I've got old Royston Ackroyd working with me until then and there wouldn't be room for the three of us. He's retiring. Off to Australia to live with his son. We'll give it six months, then if we get on all right we'll see about a partnership.'

'That will be fine. Thank you.'

'You won't thank me when you've had to get up in the night a few times. You'd better bring your wife along . . . er . . .?'

'Beth.'

'Beth. I'd like to meet her. And the baby. Next weekend if you're not working.'

'No. That's fine. I've finished my house jobs.'

He looked serious for a moment. 'What will you do for the next eight weeks? Locums?'

I said I didn't think I'd be able to get any at such short notice. In any case, I didn't want to be away from Beth any more. But money had to come from somewhere.

'I know a nice little cottage in the town that you can rent very cheaply for the next two or three months,' said Harry. 'The owner's going away.'

An idea was forming in my mind.

'Harry? How far are we from Westhaven here?'

'About eight miles.'

That was it then. If Jimmy Rustington had not told them he would be unavailable, I'd have a job waiting for me.

24

'There's one more thing,' said Harry. 'You haven't got a car, have you?' Obviously I wasn't yet in that league. 'Hhmm, well. Look, I was thinking of getting one of those little Mini cars for the practice – just a runabout, you understand . . .' A Mini! The car of the hour. Beloved of princes and pop stars. It couldn't have been better. 'But it looks rather small to me.' I hastily reassured him that it didn't matter at all. 'Anyway,' he said, 'in the event, I wouldn't mind putting up with it. But you . . .' there was a dramatic pause as he let me fully grasp the enormous generosity of his offer, '. . . can use the Riley!'

Chapter Two

'Any more fares, please?' God! It was sweltering hot. The stationary bus was packed with holidaymakers on their way to the pintables and bingo of Westhaven pier. Squeezing past the standing passengers, I rang the bell. 'Any more fares, please?'

'Is this the right one for the pier?' asked a little, round red-faced man, his open-neck shirt black with sweat. It seemed an ideal moment to tell him that the letters, about two miles high on the side of our venerable vehicle proclaiming 'SEA FRONT AND PIER' were not placed there to deceive.

'Yes, sir. That's right.'

He grinned and nodded his head. 'Grand, isn't it?'

I smiled weakly. 'That's threepence please, sir.'

He produced a crumpled, somewhat damp five pound note from his back pocket.

Despair. 'Haven't you got anything smaller, please?'

'Nay, lad. I'm sorry.'

I plunged my hand into the leather money bag and grasped a handful of coins.

'Have we reached Church Street yet?' yelled an old lady from the other end of the bus.

'No, madam.'

'Mind you don't forget to tell me when we get there. I've got people waiting.'

We wouldn't be getting anywhere at the moment. The bus was still stationary. I banged the bell again and sucked my teeth. Walter! Just my luck to get a deaf driver. Laboriously, I counted out the change for the five pounds. The sweat trickled into my eyes.

'Sixteen shillings, eighteen shillings, nineteen shillings, nineteen shillings and sixpence, and ninepence. Two, three, four, five pounds. Thank you, sir.'

I rolled off the threepenny ticket from the machine hanging across my chest.

'Thank *you*, lad ... er, just a minute ...' He reached into the top pocket of his shirt and produced a sixpence. 'Forgot about that. I *did* have some change after all. Let me give you the other money back and I'll ...'

But I was already at the next seat.

'One and a half to the pier,' said a large lady with ginger hair.

The 'half', presumably, was for the child who sat beside her – a good six feet tall, sixteen stone and hirsute.

'I'm sorry, madam, but half fare is under fourteen years of age.'

She coloured up. 'He's only thirteen.' She turned to the infant, 'Aren't you Ronald?'

'Yes, Mum,' he replied, in a deep baritone.

Oh, sod it! 'Fourpence halfpenny then, please,' I said in surrender. What on earth was wrong with Walter? We were still stationary. I pressed on the bell several times. Surely he could hear that! As I did so I looked up from the ticket machine and passengers. We were in the middle of a huge traffic jam. Cars, lorries, buses packed together the entire length of Westhaven High Street. We could not move an inch. Walter turned round in his seat and, with banana-like fingers, pushed aside the small sliding window in the partition between driver's compartment and the rest of the bus. He fixed me with a withering gaze. He looked about at the sea of vehicles. And then, in a voice dripping with sarcasm, he asked, to the evident amusement of the passengers, 'What do you want, mate? Underneath or over the top?'

I had been lucky. The job *was* still vacant. Jimmy Rustington *had* forgotten to tell the Westhaven Corporation bus company that he wouldn't be coming to work for them after all. To his own and everybody else's amazement, he had passed the second MB examination at the first attempt. No more long summer holidays and vacational jobs for him. He was now working as a clinical student on the wards. His elder brother had been a house surgeon with me and had told me all about it. I phoned up the bus company. Could they take somebody else instead? Another medical student? They were delighted.

I had brought Beth and Sarah down to meet Harry the previous weekend as he had suggested. They took to each other straightaway. Apart from anything else, it turned out that Harry was an accomplished performer on the recorder, an instrument that I did not generally associate with adults. Beth taught the recorder to the children in her class when she was working as a primary school teacher.

Albert, patient as ever, spent the whole afternoon acting as Sarah's pony. She crawled on top of him, pulled his tail and held on to his ears. All this he treated with the same forbearance that he gave to his vocabulary lessons.

I told Harry about the job with Westhaven buses.

'Splendid!' he said. 'You'll get the feel of the place, get to know your way about – not that we've got all that many patients in Westhaven.' I thought he was joking. Westhaven was eight miles away, and had many doctors of its own, but such was his reputation and his willingness to accept patients from afar that his practice covered a huge area.

'When you get a bit of free time you can come and sit in with me at some of the surgeries,' Harry said. 'You've got some gear, haven't you? Stethoscope, auriscope, ophthalmoscope, that kind of thing?'

I had to admit that I possessed only a stethoscope, no other instruments. Beth, Sarah and I had been living on four pounds a week for the previous six months, once our four-guinea weekly rent had been paid. What I had been offered by the bus company was a king's ransom compared with a house surgeon's salary. Beth had existed almost entirely on bread and marg, scrag end and rice pudding since I had qualified.

It was with the pleasurable anticipation of earning real money that I arrived at the bus depot the following Monday. Having been met by the inspector, Mr Henry, a severe-looking but kindly man with a toothbrush moustache, I was fitted out with an enormous blue jacket, a tiny cap and a Sam Browne belt on which to carry my ticket machine. And, of course, a large leather money bag.

'You'll work with a crew for three days, Doctor,' he said, as he led me towards some parked open-topped buses, 'then you'll have your own driver.' I found out later that he called all medical students 'Doctor'. I hadn't told the bus company that I had qualified in case I didn't get the job.

We stopped at a bus showing 'CLIFF TOP AND PARADISE GARDENS'.

'This is Mr Goodman. He'll show you the ropes,' said Mr Henry, introducing me to a young man with a Tony Curtis haircut. We shook hands.

'Dave.'

'Neville James . . . Neville.'

Mr Henry disappeared in the direction of the staff canteen. Dave took the cigarette butt from his mouth and flipped it away in the approved Hollywood fashion.

'I'd better take you to meet Walter,' he said. 'He'll be your driver.'

Sitting in the driver's seat was a man smoking a pipe and reading a racing paper.

'This is Walter,' said Dave.

'Pleased to meet you, Walter.' No reply.

'WALTER! ... He's a bit deaf,' Dave explained. 'WALTER. THIS IS NEVILLE!'

Walter turned. Bright blue eyes set in a face like a rockery.

'Oh.'

'He used to be a tank driver – in the war,' said Dave. 'Got blown up a few times ... USED TO BE IN TANKS, DIDN'T YOU, WALTER?'

'Yeah.'

'WHAT KIND? WHAT KIND OF TANKS?' I shouted, eager to demonstrate my knowledge of military history.

'Crusaders.'

'OH YES! VERY GOOD!

'No they weren't. They were bloody awful!' He spat out of the window. 'Tin cans.' He stuffed the paper into the side of his seat and put on his leather driving gloves.

'We'd better be off,' said Dave.

We went around to the back of the bus and I got on to the platform as Walter turned the starter. I noticed that Dave was gripping the passenger rail very tightly.

'I'd get inside if I was you,' he said.

There was a grinding scream from the engine and I was hurled the length of the bus to crash into the bulkhead behind the driver. Dave grinned.

'You'll have to watch that. He still thinks he's in a tank. A gearbox never lasts him more than a month or two.'

Before we got to the first fare stop Dave explained that he always worked with Walter. Nobody else would. Not since his previous conductor died of a heart attack.

'It is said,' Dave commented as we approached the first cluster of would-be passengers standing outside the Paradise Gardens, 'that he died on the job. In bed you know. Poor sod – didn't know whether he was coming or going!' We stopped.

'Plenty of room. Come on, ladies. I'm at your service.'

A plump young woman, her curlers covered by a headscarf, clambered up on to the platform. Dave whistled as her tight skirt pulled up over her knees.

'Especially yours, darling,' he said with a wink.

'You cheeky bugger, Dave Goodman. I'll tell your wife on you.' She slumped into the seat at the back of the bus. Just in time, as it happened. Dispensing with the clutch, Walter manhandled the tortured gearbox into first, and we lurched off down the road.

We stopped at the corner behind another Corporation bus.

'Hallo, Winston!' shouted Dave from the platform. 'You're getting a nice tan.'

Swinging from the passenger rail of the other bus, the conductor, a very tall black man, grinned at us. 'How's it going, Dave?'

'Winston Jenkins. From Jamaica. He's only been on the buses a couple of months. Nice bloke, though,' said Dave, by way of explanation as the other bus pulled away. 'Lives down your way. Just outside Amblesham.' Dave quickly collected the fares from his passengers. 'Now let me show you the various things on the machine. This here is the fare stage number, on this wheel you set the fare, the date is over here . . .'

That had been four weeks ago.

'Any more fares, please?' I had now become something of an expert. I no longer had to consult the fare-stage book before selling a ticket. I knew that Linden Road was 2, that Mulberry Close was 4, the Library was 5, St Anne's Church was 6 and that 3 to 5 was a penny halfpenny and 4 to 6 was tuppence.

31

The medical students, it transpired, were the most adept at learning these complex fare charts. Having spent hours with Gray's *Anatomy* poring over the course of the median nerve in the forearm and the relations of the left kidney, the complexities of Paradise Gardens, High Street, West Town were as nothing.

I saw a woman at the front of the bus trying to conceal her bulk in the seat. She hadn't paid. I squeezed past the standing passengers until I was beside her. 'Any more fares please?'

'Oh yes,' she said, looking rather flustered and starting to open her large handbag. The child beside her, climbing all over the seat, would benefit from losing his adenoids. Large green gobbets of infected mucus hung from his nose.

'One and a child to Cliff Top, please . . . Norman! Wipe your nose!' The child sniffed loudly and the mucus disappeared up into his nose like roller blinds.

I cranked the handle of my ticket machine. It wouldn't go around. Jammed! Damn! It was always happening at the worst of times. I banged it against the seat and tried again. No movement. I looked out of the bus window. One good thing about the snarl-up – we had stopped almost immediately outside the High Street bus office. I banged the glass behind Walter. He turned.

'WALTER!' I shouted, and indicated the machine with my finger. 'MY TICKET MACHINE IS JAMMED. I'M JUST GOING INTO THE OFFICE FOR A MINUTE.'

Walter's face remained immobile. I ran into the office. As luck would have it, Mr Henry was on duty.

'Let's have a look at it for you, Doctor.'

He took out a small screwdriver and rapidly dismantled the machine. 'Here it is.' The roll of tickets had crumpled up and was snaring on a cog. He eased it out and inserted a new roll. With a quick thanks I rushed out of the office.

Fortunately, the traffic jam had gone. So, unfortunately,

had the 'Sea Front and Pier' bus of which I had recently been the captain. I could see a bus in the distance at the far end of the High Street, perhaps that was it. I started to run down the middle of the street. As I ran my money bag bounced up and down and coins cascaded out on to the road. Every few yards I had to stop and pick them up.

'You'll have to wait for the next one, mate!' shouted someone from the grinning crowd of pedestrians on the pavement.

I had visions of Walter going on forever. Unstoppable. Like the flying Dutchman.

'Excuse me, but could you give me a lift and follow that bus?' The driver of the car I waved down might have thought I was joking, but my pathetic appearance soon convinced him I was in earnest. We caught up with the bus at some red traffic lights half a mile further on.

I tore around to the front. 'WALTER! WHAT THE BLOODY HELL ARE YOU PLAYING AT?'

'What?'

'THE BUS. YOU LEFT ME BEHIND!'

'I thought you rang the bell.'

'WELL, I DIDN'T, YOU . . .' Oh! What was the use?

I got back inside to confront my sniggering passengers. I tried to appear as though the episode had been an everyday occurrence. As the adenoidal boy got off the bus he turned to give me a toothless grin. His mother pushed him in the back. She chided him in a loud whisper. 'I told you not to ring that bell, Norman. Next time you'll get a damn good hiding.'

It was early evening when I pushed the old bicycle I had borrowed from Harry through the cottage gate. Beth was waiting by the front door.

'Had a good day, darling?'

I kissed her in a perfunctory fashion and slumped into an armchair. 'Pretty awful. I lost the bus!'

'Lost it?'

'Well, more mislaid it, I suppose.'

She fell into my lap laughing when I told her all about it.

'How have you been today?' I asked. 'OK?'

'Yes. Fine.'

'Is Sarah asleep?'

'You must be joking. She's in her cot playing.'

Sarah never slept. Well, she did. About two hours a night it seemed. And the occasional catnap every now and then. We had tried every trick. Leaving her to cry heartbreakingly, letting her stay up until all hours. In the end there was nothing for it. We had to have her in bed with us.

'I'll go and say hallo.'

Sarah was in her cot surrounded by a huge pile of plastic bricks. She took no notice as I came in.

'Hallo, Sarah.'

She looked up. 'Daddy, brick.'

I gave her a kiss.

'Daddy, brick.'

I knew what I was meant to do. In the early days of the game she had never waited until the pile I carefully constructed was more than four or five bricks high before she knocked it over with great screams of delight. Now, she would wait to eight or nine or even ten.

She had the same eyes, the same glorious smile as her mother. The smile that had made me sure as a fifteen-year-old that the girl I had met in a school play would one day be the girl I would marry.

'Supper in a minute,' Beth shouted up.

I built one more pile of bricks for Sarah to demolish and went downstairs.

'How's Walter?' asked Beth from the kitchen.

'Just the same.'

'And Dave? Have you seen anything of him?'

'Yes. He'll be driving until I finish then he'll be back with Walter again.'

'He must be some kind of saint,' said Beth.

'Yes. I suppose he is, really.'

Beth looked around the kitchen door, a steaming sauce-pan in her hand. 'By the way. Harry phoned. He said he'll be around some time this evening – he's got something to show us.'

I picked up the newspaper. It was marvellous to sit down. To be home, however small and temporary that home was. The tiny cottage Harry had fixed up for us was ideal. Two down and two up – sitting room, kitchen, one small bedroom, one very small bedroom. We washed at the sink in the kitchen. The loo was outside facing the small, overgrown garden.

The furniture was old but comfortable and there were no precious knick-knacks that Sarah could break. And there was a good, big double bed. What luxury it was to sleep together every night however late I came home from work. I would never again, I promised myself, endure the separation that hospital work involved.

Beth came in with a large tray which she placed across my knees and while watching television we tucked into great slices of bacon pudding. The plates were soon clean. We heard a car horn toot outside. I stood and looked out of the window.

'It's Harry. He's got the Mini!'

Harry unfolded his gangling frame from the front seat of the tiny, bright red car and came beaming up the path. I opened the door.

'Hallo, Harry.'

'Neville. What do you think of it?'

'Smashing!'

Beth came and peered over my shoulder.

'Hallo, Harry.'

'Beth, my dear. You look charming.' He kissed her cheek.

'Thank you, sir,' she said with a little curtsey.

'Come and have a look at it, then.'

The Mini was still something of a curiosity, more commonly seen buzzing around Mayfair than country lanes.

'I can't see quite how you could get five guardsmen into it,' said Beth, questioning the veracity of the advertisements.

'It's big enough for me,' said Harry, 'and it does nicely just to get from here to there. Not really a proper car.' But it was clear he was delighted.

'Come in and have a cup of tea,' said Beth. 'We've just made it.'

Harry looked at his watch. 'Well, I haven't got much time. Red Cross lecture this evening and I mustn't be late. They're dead keen ... but I'll pop in and have a quick one.'

'You can have a piece of bacon pudding if you like, Harry. It's a bit cold and there's only the end bits with no bacon in. But you're welcome.'

Harry declined politely. Though if we could wrap it up in a piece of paper he'd take it back for the geese.

'Thank you, Beth.' He put his cup on the arm of the chair and got out his pipe. After an age it was going like a damp bonfire.

'I'm sorry that I haven't had you around to the surgery but things have been pretty busy. Poor old Royston has slowed up a good deal. I can't wait for you to start. How are things with you?'

'We're fine, Harry,' I said.

'And Sarah?'

'Quiet – just for the moment,' said Beth.

'And the buses, Neville? You're getting to be something of an expert?'

I told him about my latest adventures with Walter. How we had been saying that Dave was something of a saint to put up with him all the time.

'You'd be surprised how many saints there are about the place,' said Harry. 'I didn't fully appreciate it until I started in general practice. Astonishingly good people. Looking after their aged relations – sometimes only distantly related. Disagreeable, incontinent, demented. A thankless task. You ask them why they do it and they just say "There's nobody else to look after them". More often than not, nobody else will.'

Beth offered him a biscuit.

'Not now, thank you, my dear. Last month, for example. I went to see an old friend of mine, Mildred Crowfield. I'd been looking in at her old mum for years. Lottie Crowfield – she had a series of strokes five or six years ago and she's been a complete vegetable ever since. Quadriplegic. Couldn't move a muscle. No speech. Doubly incontinent. Mildred, who'd never married, gave up her work – she was a nurse, as it happened – to look after her mother.'

'How on earth did the old lady last that long?' I asked Harry. 'She must have developed bed sores or pneumonia?'

'Good nursing,' said Harry. 'Mildred got up every two hours in the night to turn her. Continual nursing. Day and night for five years.'

'Couldn't she have got her mother into hospital?' asked Beth.

'Wouldn't hear of it. Mildred said that her mother hated hospitals and in spite of how she might appear to me, she was sure the old lady was aware of where she was. In her own house. Where she would wish to be. Mildred might have been right, of course. Who's to say?'

'And no chest infections?'

'Nothing serious until a couple of months ago. Minor ones, of course, that she got over unaided. In spite of everything, she was a tough old thing. I wouldn't have liked to have given her antibiotics and Mildred never asked for any. Sometimes you can be in a very difficult position. Some relatives of hopelessly disabled old people insist on them having antibiotics however much it seems that a gentle death would be a kindness. Pneumonia isn't called "the old man's friend" for nothing.'

'But she did get pneumonia in the end?'

'About six weeks ago. I was beginning to get worried about Mildred because the strain was telling. She looked poorly and had lost weight. Exhausted, I presumed. Anyway, the old lady just passed away.'

He blew in his pipe and tapped it out on the fender. 'I went back to see Mildred, as I said, a week later. She was in her dressing gown. She said she thought she'd stay in bed for the day because she didn't feel very well. I told her that I'd better check her over. She sat on the bed, I lifted up her nightie and there it was.' He gave a long sigh. 'A huge fungating cancer of the left breast. Must have been the size of . . . this saucer. She had glands in her neck and in her axillae, there was a lump in the right breast as well. It was all over the shop. She must have had it for months – years possibly.'

'Why didn't she say something about it?' I asked. 'Didn't you say she was a nurse? She must have known!'

'Of course she did,' said Harry. 'As soon as she first felt a lump. I asked her, of course. The answer was quite obvious. This good lady, this extremely good, dear lady, knew that if she did tell anybody about it she would be pressured into going into hospital for a mastectomy. Her mother would have gone to the geriatric unit.'

'And she didn't want that,' said Beth.

'No. So Mildred sat it out. And mother went on and on . . . and the cancer grew bigger and bigger.'

'And inoperable,' I said.

'Absolutely,' said Harry. 'The whole illness was too widespread even for radiotherapy to make any difference. But still, there we are. I sent her into hospital. She was quite happy to go. She died yesterday.'

He shook his head and gave a sad smile. 'But there's a funny thing. That day – when I found she had the cancer – I came out from her house, sat in the car and burst into tears. Daft, really. But I suppose I was just overwhelmed by the . . . grandeur of her sacrifice.'

We were silent. Suddenly, Harry stood up. 'Good Lord! Look at the time. I shall be late for that lecture and get drummed out of the corps . . . and I haven't even told you what I really came for. Am I right? Did Beth tell me that you've got the whole day off on Friday?'

'Yes, I have, Harry. You'd like me to come and sit in at your surgery and . . .'

'Good heavens, no! All work and no play and that kind of thing. It occurred to me that Beth, and Sarah if it comes to that, haven't seen much of the country around here. Westhaven even, Beth?'

Beth shook her head.

'Then why don't you borrow the Riley, Neville, and take Beth and Sarah out for the day?'

'That would be lovely, Harry.'

'Good then, that's settled,' he said. 'See you next Friday . . . and another thing. As soon as you get a Sunday free Ron Godden's asked if you would like a game of cricket for the Sunday eleven. They're pretty short. People on holiday, you know.'

'Yes, that would be nice.'

'And next week, I'll get you into the surgery for an evening or two.'

We stood at the door and waved goodbye as the Mini busied its way up the lane. Beth went upstairs and almost immediately came down again.

'Time for bed,' she said.

'But it's only eight o'clock!'

'I've just looked in at Sarah. She's asleep. It won't last more than an hour or so ... but perhaps you'd rather watch "Panorama"?'

I got out of my chair and switched off the television.

Later that night, as we lay in bed with Teddy, Big Ears, several large picture books and Sarah fast asleep on the pillow between us, Beth looked over at me. 'That was very sad, wasn't it, that story Harry told us about the lady? I hope you'll always be able to cry.'

Chapter Three

It *had* to be a rodent ulcer. There could be no doubt. I first spotted it between Fingelli's ice cream parlour and Promenade Mansions on the seafront. A little scabby lesion about a quarter of an inch across. On the bridge of an old man's nose, a very large red, bulbous nose. Just about where his spectacles would have rested had he been wearing any. I knew that I could, no longer, resist the temptation to intervene.

I was now in my seventh week on the buses, the early morning seafront run. My favourite. No crowds of holiday-makers yet. They were still tucking into the egg, bacon, sausage, fried bread and HP sauce. Just the salty, sea-weed smell blowing up from the shore. Cliff Top, sparkling white and clear in the morning air. Not as majestic as Eastbourne's Beachy Head further down the coast, but spectacular, nevertheless.

There weren't many other passengers on the bus. I tried, in vain, to catch the old man's eye. There was nothing for it. I had to take a direct approach. 'Excuse me.' He continued to look out of the window. 'Excuse me!'

He turned. 'Yes? I've bought my ticket!'

'I'm sorry, sir. It isn't anything to do with that . . . I just wondered whether you've been to your doctor recently?'

'Have I what?'

'I know it seems a strange thing to ask but I wondered whether you'd seen your doctor in the last few weeks?'

'What business is it of yours?'

'Well, you see . . .' I stammered. 'It's your nose.'

He coloured up. I realized I had touched a very sensitive area.

'What the hell do you mean?'

'Your nose. That little crusty spot. There.' I pointed with my finger. He pulled his head away. 'You should tell your doctor about it if you haven't done so already.'

He looked about ready to explode.

'I know about these things,' I explained before he could interrupt me. 'Actually, I'm a doctor myself and I can tell you that spot is almost certainly . . . well, er . . . it's malignant in a kind of way and you should have it removed.'

'Are you mad?' he shouted and stood up.

'No, really. I'm very sorry, I . . .'

'Let me off. Stop the bus,' he said. Fortunately we were just approaching a compulsory stop. Even before the bus had come to a halt he jumped off in a surprisingly agile way and walked off muttering.

'Not *very* malignant,' I shouted after him.

I had wanted to give the benefit of my medical knowledge to my passengers on numerous other occasions. Overactive thyroids, anaemias, several cases of German measles, mumps and chicken pox. But I had demurred.

'It's never a safe thing to give advice where it's not sought,' Harry told me on one of the evenings I had by now spent with him at his surgery. 'If you're right, the patient is unlikely to admit it and if you're wrong, he will never forget it.'

Harry was full of such homilies. As he examined each patient he would lace the demonstration of his obvious clinical skill with some small piece of philosophy.

'And remember. If patients *do* make a diagnosis of their own condition try and agree with them as far as possible. It gives them confidence in their ability to cope. If they say they've got fibrositis, whatever that's supposed to be, don't argue. You are unlikely to come up with anything better.'

My thoughts were broken by a loud grinding noise. It was coming from the back wheel of the bus just in front of the platform upon which I was standing. We stopped and picked up a few passengers. I took their fares. The noise returned, louder this time, and the lady facing me on the back seat raised her eyebrows in puzzlement.

Walter, in a series of juddering gear changes, was taking the bus off the seafront into Westhaven High Street. We stopped at the traffic lights and I went to the front of the bus and knocked on the glass. He pushed back the sliding window.

'What is it?'

'WALTER! THERE'S A VERY LOUD NOISE COMING FROM THE REAR NEARSIDE WHEEL.'

'I can't hear it,' said Walter, and pushed the window closed.

The lights changed and we pulled away. The noise was getting very loud indeed. Leaning out from the bus by hanging on to the rail, I tried to see if there was obviously anything wrong. I thought I saw a puff of smoke.

We were well down the High Street alongside a pavement filled with early morning shoppers when it happened. There was a loud explosion from almost under my feet. The bus slewed round and a large, red hot chunk of metal shot out from the middle of the wheel and skittered across the pavement, missing a dozen pairs of ankles by inches to crash into the wall of a bank. Walter, visibly shaken, came around to the back of the bus to see what had happened. We were in trouble.

'The transport manager will see you now,' said Mr Henry.

Walter and I followed the inspector into the office.

'We were lucky nobody was crippled for life,' said the manager. 'It was the half shaft, I understand. God knows what would have happened if it had hit somebody.'

He turned to me. 'Wasn't there any warning? You should have stopped earlier!'

'Well . . .' I said. I could feel Walter looking at me. 'I *did* hear something but I didn't know it was anything serious. It all happened rather suddenly.'

Mr Henry stepped in. 'It's a very uncommon occurrence, Mr Wigley. I can't see how . . . er . . . Mr James could possibly have known. It was going to happen. What did . . . as it were.'

The manager thought for a moment then looked at me. 'If you ever do hear anything strange like that again you *must* let the driver now. He'll know what action to take.'

'Yes, sir,' I said.

'Thank God nothing happened,' said Mr Henry as we left the office. 'You can take Mr Bolton's bus when he gets back to the depot. He's on a split shift.'

Walter and I went down to the canteen. We were alone. We bought a cup of tea and, used to the silence on such occasions, I took a crumpled newspaper from my pocket. Before I could start reading he leant over and touched my arm.

'Thank you, son. That was very good of you.'

'THAT'S ALL RIGHT, WALTER, I . . .'

Walter shook his head and looked around furtively. When he was sure he was not seen he pulled an earpiece and cord from inside his jacket. Obviously it was connected to a hearing aid. He screwed in the earpiece, adjusted a hidden volume control, and the shrill whistling ceased.

'I don't like people to know that I'm deaf,' he said, 'so I don't let them see me wear this . . . I might lose my job.'

'I never knew that you had . . .'

'No. Most people don't. It came on during the war. I got blown up a couple of times. The doctors thought the nerves

44

to the ears had been damaged. They didn't think anything could be done about it.'

'Your doctor got you the hearing aid, though, didn't he?'

'No. I never go to the doctor. I bought this one in a shop. Bloody expensive it was. It's all right just speaking to one person like you . . . now. But it's no good at all in a crowd.'

I nodded.

'Anyway,' he said, 'thank you for keeping quiet about — you know, and I'm sorry that I'm such a miserable devil a lot of the time.'

'No, Walter, you're not. You're . . .'

'Yes I am. Being deaf can do that to you. It makes you keep to yourself, not bother with people. I can see it when other blokes make a joke and that. They don't think I've got any sense of humour. But I just don't hear it. Still, as I said, thanks.'

He smiled. 'You've got the day off tomorrow, haven't you? Friday?'

'Yes. I'm taking my wife and my little girl out for the day. Probably end up in Westhaven.'

'That will make a nice change for you,' grinned Walter. 'This time of year you . . .'

I heard someone come into the canteen behind me. Walter hurriedly removed the earpiece and concealed it in his jacket. Once again, back in his world of silence.

'Alfriston, you say. That's one of the local beauty spots, isn't it?' asked Beth. We chugged along the narrow road whose flint walls threatened to scratch the less than immaculate paintwork of the Riley. Beth, able to see out of the window by courtesy of three large cushions on the passenger seat, had Sarah sitting on her lap.

'Yes. Harry said it was really worth seeing.'

There was a slight incline, a further narrowing of the

road into a double bend, and we were in the village square. There was a market cross and on all sides the daub-and-wattle walls of Tudor buildings.

'It's so pretty!' said Beth.

It certainly was. The little High Street. Tiny shops. A chemist, a grocer, a butcher.

'You see that butcher's there?' I pointed it out to Beth. 'Harry says they make the best sausages in England – Sussex anyway. And that's much the same thing according to him.'

'Can we look around for a few minutes?' Beth asked.

We parked the car and walked down a narrow passage to the River Cuckmere. Sarah loved the little white footbridge and made stamping noises on the boards. We played Pooh Sticks with pieces of dead grass floating on the slow-flowing river.

'That's a lovely church,' said Beth. 'It's a very unusual shape.'

'Cruciform . . . like a cross,' I explained.

'Thank you, dear,' she said, in a voice heavy with admiration.

'No, seriously. The local legend, Harry tells me, is that the medieval architect who designed the church saw four cows lying in this field, at right angles to each other. Whence the shape of the church. The Cathedral of the Downs they call it.'

We walked up through the lych gate and into the cool, musty interior. Bell ropes hung down right into the middle of the building. Three sets of pews and the altar made up the four points of the compass. There was a feeling of peace everywhere. Above us, on the wall, carefully drawn on a large sheet of paper, was a list of baptisms. There were very few names.

'When we have another baby,' whispered Beth, 'we'll have the christening here.'

It wasn't until we drove out of Alfriston, on to the top of High and Over Hill, that we fully realized for the first time the true loveliness of the area into which we had come to live.

'Neville, it's beautiful. I had no idea.'

On all sides, the Downs surrounding us plunged down to the patchwork quilt of the Sussex Weald. That in its turn stretched almost as far as the eye could see to the ridge of Ashdown Forest in the distance. It would be impossible to imagine anything more quintessentially ... English. We stood spellbound, and there was nothing to hear but the rustle of the wind in the long grass and the song of the skylark high above our heads. We turned, to the south. Covered by a slight grey haze was the sea, and everywhere a gentle soft beauty.

'We'll come out here for a picnic,' said Beth. 'Look down in that field. It's full of flowers.'

As we approached the outskirts of Westhaven the traffic thickened. Sarah was bouncing up and down on Beth's lap, helped in large part by the Riley's creaking suspension. There was the whir of an electric motor from under the dashboard.

'Why have you put those on, darling?' asked Beth.

'I didn't,' I said. Nevertheless the windscreen wipers were whizzing frantically backwards and forwards in front of our eyes.

I pulled and pushed the wiper switch. Nothing. There was no response. We were now in the town traffic and I noticed one or two pedestrians looking at us with curiosity.

'I'll see what I can do as soon as we get to the car park.'

When I switched off the engine the wipers continued to sweep at the phantom raindrops.

'Can't you leave it?' asked Beth.

'The battery will go flat if I do.'

I took a perfunctory look under the bonnet but I have never understood anything mechanical. Now was no exception. Mercifully, I saw a telephone box on the other side of the street.

'Doctor Brinckley speaking.'

'Harry! Thank goodness. This is Neville.'

'Neville! How extraordinary! I've just this minute been wishing I could get in touch with you. Are you in Westhaven?'

'Yes. But, Harry – it's the car.'

'It's all right, isn't it?' he said with some anxiety. 'It was fine yesterday.'

'Oh, nothing serious. The windscreen wipers have started and I can't get them to stop.'

'They do that sometimes,' said Harry. 'I've done a temporary repair. Look under the bonnet and on the left-hand side near the dashboard, you'll see a small piece of wood wedged in. It's got cigarette packet foil wrapped around it. There are two wires taped to it. Could you find them?'

'Yes.'

'Well, unstick the wires and the wipers will stop, but if the weather changes you'll have to put them back again.'

'OK then, Harry.'

'And, Neville ... there is one thing. Providence has obviously taken a hand. I wonder whether you could possibly do a visit for me. Paradise View. It's a boarding house. A green and white building just opposite the entrance to Paradise Gardens. The owner's a patient of ours.' 'Ours' I noticed. 'One of her staff's not well, she says. Abdominal pain.'

I knew from my recently acquired encyclopaedic knowledge of Westhaven's geography that Paradise View couldn't be more than a few hundred yards away.

'I'll go, of course, Harry. But I haven't got any gear.'

'No problem,' said Harry. 'You'll find a spare doctor's

bag in the boot of the Riley. I always carry it. Everything you could possibly want.'

'Well . . . all right. I'd be happy to do it.' Happy was perhaps a bit strong.

I told Beth. She said she'd take Sarah to Woolworth's to look at the toys. I could meet her there.

'We'll go to lunch after, Beth. At Joe Lyons.' Beth looked very impressed. 'The last of the big spenders,' she said.

It took only a minute or two to get to the boarding house. The front door was open. I went in. There was nobody to be seen.

'Hallo,' I called and rattled the small brass bell on the desk. 'Hallo?'

A short, fat lady wheezed into view drying her hands on the front of a large, flowered apron.

'We've got no vacancies, I'm afraid.'

'It's not that . . . I'm the doctor.' My Hawaiian shirt and flip flops were not exactly Harley Street. Neither was the Gladstone bag, green with mildew. 'Doctor Brinckley asked me to come.'

The lady smiled and shook my hand. 'Doctor Brinckley! Bless him. He's a dear. You must be his new assistant. I knew he was looking for one. I'm very pleased to meet you.'

'Thank you, Mrs . . . er, Mrs . . .?'

'Call me Doris. Everybody does. Well, in Amblesham anyway. I lived there for years. Used to work behind the bar of The Duck and Donkey. Until I met my husband. Then we bought this.'

Her eyes scanned, lovingly, the small entrance hall. Regency stripe and bullfighter posters. 'But he wasn't spared to enjoy it for long.' She gave a loud sigh.

'Still, you'll have come to see Caroline. She's a maid here. From the North. Comes down for the summer.'

I followed Doris up two flights of stairs to the end of a small passage at the top of the house.

'It's a bit cramped,' she apologized as she opened the door of a tiny, dark room. 'I'm afraid we have to let out all the proper accommodation in the high season.'

The only illumination was a tiny skylight in the sloping ceiling. A young woman lay on a camp bed.

'It's the doctor come to see you, Caroline.'

The patient looked up at me with some surprise, then vomited in the plastic bucket at her elbow.

'I'm Doctor James,' I explained. 'Doctor Brinckley's . . . I work with Doctor Brinckley.'

'Oh,' she said.

'What's the trouble?'

'I've got this terrible pain . . . here.' She pressed her fingers into her abdomen and winced.

'Have you been sick many times?'

'Lots.'

'Let's have a look then.'

I knelt down beside the low bed, pulled up her dress and struggled to lower her roll-on. Her abdomen was flabby and covered with white stretch marks. The legacy of past pregnancy. She anticipated my next question.

'I've got two children. June and Brian. They stay up with me mam in Liverpool when I come down here for the summer. Me husband's . . .' She broke off to vomit once again.

There was no doubt about the diagnosis. I pressed gently into the lower right half of her abdomen. The muscles were rigid and she groaned.

'Acute appendicitis,' I said as I stood up. 'I'll get you into hospital straightaway.'

Using the phone in the hall I spoke to the admitting house surgeon at Westhaven General Hospital and then called an ambulance. I returned to Caroline's bed and told her what I had fixed up. My first home visit as it were. It had all been pretty decisive stuff. No fuss. No delay.

Caroline cleared her throat. 'I didn't know they could grow again, Doctor.'

A looseness gripped my bowels. The appendix is the only single organ in the body that habitually occasions the pronoun 'they'.

'What?' I said. Already knowing.

'The appendix.'

'No . . . why?'

'I had mine out when I was twelve.'

'Ah . . . yes . . . well . . . I meant not *actually* the appendix itself . . .' I peered at the abdomen again. Yes. There it was, hardly visible in the gloom, among all the wrinkles and striae. A tiny, fine white scar. Blasted keyhole surgery.

'I meant something *like* appendicitis. You know – inflammation.' I smiled at her reassuringly. 'They'll soon sort it out at the hospital for you. The ambulance will be here in a minute.'

I went to the door. 'Excuse me just a minute while I wash my hands.'

Once out of the room I tore down the stairs to the phone.

'Is that the admitting house surgeon?'

'Yes?'

'This is Doctor James again . . . I was on the phone to you just now. Did I by any chance say that I was sending in a case of acute *appendicitis*?'

'Yes.'

'Ha! Ha! Oh my goodness me! A slip of the tongue, I'm afraid. I meant to say acute *abdomen*.' I heard him suck his teeth. 'Acute abdomen' is a general term that can mean almost anything. '. . . It could be a perforation . . . or a twisted ovarian cyst. Something . . . definitely.'

'Oh.'

51

'Anyway, you'll be seeing her in a minute. Nice girl. I'm sure you'll get her sorted out.'

As I sat with Caroline and wrote the referral letter I felt her staring at me.

'I've seen you somewhere before.'

'Oh, really?'

Suddenly she remembered. 'I know! On the buses! In the morning when I go down to get the groceries!' I felt my ears go red. 'You must travel on the same bus as me. That's where I've seen you. On the way to the hospital I expect.'

Beth was waiting outside Woolworth's.

'You were a long time.'

'I had to get this girl into hospital ... acute abdomen of some kind. Couldn't leave it.'

Beth smiled at me proudly, and then we were off to feast on shepherd's pie, chips and peas.

'Right here. In my belly button, Doctor. Sore. And it smells something horrible.' I looked over Harry's shoulder as he stooped to examine the man's inflamed navel. 'My missus says that the poison will go right through into my stomach if I don't have something done about it.'

Harry turned to me. 'The umbilicus is the seat of more anatomical misunderstandings than any other part of the body. It won't go anywhere, Joe, but you've got some infection right enough. We'll soon clear it up for you.'

He sat down and took out a prescription pad. 'What would you give for this, Neville?'

I didn't have the first idea. 'Antibiotics? Penicillin V?'

'Yes. You could do that. There is a little cellulitis. But what would you use as a local application?'

Well, at least that was obvious. 'Some kind of cream.'

'Ear drops,' said Harry. 'Best thing by far.'

'*Ear* drops?'

'Absolutely. The kind with antibiotic and steroid. Ideal. The dropper goes right down into the umbilicus and the drops can creep into all the little crevices. Here you are, Joe. Put these in your navel three times a day. Fill the dropper about half full.'

'Thank you, Doctor Brinckley.' He smiled and walked to the door.

'And, Joe, it will say "ear drops" on the bottle. But you do understand where they're to go?'

'I do, Doctor. Annie will do it for me. She's good at that kind of thing. Always reads the instructions. Likes to get things right.'

Harry stood up to open the door for him. 'You don't want to be like the old farmworker who was given suppositories for his asthma, Joe. Came back to the doctor a week later and said he was no better. "I've taken one with a cup of tea twice a day, regular, for the last week," he said, "and for all the good they did me I might just as well have stuffed them up me bum!" '

Joe was still laughing at this old medical chestnut when he went out through the front door. The waiting room was empty.

'I'll just make a few notes, if you'll excuse me a moment, Neville.'

I would be working with Harry full time from the next Monday. The evenings spent with him at the surgery had been invaluable. General practice was totally different from anything I had done in hospital, but it did not take long to realize that I was in the presence of an exceptional doctor. Harry examined everybody and always noted down his findings. 'You never know when you might need them,' he said.

With his patients he was hectoring, compassionate, worldly wise and loving. He said that kindness never cost anything, was better than most medicine and, apart from anything else, if you were wrong – and kind – people forgave you. Harry need not have worried; his clinical acumen, his attention to detail and his interest were more than enough.

'Never forget the rare diseases,' he told me. 'They're very common. Not individually of course, but lumped together.' Indeed, I had already seen more 'rare' diseases in a few evenings in the surgery than in months at the hospital.

There was a tap at the door. Harry looked up from his notes. 'Come in.'

'Hallo, Harry!'

'Ron! You've met Neville, of course. First day he was here. You remember Ron, Neville – with the thoracic disc lesion? Manipulated it for him.'

'Nice to meet you again, Doctor.' Ron shook my hand warmly. 'I hope you've given the old man a few tips,' he said.

'Starts here properly on Monday,' said Harry. 'Now Ron, what brings you here? Nothing to do with the accounts, is it? If it is, don't bother. I haven't got any money.'

'No,' laughed Ron. 'You *asked* me to come in a month or so to check my back. It's nearly eight weeks, but I thought I'd better come. It's fine. I'm a complete fraud.'

'Good,' said Harry, as he got Ron to rotate his trunk and take some deep breaths. 'Fine.'

'I did want to see you anyway, Harry. I wondered whether you could play for the Sunday eleven this week. We're very short.'

'Afraid not,' said Harry, 'I'm on duty . . . though Neville will play. Won't you, old lad?'

'Well . . . er . . . it's been a long time since I picked up a cricket bat . . . but, all right.'

'That's settled it, then,' said Ron. 'You can bring your

wife and nipper down and we'll have a good afternoon. Beth and Sarah, isn't it? Sylvia thinks she's met them in the supermarket but she didn't introduce herself.' Beth had said that she'd met a lot of friendly folk locally. 'Anyway,' said Ron, 'have you got any whites? . . . No . . . I'll bring a pair of cricket trousers for you.'

Harry looked at his watch as Ron left. 'Seven thirty. Splendid!' Harry rarely finished on time. 'Old Royston said he'd cover me this evenng. I'll just make the last house at Westhaven Odeon. *El Cid* – they say it's magnificent. Last night tonight. I've really been looking forward to that. I'll just lock up.'

The waiting room was not empty. A young woman sat on one of the plastic chairs amid the piles of *Punch* and *Illustrated London News*. She was sobbing. Harry went over to her.

'What's the matter, my dear?' he asked softly.

She looked up. Her eyes were red and her face smeared with tears. Her head dropped again.

'You'd better come in here,' he said, taking her elbow and gently leading her into his consulting room.

'Sit down. That's it.' He picked up a large packet of paper tissues and put it on the desk beside the young woman. She took one and wiped her eyes self-consciously. Harry said nothing. He took his pipe from his pocket, filled it carefully and soon the room was full of aromatic smoke. He leant forward and touched her arm.

'Now. Tell me all about it.' There was not a hint of disappointment – or haste – in his manner. 'We've got all the time in the world.'

'Last day today, then, lad?' said Walter, as we took a lunchtime break under the trees of Paradise Gardens. 'I'll miss you. Though Dave will be back on the platform next week.'

I gave Walter one of my egg sandwiches in exchange for one of his pilchard and tomato.

Our off-duty periods had been entirely different since Walter had let me into the secret of his hearing aid. He would reminisce about his experiences at Dunkirk, in the Eighth Army, at El Alamein . . . 'You said your Dad was there . . . regular was he? An officer I suppose?'

'No,' I said, 'he was a coal miner originally. From the Rhondda Valley. Came up to England during the Depression. Joined the Territorials. Lots of people did. For company, I suppose.'

Walter offered me another pilchard and tomato. I declined.

'Where will you go from here? Back to college?'

'No, Walter. I've got a job in Amblesham.'

Walter looked concerned all of a sudden. 'You're not giving up your studies? That would be silly.'

'No. Not that at all. I've finished with the college part of it. I'm going to learn to be a GP . . . a general practitioner.'

'Perhaps I'll see you again? Like you might be a passenger, but you're more likely to have a posh car.'

He munched on in silence. I took something from my pocket that I had borrowed from Harry.

'What's that?' said Walter.

'It's a tuning fork.'

'Rum-looking tuning fork. It's got a flat end.'

'It's a special tuning fork for testing different types of deafness.'

'Go on,' said Walter.

'I just wondered if I could try something on you?'

'If you want.'

'Could you take out your hearing aid for a moment?'

Walter took out the earpiece and stuck it in his top pocket. I struck the tuning fork on my knee and held the vibrating prongs by his ear.

56

'Can you hear . . . CAN YOU HEAR THAT, WALTER?'

'Only faint.'

I took away the fork and then placed the flat base on the mastoid bone behind his ear.

'Christ almighty!' Walter shouted. 'What the hell did you do then?'

'WAS IT LOUD?'

'I should bloody well say it was.'

That was it then. The sound was bypassing Walter's damaged middle ear. Conductive deafness. There was nothing wrong with the nerve. I indicated for him to put the earpiece back in again.

'Walter. I think it's just possible someone might be able to do something for your deafness. Do go and have a word with your doctor. He won't mind. Tell him what happened.'

Mr Henry was waiting for me in the office when I went to return my equipment. 'We'll be sorry to see you go . . . Neville. I don't expect you've found it very exciting working here. After what you're used to.'

What could I say without sounding patronizing? That I had learnt more really important things in my two months on the buses than I could have learnt in six at medical school. How to speak to people – all kinds of people. The kind, the irritable, the obnoxious, the lost, the confused, the young, the old, the happy, the drunk.

How to cope. There are few medical emergencies that require as much presence of mind as that needed to deal with a crowded bus. I had met men whose conversation and company were a joy and who were far better bus conductors than I would ever have been if I were to do the job for thirty years, and people like Dave who demonstrated a level of tolerance that I would be quite unable to match.

'Well, you'll be working in a hospital now, I suppose,'

Mr Henry said, and quickly explained, 'I knew you was a real doctor all along. From the first day when your insurance cards came through. Didn't tell anybody, though. I thought you must have some reason for not saying.'

'In Amblesham, Mr Henry. As a GP. I've finished with hospitals.'

'Well, that's *nice*. I wish you all the best. You'll come and see us, won't you?'

As I walked away, I think that I have rarely felt more proud than when Mr Henry shook my hand in farewell. 'If things don't go right in the practice, Doctor,' he said. 'Any time. You can always come back here. We'd be happy to give you a job as a *proper* conductor.'

Chapter Four

'Piles, Mrs Smetherley.' Harry bent over his prescription pad and began to write.

'Piles, Doctor?'

Harry looked up at the middle-aged lady seated, uncomfortably, opposite him. 'Piles.' His pen returned to writing 'Anusol suppositories'.

The patient looked at me. 'I'm very worried, Doctor.'

This time Harry did not look up. 'I can assure you that there is nothing to worry about,' he said as he signed the prescription with a flourish.

The patient cleared her throat, nervously. 'I would like,' she said, 'a second opinion.'

Harry looked up and smiled, obligingly. 'Certainly, Mrs Smetherley. Pop up on the couch and I'll have another look.'

Harry's philosophical approach to medicine seemed to prevent minor conditions being elevated to the realms of major illness. Mrs Smetherley hesitated for a moment.

Harry leant forward and patted her on the shoulder. 'Don't worry, my dear. It will be all right. Come back in a week's time and I'll make sure everything's going on satisfactorily. But it will be OK, I promise.' The woman relaxed.

This would be the last occasion on which I would sit in with Harry. There was only a scattering of patients. People had too many other things to do on a Saturday morning. It had been a different story the evening before last. We hadn't finished until 8.30. Harry had missed his film but the sad lady had eased her heart a little. The bully of a husband. The money problems. Too many children, another on the way. 'He won't use anything, my old man.' She said that she couldn't face another pregnancy. It was a mess. Could the doctor give her something to bring her on? He had to say no. There was little he could do but lend a sympathetic ear. Harry had said that he'd send her to the family planning clinic after the confinement.

As Mrs Smetherley left the surgery the sound of a child crying came in from the waiting room.

'Otitis media,' said Harry. 'I'll bet you a quid it's an ear infection . . . Always is . . . COME IN!' he shouted.

The mother had the child wrapped in a shawl. The little girl whimpered. She had her right thumb in her mouth and her left hand over her ear.

'Dear, oh dear, oh dear,' said Harry. 'You do look a poorly thing.' He reached into a jar of sweets on the trolley and found a jelly baby. The little girl took it from him.

'Now, let's have a look.'

The mother fidgeted. 'It's the other ear, Doctor.'

Harry smiled. 'No. We always look in the one that *isn't* hurting first.'

He showed me the bulging red eardrum. To the mother he gave a prescription for penicillin and nose drops.

'They're not ear drops,' he explained. 'They *are* nose drops. To go down the nose. They open the air passages and make the ear better. Keep Alison sitting up, the ear won't hurt as much as if she were lying down . . . and get her some children's painkillers from the chemist's.'

'You have to tell the parent that,' explained Harry, as mother and child left, 'otherwise they think that the antibiotic will get rid of the earache by itself – which, of course, it won't . . .' He looked past my shoulder towards the door.

'Hallo, Arthur. My goodness. You *do* look well!'

'Then my looks don't do me no favours,' said the sturdy, middle-aged man. A picture of abject misery, he eased himself into the patient's chair with some difficulty and sat with his legs straight out in front of him.

'It's my back, Doctor Brinckley. Murder. Murder it is!'

Harry went to the filing cabinet that all but covered the end wall of his surgery and removed a very fat record envelope.

'Back you say, Arthur?' he said, taking out a thick bundle of cards and letters.

'Yes, Doctor. It's agony.'

'Let's have a look, then.'

Arthur stood with difficulty and removed his jacket. As he turned to get on to the examination couch, Harry, standing behind him gave me the slightest grin.

'Does it hurt when I lift this leg?'

'Aaaaarggghhh! Yes! Yes!'

'And this leg?'

'God! Oh, that's terrible!'

I was rather surprised at Harry's somewhat carefree manner as he seemed to put his patient through some agony. The grossly reduced ability to lift the straightened legs showed that the poor chap had without doubt got an acute lumbar disc lesion. A slipped disc.

'And what about when I lift your left arm?'

'Oooohh,' groaned Arthur. 'It goes right through to the top of my head.'

'Does it get worse when you blow your nose?'

He thought for a moment. 'Now you come to mention it, I think it does.'

Harry asked a few more questions, each more bizarre than the one before.

'And you *have* found that your vision blurs slightly when you pass water?'

'Absolutely.'

'Well,' said Harry. 'We'll have to do something about that.'

Arthur dressed with difficulty and resumed standing. 'Is it serious, Doctor Brinckley?'

'No. I'm absolutely sure it isn't, Arthur. But you *do* need some fairly intensive treatment. Physiotherapy, I think.'

Arthur looked interested. 'At the hospital?'

'No, we'll be able to do it here.' Harry opened his desk and took out a sheet of paper. It was headed 'PHYSIO-THERAPY SESSION. SATURDAY'. The list of names written on it reached halfway down the page.

Arthur looked a little concerned. 'I won't have to miss any work, will I? They're very busy down the factory at the moment.'

'Not at all, Arthur. Come here next Saturday at ten a.m. sharp. Wear some old, loose clothes. I shall be instructing you in a special course of exercise.'

'Thank you, Doctor . . . but what about the pain, now?'

'I'll give you some tablets for it.' Harry wrote a pre-scription for Acetylsalicylic acid tablets. BP. 'Just one, three times a day.'

Arthur marched happily, and quite briskly, to the door clutching the document that instructed the chemist to give him a twopenny's worth of aspirin.

'Dear old Arthur is a lion,' said Harry when the door closed. 'Got the Military Medal at Normandy. Do anything to help anybody. But he does get a touch hypochondriacal from time to time. His mother and father both died when he was a kid. Now he's always waiting for the axe to fall.'

'Do you do these physiotherapy sessions very often?'

'Only occasionally. Come along next Saturday and have a look.'

Three sore throats and a cystitis were followed by an elderly gentleman in an unseasonably heavy, long black coat.

'It's about those tablets you gave me for the water,' he said grimly. 'Can you drink with them? . . . Alcohol?'

'You can, Zebedee. But I didn't know that you drank.'

'I don't, Doctor. I hate the stuff – we've never been a drinking family. But the pensioners have got an outing to the Isle of Wight tomorrow and before we have our dinner we have a glass of sherry. It's free. I don't want to waste it.'

'That will be perfectly safe, Zeb. You go and enjoy it.'

He pulled a face as he left. 'I certainly won't do that!'

'Last one, Doctor Brinckley,' said the next patient, an attractive girl in her mid-twenties.

'Hallo, my dear. Neville. Let me introduce you. June – Mary's niece.'

I had heard Harry's housekeeper talking about her. She smiled a greeting.

'Now, June, what can I do for you?' asked Harry.

I noticed that he nearly always asked, 'What can I do for you?' It implied that he was ready to do his patient a service rather than that they had to ask him a favour.

'It's silly. But I think I've caught German measles. I was babysitting for the neighbour's children two weeks ago and they'd just had it.' She was covered in small pink spots and there were large glands behind her ears.

'I'm sure you're right,' said Harry. 'I've seen several people with it this week.'

He turned to me. 'It's not always that easy, Neville. Scarlatina can look very much like rubella . . . German measles,' he said in an aside to the patient. 'And there are a load of viruses that can give you an identical rash. Sometimes you see babies who appear to have several attacks one after the other.'

He turned to the woman again. 'There isn't anything you can do about it. You're not expecting are you? Period late or anything? . . . Good. But don't get too near anybody

63

who is. Stay at home for a few days. Keep away from shops and the like.'

June was, indeed, the last patient, and after she left Harry went off to the kitchen to make us a cup of coffee. I looked around his consulting room once more. It was . . . homely. Cluttered. But everything was to hand. An examination couch with a small sliding curtain, a large desk and swivel chair, a comfortable padded seat for the patient, a glass trolley holding not only all his instruments, needles, sterilizer, but all manner of other treasures – free samples, assorted paperweights and diaries given to him by the drug companies – and the large jar of sweets for children. And a large packet of paper tissues.

'If you don't get through a packet of those once a month,' he had told me, 'then you're probably not giving your depressives a fair crack of the whip.'

The walls were covered with pictures. English country scenes, warships, railway engines, an old photograph of Harry in naval uniform with three other young officers. Old young faces. All laughing – a joke frozen in time. On the desk a photograph of an attractive, dark young lady with a small white dog – a West Highland White, it appeared. Dominating one end of the room were grey metal record cabinets.

Harry had over three thousand patients. He had set himself up in practice in Amblesham. 'Squatting' it was called, particularly by the doctors in the old-established practice which had its premises in the centre of the town. Harry's practice had become much too large for him to manage comfortably by himself. Old Royston Ackroyd had been a godsend when he had come to live in Amblesham in semi-retirement. He did a number of surgeries and covered for Harry's occasional night off. More than that, he took the phone calls when Harry's housekeeper was on holiday or staying with her daughter in Brighton for a few days.

Harry's situation as a bachelor made it very difficult for him to function as a single-handed GP. If he had to go out on a call it was essential, after all, that someone was still at his number to answer the calls. He had to switch the phone through to Mary in her flat above the garage. The NHS demanded a twenty-four-hour cover, 365 days of the year.

He had mentioned to me before that he exchanged duty on alternate weekends with another single-handed GP, Jim Grastick, who had a practice in a nearby village. They covered each other's calls from lunchtime on Saturday until Sunday at ten p.m. Effectively, this meant that Harry was on call thirteen nights out of fourteen. There was no wonder that the life expectancy of a single-handed family doctor was one of the lowest of any occupation. When I joined the practice he would only do every other night.

'Here we are. Two sugars, isn't it, Neville?'

I smiled and took the cup. Albert came padding into the room, tail wagging massively.

'Thank you, Harry. How's Albert been going with his lessons?'

'I'm not sure. The other day – perhaps I'm imagining it – he made a funny growl each time I showed him certain pictures. I'm sure he recognizes a few more words now. Don't you, old boy?' He slapped the dog on his flanks and bent down to have his ear licked.

Harry looked up. 'You think you'll like doing general practice then, Neville?'

'I'm sure I will. I've got a lot to learn, though.'

'You'll pick it up as you go along. I'll nearly always be around. Won't be taking a holiday until next spring. Try a bit of skiing then, I think. You've got plenty of time.'

He took out his pipe and started to fill it with tobacco.

'By the way. How much longer have you got the cottage for?'

'About three weeks. We haven't had much chance to look around yet and . . .'

Harry held up his hand. 'Well, Neville. There was *something* I was thinking about as a possibility. Just an idea.'

From among the accumulated junk on his examination trolley he found a street map of Amblesham and unfolded it on his desk.

'I think I know where you mean,' said Beth, without any great enthusiasm. 'In Sangster Road. Big. Seems to be completely covered in ivy. It's in the local estate agent's.'

'Yes. That's the one. It has a lovely garden, I'm told.'

'I'm sure it must have,' she said, 'but it's rather large, isn't it?'

'That's the whole point, you see. Harry said we could turn the side part of it into a surgery. My surgery. We've got a lot of patients in the Sangster Road area. Half the practice nearly. I could look after them there. We'd expand. No question, Harry says.'

Beth still looked worried. 'But how much will it cost?'

'Six thousand pounds.'

'Six thousand! You'll hardly be earning a thousand for the first year or two.'

'Harry says it will be all right. There'll be lots of extras. Insurance examinations, that kind of thing.'

Beth had always made sure we were never in debt even when we only had four pounds a week to keep us. I was the profligate one. Coming home with an armful of flowers – half price from the Covent Garden barrows at the end of the day – when Beth would have given an arm and a leg for a piece of steak.

'And you'll have to get yourself a car.'

'Harry said I can borrow the Riley for the time being.'

'I have no wish,' said Beth, 'to be a widow ... Not until we've got enough money for me to be merry with it, anyway.'

She was right. It was an absolute deathtrap. With each journey the indestructible engine was shaking the frail body to pieces.

'Let's go and look at the house,' said Beth. 'I'll get Sarah's pushchair.'

The house with the 'For Sale' notice had, clearly, been empty for some time. It was difficult to determine its exact structure beneath the dense covering of ivy and other creepers, 'Probably a good thing,' commented Beth. An elderly lady clipping the top of the hedge next door inspected us from under the brim of an enormous straw hat. We went to the side gate of the house. It was locked.

'There's nobody there, I'm afraid.' The old lady had the clipped society twang of an early thirties movie. Harrods out of Belgravia.

'No. We know,' I said apologetically. 'We were just looking ...'

'It's very big. The last man who lived there had a large organ.' It seemed that she knew the previous occupant very well. 'Lived on his own, you see. Used to play with it all the time. That's why it's a funny shape. The house. You can see from the back.'

She disappeared. I thought, for a moment, that she had fallen over.

'If you like you can come around to our back garden and look over the fence.'

We turned. The voice was from behind us. The elderly lady was now in the driveway we had just entered. She was tiny. She must have been standing on a box while cutting the hedge.

'Thank you,' said Beth, 'that would be most kind.'

We followed the diminutive figure, striding along in

her enormous Wellington boots, around to the back of the bungalow.

'I do the gardening from here to the plum tree,' she said, indicating an expanse of razor-cut lawns, neat flowerbeds full of blooms, trim hedges, 'and Soames is responsible for the garden beyond that.' A jungle – vast, towering weeds, thistles, cow parsley. 'Through here, look. You can see through the gap in the hedge.'

The garden of number twenty-seven was not as wild as Soames's patch and one could differentiate between lawn and flowerbed.

'Look over there,' said Beth. 'A swing and a sand pit. And there. That's a cherry tree, isn't it?'

'Beautiful in the spring,' said the old lady. 'The blossom is quite glorious. Can you see how the house has been extended?'

The house from the back was much more attractive than the front, with small windows and various roof levels.

'That room with the French windows is where he had the organ. The room above was the organ loft. But there's a floor been put in now. Not many people would have wanted a room that shape.'

Beth held Sarah so that she could look into the garden.

'It's four o'clock and I haven't had my tea!' A man's voice from behind us. Exactly the same accent as the lady but heavy with irritation. We turned. A large fat man was standing at the back of the bungalow. In spite of the hot weather he was wearing a heavy three-piece suit. In his hand the unmistakable pink of the *Financial Times*.

'I'm just coming, Soames,' said the lady. The man disappeared back indoors. 'Soames gets very cross if his tea is even a minute late.'

It was obviously time to go. We made for the front of the house. Beth turned. 'It's very kind of you to let us have a look at next door. I'm sorry that we have made you late with your husband's tea.'

'Good Lord!' said the lady. 'Soames isn't my husband. I wouldn't marry him for a million pounds even if I could.'

'We could go around to the estate agent and ask for the key,' I suggested.

'They won't be open until Monday,' said the lady.

'We'll come back then.'

For the first time the lady smiled. 'It really is quite a nice house. It would be very . . . nice to have someone living in it again. If you do come on Monday, please join us for coffee. We have so very little opportunity to entertain these days.'

'That would be lovely,' said Beth. 'Thank you, Mrs . . . er . . .'

'Tarrington-Bagford. Miss Tarrington-Bagford. But my friends call me Millie. Perhaps you would.'

'Thank you . . . Millie. I'm Beth. This is Neville. Neville James.'

'How do you do, Mr James. Will you be working in Amblesham?'

'Er . . . yes. I shall be in practice with Doctor Brinckley.'

'A doctor! How lovely! Imagine, we could be living next door to a doctor!'

As we walked down the road, Sarah fast asleep in the pushchair, Beth turned to me.

'Did you notice? That man Soames. He was wearing spats. I've never seen anybody wearing spats before.'

Now she came to mention it, neither had I.

Sunday afternoon. It was warm and fine as I waited to bat for the Amblesham cricket team. The 'whites' Ron had lent me were as yellow with age as the ancient cricket bat I had found in the broom cupboard back at the cottage. On each leg I wore a left pad.

'That's Ernie, daft bugger.' I had been told about the

stout gentleman now at the crease. 'Always wears two right ones.'

My team mates were the glorious mix of any small country-town cricket club. Vic Wheeler, sixty years old, who was Lady Westhaven's head gardener and our spin bowler, Griff Thomas, the local police inspector and opening bat, Joe Tusker, the local charcoal burner, a retired stockbroker and two lanky seventeen-year-olds, glowing with acne, who were our fast bowling attack.

Apart from Ron, I had not met any of them before, but when I saw the Nomads – the opposing team – I recognized their star bowler straightaway: tall and resplendent in gleaming white flannels and dark blue blazer, decorated with a silk and filigree gold college badge.

'Neville, it's good to see you, man. I never knew you were a cricketer.' He put his arm around my shoulder and laughed.

'Neither did I, Winston.'

I believe that it was the Welsh Fusiliers who stood up so bravely to the charge of the Zulu Impi at Rorke's Drift. Griff must have had the same feeling as he faced up to the opening ball of the innings. Exchange cricket ball for assegai. Winston was all warrior. With a long, loping run he accelerated up to the wicket and whipped over his arm. The first thing Griff knew about it was the leathery 'smack' as the ball slapped into the wicketkeeper's gloves some twenty yards behind him.

As it turned out, Winston was more danger to life and limb than to the wicket and eventually he was taken off to be replaced by the slow bowlers. Runs mounted and wickets began to fall. There was a loud click and a shouted appeal. Ernie Boggins trudged disconsolately back to the pavilion. It was my turn. Never mind, the bowling was slow to the point of friendliness. It was, however, the end of the over. Their captain had the ball.

70

'Winston!' he called.

My stomach fell about eighteen inches. At least the redoubtable Ron was facing.

I heard the crescendo-stamping of Winston's feet behind me and the loud grunt as he launched the projectile towards our captain. Ron, with what seemed like all the time in the world, played a broad edge through the covers and we ran two. The ground shook as Winston thundered up again. The ball was short and bounced shoulder-high down the leg side. With impeccable timing, Ron stepped back almost to his wicket and hooked the ball to the boundary. The opposing captain stood at first slip. 'Good shot, Ron,' he growled.

Winston was poised again. The run-up faster still. He pitched the ball in almost exactly the same spot. Once again, Ron stepped back and shaped to hook. This time, however, the ball cut back inside and gave him a glancing blow on the shoulder. Ron, off balance, tripped and fell, spreadeagled, across the stumps.

The umpire lifted his finger. Ron did not get up but sat by the shattered wicket rubbing his left side. He looked in some distress. I ran down the wicket as fast as my flapping pads would allow. Winston got there first but stood aside for me.

'Are you all right, Ron?' I knelt down beside him.

'I think so. Took the wind out of me. Felt a bit funny for the minute.'

He took two or three deep breaths, rubbed his shoulder and grinned wryly at Winston.

'By God! You moved that one.'

'I'm very sorry,' said Winston. 'I . . .'

'Oh. No, no, no, no,' said Ron. 'My stupid fault entirely. I'll be all right in a moment.'

He got up gingerly and walked up and down a few paces.

'That's a bit better.' Looking down at the devastated

wicket, he added, 'Don't think there's much doubt I was out.' He walked, rather shakily, from the field, dragging his bat behind him.

The spring had gone out of Winston's step as he walked back to bowl to the new batsman. If the delivery was any slower, however, I didn't notice. The ball bounced out of the wicketkeeper's gloves and with extreme reluctance I called for a bye and took my place at the batting end.

Heart pounding, and with a feeling of impending incontinence, I saw the blur leave Winston's hand. Leaping backwards, I left my bat dangling in front of the stumps. There was a crack as the ball hit the top edge, flew over the heads of the slips and reached the boundary fence in two bounces.

'Well done,' shouted a voice from the pavilion. It was Beth. She liked cricket. I would have happily exchanged places with her.

Having survived the rest of the over, I was mightily relieved when we all left the pitch for tea. I went straight to find Ron. He was looking at the score book.

'Good knock, Neville.'

'How are you, Ron?' He still looked rather shaken.

'Not too bad. Bit bruised.' He pulled up his shirt. There was a graze and some bruising on his left side where he had fallen on the stumps.

'It's not much,' he added. 'The shoulder's sore. But I'm feeling better already.'

I sat down for tea next to Winston.

'Is he all right, Neville? Your skipper? I'm sorry about what happened.'

'Don't worry, Winston. Just one of those things. Tell me. How do you come to be playing for the Nomads?'

'Oh that. I met one of the team when I was coaching his son.'

'Cricket?'

72

'No. Maths. For the GCE.'

'Maths?'

'Yes. I taught maths in Jamaica, for a spell, after I left college.'

'College? Then how . . .?'

'How did I come to be here? There weren't many prospects at home and Chrissie, my wife, got an offer of a nursing job in England. At Westhaven General. So I'm working on the buses until something else comes up.'

A lady with a large teapot topped up our cups as she passed. We heard her voice as she moved down the table. 'Come on, Ron. You usually eat enough for three.'

I looked up. Ron was declining a sandwich with a shake of the head. He still looked a little groggy.

We gathered outside the pavilion before going out to field. Ron had declared our innings. The Nomads needed 171 to win. It should be a good match. As we walked out to the wicket Griff came up beside me.

'They've only got one really class batsman,' he said. 'That stocky bloke with the ginger hair. Mustard, he is, mind. Get rid of him and we're home and dry.'

We took our places in the field, Ron keeping wicket. The batsman Griff had described was opening and taking strike. He hit our fast bowler for a two and a four in the first two balls. The third ball was short and should have followed the previous one to the boundary. It did not. Hitting a rough area of pitch, out of which Winston's mighty feet had already carved a few divots, it flew down the leg side catching the inner edge of the bat. Ron launched himself to the left, and, crashing to the ground, took a brilliant one-handed catch.

'Well caught, Ron!' The shout went up. I ran with the rest of the fielders to congratulate him. He lay motionless on the ground.

'Ron? Ron?' I bent over him. He was deathly white.

I felt his pulse. It was fast and thready. He groaned and turned slightly.

'God! I feel terrible. So faint. And my side hurts again.' He winced as he tried to put his hand to his left side. There was a dew of cold sweat on his forehead. The pallor. The pulse. He sounded breathless. The sweat. He was in shock. From . . .? Of course! Quite suddenly I felt sick. Memories of a rugby match. A winger who had insisted on playing while still recovering from glandular fever.

I lifted Ron's legs into the air to get some more blood into his depleted circulation.

'Vic. Hold Ron's legs up like this. Griff. A word.' I hurried Griff a few paces away from Ron. Out of earshot.

'Griff. I'm afraid Ron could be really ill,' I said hoarsely. 'We must get him into hospital straight away. Can we go in your car? It would be quicker than waiting for an ambulance.'

Griff looked shaken. 'Well, of course. But . . .'

'I think he's got an internal haemorrhage. From a ruptured spleen. He must have done it when he fell on the stumps. He could die . . . very quickly, Griff.'

'Christ!' He turned and ran to get his car. Sylvia was now at Ron's side.

'I'm going to have to get Ron into hospital straight away, Sylvia.'

She didn't ask why. Ron's appearance was enough.

Griff drove his car across the pitch. We lay Ron down on the back seat. I sat beside him holding his legs up. I turned to Griff as he was getting in, Sylvia beside him.

'It's a summer Sunday. The roads will be terrible.'

Griff thought for a moment. The other players had crowded round.

'Vic. That woman in the front garden of the house over there. She's bound to be on the phone. Dial 999 and ask for the police. Say that it's for Inspector Thomas. Tell them

74

that I'm bringing a very seriously ill man from Amblesham to Westhaven General. I'll be in a black Morris Oxford, FPN 404. They're to meet me with a patrol car at the Green Man roundabout and escort me through the traffic.'

'Right.' Vic began to jog towards the house.

'And, Vic,' I called after him.

'Yes, Doctor.'

'When you've done that. Phone up Westhaven General casualty department and tell them that a doctor is bringing in a man with a ruptured spleen. A ruptured spleen, got it? Tell them he's in shock.'

'Right.'

Griff accelerated away from the recreation ground. A few minutes later we were at the Green Man roundabout.

'There they are,' he shouted. The patrol car flashed its lights and led us through the streams of cars, bell clanging.

Ron was still conscious but looked ghastly.

'My shoulder's worse,' he whispered. Of course it was. It wasn't the blow with the cricket ball that had caused all the discomfort in the shoulder. Part of it would have been referred pain from the spleen as blood had collected under the diaphragm.

Sylvia looked back at us over the front seat. She was near to tears.

'He'll be all right, won't he?' she asked softly. I nodded and smiled but with no great conviction. Ron's pulse was getting faster and more feeble. As we arrived at Westhaven General casualty there was a doctor and a handful of nurses and porters waiting at the entrance. I jumped out of the car.

'Give us a hand.'

The porters gently lifted Ron out of the car and placed him on a trolley.

'I think he's ruptured his spleen.' I said to the casualty officer. 'Fell on some cricket stumps. Was OK. Then banged himself again a bit later and went straight into shock. His name's Ron Godden. Aged thirty-five. No other medical history.'

I followed Ron and the doctor in to casualty.

'He's in shock,' said the doctor to the sister. 'I'll take blood for cross-matching. Then we'll put up a bottle of 0 negative in the right arm and dextran in the left.'

A tall man in surgical greens came into the casualty room. 'This the chap, Tim?' he asked the casualty officer who was taking a sample of Ron's blood.

'Yes, Dick. I'm sure it is a ruptured spleen. Impaled himself on a cricket stump. Doctor James here brought him in.' There was no time for formalities. The man in green was clearly the surgical registrar. He looked at Ron's abdomen. There was now extensive bruising all down his left flank. He placed a hand lightly on Ron's left side.

'You can feel the fullness in the left upper quadrant. What's his blood pressure?' The nurse with stethoscope and sphygmomanometer shook her head.

'We've got to get his volume up bloody quickly, then.'

The nurses arrived with two drip stands. 'Put the I/V into the big veins in his cubital fossa,' said the registrar. 'And use the pump. Push the blood in fast. As soon as the drips are up wheel him along to theatre.' He leant down to Ron and said with surprising gentleness, 'We'll soon have you sorted out, old son.' Ron managed a slight smile.

'Are you coming to have a look, Doctor?'

I realized the registrar was addressing me.

'Yes . . . Yes, thank you.'

I couldn't say that I didn't really want to watch, nor could I think of an excuse not to. I never minded dealing with things myself, nor assisting at an operation, but just being an onlooker was a different thing altogether. Like a surprisingly large number of doctors, I had a nasty tendency to feel faint at the sight of blood. Strangely enough, it was worst of all if it was on film. Several times in the past I had had to leave a cinema when the technicolour blood started flowing.

The transfusions were up within a few minutes, and Ron, the bottles swinging above him, was pushed through the doors towards the operating theatre. I turned as I felt someone touch my arm. It was Sylvia.

'What's happening, Neville? I signed a consent form for surgery on Ron but nobody's had time to tell me anything about it.'

I took a deep breath. 'When Ron fell on the cricket stumps they must have stuck up under his ribs and damaged his spleen. It's a soft, roundish organ tucked up under here.' I tapped my left rib cage. 'It mainly acts as a kind of waste disposal for old blood cells. If it's damaged and starts to bleed the only thing to do is take it out. Otherwise the person will bleed to death. It isn't a vital organ and you lead a perfectly normal life without it.'

'But he seemed all right after he fell on his wicket.'

'Yes. That's not uncommon. It would have started to bleed then, but if the capsule of the spleen – the skin around it, as it were – wasn't damaged, the blood would have been contained for a while. Until it burst or until he had another knock.'

'Like that fall?'

'Exactly. Then the collection of blood, the haematoma, broke and he started bleeding freely. And he suddenly got worse. Went into shock. Sometimes people go into that stage straight away. We had a student at our medical school do that after a rugby tackle. Mind you, he had glandular fever at the time and you can be much more prone to a ruptured spleen if you're injured when you've got that.'

I caught up with Ron in the anaesthetic room. With no delay he was anaesthetized, intubated, and pushed into the operating theatre. He was lifted on to the operating table. The surgical registrar was to his right, the surgical house officer, opposite, to his left.

'We won't hang about,' said the registrar. 'Midline incision and go straight for the spleen. We'll tidy up later.'

As soon as the drapes were in position he took a scalpel and made an incision from the end of the breastbone to the navel. Cutting through the fibrous tissue beneath, he opened the abdominal cavity in moments and plunged his right hand into the wound.

'Now what we do is place the right hand so, go up under the left diaphragm and . . . find the damaged spleen. I have it . . . in the palm of my hand. And then . . . pull it to the right . . . and deliver it, like a baby, through the incision.' So saying, he pulled out the soft, purplish, haemorrhagic ball of tissue. 'And with any luck the splenic artery will have been kinked in the process and the bleeding will have stopped. Swab please, sister. As it has. Ladies and gentleman, the tap is turned off. We'll just clamp it to make sure . . . avoiding the tail of the pancreas. Now we can all have a fag and a cup of tea . . . not really, Susie,' he added, as he saw the look of alarm in the eyes of a young theatre nurse, 'but the worst is over. How is he, Fred?'

'The anaesthetist nodded. 'OK.'

At this point, I heard the familiar whistling in my ears and knew that, whatever the state of Ron's blood pressure, mine was certainly falling rapidly. I went into the anaesthetic room and lay down on a trolley. As the feeling passed I could hear from the registrar's continuing commentary that the spleen had been removed and careful examination of the abdominal cavity had revealed no damage to any other organ.

'Spencer Wells, please, sister.' The registrar asked for the most famous of all named clamping forceps. 'And again . . . And again . . . Sister, do you know who was the first

surgeon to remove a spleen for haemolytic disease? No?
. . . Anybody? No? . . . Mr Spencer Wells!'

I found Sylvia in a small waiting room, talking to a
black nurse and Winston.

'How is he, Neville?'

'I'm sure he's going to be all right, Sylvia.'

'Thank God.' She broke down in tears and the nurse
put an arm around her shoulders.

Winston shut his eyes and was silent for a few moments.

'Yes. Thank God.' He looked at me. 'Neville. You've
not met Chrissie, my wife.'

She smiled. 'I'm pleased to meet you, Doctor James.
I've heard Winston talk of you.'

Ron came around later that evening. He was pale and
very weak. A transfusion still ran into his arm. A naso-
gastric tube was taped to his cheek. There was a drain
running from the wound. But he was stable. He would
get better. The hospital staff had saved his life.

Sylvia was at his bedside. As was Winston. Ron looked
at Sylvia.

'I'm sorry I couldn't eat any of those sandwiches,' he
whispered. 'They looked very nice.'

She leant down and kissed him. Over her shoulder
he spied Winston.

'I don't suppose,' he asked, 'you've thought about playing for us?'

Chapter Five

'I heard all about the cricket match, old chap. My goodness me!' I'd hardly put my foot in through the surgery door when Harry clasped me around the shoulders. 'A ruptured spleen!'

'That's right, Harry. Fortunately, it was pretty obvious in the end. I'd have hated to have made a fuss about nothing.'

Harry's face suddenly became serious. 'Not at all. Not at all. You mustn't think that. If you're afraid of making a fool of yourself, then you'll never be any good as a doctor. Not a GP, anyway.'

He lead me through into the kitchen. 'I expect you could do with a quick cup of coffee before you start.' He put some instant and hot water into a mug. 'No, Neville. If you're not sure, always assume the worst then you won't get caught out. Nobody minds being sent into hospital for nothing – not much, anyway – but there are some tragic cases about, that nobody wanted to make a fool of themselves over.'

He smiled again. 'And after all, with Ron Godden gone who'd have kept wicket for us? More important, who'd help me look after all my money?'

He stopped for a moment. 'That reminds me. I've got the tax inspector coming this afternoon – usually does at this time of year. Sorts out the practice expenses, you know. He won't want to see you until next year.'

I felt a scraping down my leg. It was Albert's paw.

'You can't have another one, Albert. Always trying it on,' said Harry. 'Wants a biscuit and you've already had one, my fat friend.'

Albert looked up. Eyes black with all the suffering of the world. He whined softly.

'All right then. Just one more.' Tail wagging, Albert trundled out of the surgery, the biscuit turning his face into a broad smile.

'He won't eat it,' said Harry. 'He never does, the second one. He'll hide it behind the potted plant in the lounge. I'll pick it up later and put it back in the box. Then I'll give it to him again tomorrow morning. A process of recirculation. You've heard of the nitrogen cycle. This is more of a Bonio cycle.'

We went into the surgery. I could already hear the scratching of the chairs on linoleum from beyond the door that separated us from the waiting room.

'You take surgery this morning, Neville, and I'll do the visits, and after elevenses you can go down to the estate agent's. You take the calls this afternoon and I'll do the evening surgery. Will that be OK? Good. One thing — a little favour. I have to go to Westhaven this evening for a Local Medical Committee meeting. Could you give the Red Cross lecture at St Mark's church hall?'

'If you think I . . .'

'Of course you can. They'll be delighted to see a new face. I'm sure you'll be absolutely splendid. They'll tell you what to talk about when you get there.

He rummaged in his desk and produced a slim volume. 'I just use their handbook as a crib . . . read out large chunks of it, like doing the lesson in church. It's a bit of a religion with some of them, after all. Not that I've yet met a doctor who could put a bandage on a finger so that it didn't come off.'

He handed me the book and picked up a piece of paper on the desk. 'Let's see what we've got on the visiting list.'

It was written in Mary Brewer's neat hand. Harry copied the names down into his visiting book.

'Mrs Newbolt, 46 Martlett Street. That will be her varicose ulcers. Remind me to tell you a story about her one day. Ah! Rosalind! Bellyache. If she goes on getting it we'll have to have a look at her gall bladder. Heather Trimble. That will be her tonsils. She's waiting to have those out. Alf Hawkins. Chest pains? I'd better do that first. Nellie Baker, Walnut Tree Cottage. That's a pretty little place.' He put the list in his pocket.

'I'll phone you in an hour or so to see if there are any more.' Having found a fresh prescription pad and picking up his stethoscope, he put both in his bag and snapped it shut.

'It's all yours now, Neville. Good luck!' He smiled and was gone.

I looked at my watch. Eight thirty. Harry liked an early start. I went to the door to the waiting room. There were a dozen or more people. Most eyed me with curiosity. There was no appointment system. First come, first served.

'Come in please.'

A short lady with a prize-fighter face and a Barbara Windsor beehive tottered in on four-inch heels. Flopping down in the chair she rummaged about in her handbag, found a cigarette and lit it. As an afterthought she offered the packet to me.

'No, thank you.'

'I'm Mrs Littlebone. You're Doctor Brinckley?'

'No.'

'Oh!'

'I'm Doctor James. I work with Doctor Brinckley.'

'Well, I suppose you'll have to do.'

She disappeared once more into her handbag and produced two letters which she thrust into my hand. One was from the Executive Council telling the Littlebone family that their doctor had asked for them to be removed from his list. The other, from the same source but posted some time later, told them they had been allocated to Doctor Brinckley.

'I don't know why old Morgan did it,' Mrs Littlebone said. 'We always got on. The kids loved him.'

Knowing that their previous doctor was a very tolerant man, I suggested that he must have been deeply upset to refuse to treat them any more.

'Something must have happened?'

'Nothing, Doctor. Honest to God! Except the last time I saw him. I did get a bit overexcited.'

'Overexcited?'

'Yes. We had words. He wouldn't give me a letter for the Welfare. For my husband's eggs.'

'Eggs?'

'He has to eat a lot of eggs. A specialist told him. Vitamins. Gives him stamina.'

'And you took exception to that?'

'I suppose I did. I threw a tin of pears at him. South African.'

'You *what*?'

'It missed him. Nothing happened. It went through the window.'

A sense of unreality crept over me. 'You didn't take it with you to throw at him?'

'No! Don't be daft. It was for our dinner. I was so mad. I picked it out of my shopping bag when I was going out of the door . . . Anyway. Here.' She gave me a dog-eared brown bundle. 'Here's our medical cards. The kids. Eight of them. Mine. And my old man's.'

She started to leave. 'He'll be in to see you in a day or two to tell you what he wants.' Then she was gone.

'My hoat's no better,' said the leather-jacketed youth who came in next. He struggled with his consonants and the effort to speak made him wince with pain. 'I've had henicillin. No good.'

There was little doubt about the diagnosis. I looked in his mouth. The back of the throat was covered with a white cheesy exudate. I could feel large glands in his neck. It was interesting to think that twenty years before it could have been diphtheria. But not now. Not with immunization. I took some blood for a Paul Bunnel test but I was sure it *was* glandular fever.

I gave him a certificate for a fortnight off work – he'd need all of that and probably more. There was nothing I could do for him more than his sensible mother who was already giving him two aspirins every four hours.

'I wanted to see Doctor Brinckley,' said the old lady who shuffled in next. 'He knows all about me.'

'I'm sure I can be of some help, Mrs . . .?'

'Rowbuck. I'm sure you can't, sonny.' Sonny! I coloured up. Was I not the hero of the Amblesham Cricket Club? A fully qualified doctor? 'But there again,' she continued, 'I don't think that anybody can. Not even Doctor Brinckley. God bless him. I'm a martyr to them.'

'I'm sorry?'

'My feet!' She stood. 'Just look how I walk.' She slouched in a small, tight circle around the consulting room. 'I used to be able to walk like this . . .' She suddenly broke into large measured strides. 'But now . . .' she changed back to slow shuffle, 'I can only do this!'

Having looked at the neat and copious notes with which Harry had filled her record envelope it was obvious that she was right. I couldn't really help them. She gratefully accepted a repeat prescription for some salicylic acid paste to soften her corns. I did not exactly feel I was making any great inroads into the relief of human suffering.

'I hear that you were working at the hospital before you came here. Training to be a specialist.'

'Not exactly, Mrs . . . er, Rowbuck.' It was only just over a year since I had been a medical student.

'Well, my friend Mrs Walters was talking to Doctor Brinckley in the post office and that's what he told her. He said that he was lucky to get somebody so specialized.'

Harry was obviously working to set me up as an acceptable, if not preferable, substitute.

There followed a sore throat, dermatitis, certificate for a broken leg (motorcycle accident), ingrowing toenail, earache and . . .

'Hallo, Doctor James. I heard it was you.' A familiar face at last. A young, attractive woman. But who was she?

'We met on Saturday. You probably don't remember with so many patients. German measles.'

'Of course . . . June, Mary's niece.' I smiled and looked at her closely. 'The rash has gone'

'Yes. But look at this.'

She held out her hands in front of her. Her wrists and finger joints were grossly swollen. 'I can't even hold a cup.'

It was the most acute arthritis I had ever seen. Rheumatoid? The phone rang.

'Neville?'

'Harry.'

'Any more calls?' I looked for the piece of paper on the desk.

'Two. Mr Spencer of 27 Oaken Way. He says it's his heart and you always call . . . and some lady was on about her son. Clive. Lives in the house opposite you. She was a bit cagey. Said he had stomachache.'

'Of course. I know her well. Thanks. I'll take those and I'll see you later at about . . .'

'Oh, Harry. Before you ring off, I've got June sitting in front of me.'

'Give her my regards. How's her rubella?'

'That's the point, Harry. She's got no rash or anything but she's developed a really severe painful swelling of her

85

wrists and fingers.' I looked nervously at June. 'I wondered whether it could be an acute rheumatoid arthritis.'

'Well I never!' said Harry. 'Isn't that remarkable ... You didn't see it then?'

'What?'

'That article in the medical press a couple of weeks ago, about acute arthritis following rubella. Pretty rare. But there it is, right under your nose.' He chuckled. 'Do you remember what I said about rare things being common?'

'Yes Harry, but what on earth am I going to do about this?'

'Nothing. It gets better by itself in a few days, apparently. Tell her to take some aspirin, that's all ... Anyway, I'd better be going. Fascinating!'

June was suitably reassured by Harry's timely intervention. And, as if to confirm what he had said, two of the next four patients turned out to be under the local hospital for conditions I hadn't even read about in the small print. There was a lot to learn.

Just before eleven Harry came bounding in. 'Fantastic! Visits done. Surgery finished. This is going to be the life, Neville!'

Mary came in with a tray of tea. Albert appeared. He had heard the rattle of the biscuit tin. Harry filled his pipe and bubbled contentedly.

'How did it look? The house?'

'We haven't seen it inside, of course, not till we get the keys from the estate agent this morning. It looked very nice. We've already had an invitation for coffee this morning from our new neighbours to be, Barrington-Faggot or something.'

'The Tarrington-Bagfords. Of course, I'd forgotten they lived next door.'

'You know them, then?'

'Patients of mine for years.'

Harry was not satisfied with his pipe. He emptied the tobacco on to his prescription pad, picked up a scalpel from the trolley and began to scour out the bowl. Seemingly satisfied, he blew down the stem and a shower of ash fell down the front of his sports jacket. He dusted it off with a flick of his hand.

'But they're not actually married, I understand.'

'I should hope not,' said Harry. 'They're brother and sister, though you wouldn't think so to look at them. Millie's been married, of course, twice I believe. Used to be an actress. But Soames hasn't – been married I mean. Millie came to live with him after her second husband died. Always kept her maiden name. Something to do with the stage, I suppose.'

'They seem slightly . . . eccentric.'

'How hath the mighty fallen, really,' said Harry. 'Soames took early retirement from some high-powered City job in 1932 on the princely income of six hundred pounds a year. He moved to East Sussex and bought a bungalow in the middle of a delightful stretch of woodland . . .'

'Sangster Road?'

'Quite. The woodland is no more. And the six hundred hardly pays his tailor's bill. They are as poor as church mice but Millie keeps it from him . . . Ah, two things I meant to tell you from the visits. Interesting . . .' Harry sensed that I wanted to be off.

'Only take a second. One. Alf Hawkins. Nice man. Runs the newsagent round the corner. Only forty-five. Had this chest pain. Nearly better when I got there. BP, pulse, everything OK. But it had lasted a couple of hours and had radiated into his arms. Typical coronary. He won't have it. Says he knows it's indigestion and won't consider going into hospital, so I'm getting a domiciliary on him. I've told you about those?'

'That's where you get the consultant to come and see the patient at home?'

'That's right. On the NHS – no cost to the patient. Very good service. I gave Peter Fairling, our cardiologist, a ring. He'll pop in and do an ECG this afternoon, then we'll know where we are . . . But if Alf Hawkins gets more pain in the meantime he'll just *have* to go in.

'Two. That little lad, Clive. My neighbour's boy. You said the mother was a bit cagey. Stomachache, she said. Didn't know how to tell you I expect. He had one testicle twice the size of the other. Diagnosis?'

'How old is he?'

'Quite right. Always the first question. Seven.'

'Must be a torsion,' I said, referring to a twist in the spermatic cord that would deprive the organ of blood and destroy it if not rapidly corrected by surgery.

'Absolutely. I sent him straight in. They're sometimes missed you know. The doctor just thinks it's an infection and gives antibiotics. Day or two later he or she realizes they were wrong. Too late. Poor little devil's only got one ball left. At seven, always a torsion – at twenty-seven, of course, nearly always infection or worse.'

I had to go. Harry could have chatted all morning. He seemed to be interested in every case.

I told Beth about Soames and Millie as we pulled up outside 27 Sangster Road. Pulling up now in the Riley was very much something you had to consider well in advance. Millie was waiting. Her head bobbing over the front hedge.

'Ah. There you are, my dears,' she said.

She was wearing a mauve chiffon dress and high-heeled shoes with straps across the instep. Seeing her for the first time without a hat, it was fairly startling to discover that her head was covered in tight canary-yellow curls. A neat cupid's bow of vermilion was painted on her mouth, and from ears and around her neck hung clusters of jet.

'Millie.' I shook hands but Beth got a kiss. 'Perhaps we should look around the house and . . .'

'Nonsense,' said Millie. 'First you must come and have some refreshment.'

As soon as she opened the front door of the bungalow we were met by the aroma of percolating coffee.

'This way,' called Millie. We squeezed past an enormous hall stand, relic of some previous grander abode, no doubt, and then had to stoop slightly to avoid several pairs of assorted roebuck, wildebeeste, antelope and the like that appeared to be trying to stare each other out across the narrow passage with glassy unblinking gaze. Above the door at the end of the hall a leopard snarled, motheatenly.

We were shown into the living room. Soames faced the door sprawled in a large leather chair. Sutherland's Churchill; disgruntled and unwelcoming.

'You remember Doctor James and his wife, Soames?' said Millie.

'Please don't get up,' said Beth. But it was apparent that there had been no such intention. The man of the house did little more than grunt and lift his hand in grudging welcome.

'Perhaps you would sit on the sofa,' said Millie, 'while I fetch the coffee.' We sank into the leather cushions with a loud hiss and looked about the room. It was, in its own way, remarkable. No ornaments, pictures or pieces of furniture dated beyond 1940, few beyond 1930 and none before 1920 – from the sunburst mirror over the yellow tile fireplace, to the green racing car teapot on the walnut sideboard. The prints on the wall were of tight-hatted women on the arms of brilliantined men. Men with centre partings and Ronald Colman moustaches. Toppers and tails. The men of Millie's heyday.

'You've lived here quite a long time, I understand,' said Beth.

'Yes,' said Soames. He picked up the *Financial Times* from the glass and chrome table beside him, unfolded it and disappeared from view.

Beth looked at me, a smile playing at the corner of her mouth. Sarah sat on her lap in awed silence, fascinated by the ticking of the ebony and silver clock on the mantelpiece.

'Here we are,' said Millie, clinking a large tray on to the glass table. Apart from the coffee, there were slices of fruit cake, jam tarts and fairy cakes. Sarah leant forward from Beth's lap and stuck her fingers in the cream.

'Sarah!' Beth pulled her away.

'Never mind,' said Millie. 'Here, let her have this one.' Sarah took the cake from her in both hands and, in seconds, smeared jam, cream and crumbs down the new smocked dress that Beth had bought for her two hours earlier. Millie poured the coffee and handed Sarah a glass.

'Will blackcurrant juice be all right for her?' I could feel Beth's inward wince. She hadn't bought a bib.

'That will be lovely, thank you.'

Millie sat back in her chair.

'Have you worked in this area long as a doctor ... Neville? May I call you Neville?'

'Certainly you can. No. Not before joining Doctor Brinckley.'

'A charming man,' sighed Millie. 'Not that I wasn't somewhat upset with him last year. I had a little trouble. Internal, you know.'

'Oh yes?'

'He absolutely *insisted* that I went to see a specialist at the hospital. It was really dreadful. I had all manner of things poked up my jacksie!'

There was a spluttering sound as Beth's coffee went down the wrong way.

'Are you all right, my dear?' Millie asked with concern. Beth nodded, her eyes still watering.

'Most extraordinary affair altogether,' she continued. 'I said to the doctor, "I don't know what you're doing down there, young man, but there's a light shining out of my left nostril." There wasn't of course. But I felt as though there should have been.'

Beth, fully recovered, grinned from ear to ear. Millie solemnly sipped her coffee, her little finger raised delicately.

'It's one of those things we women have to bear,' she added, picking up a piece of fruit cake. 'I'm sorry to give you cake at this time in the morning. I did purchase some Bath Olivers but someone has eaten them.' She nodded, meaningfully, towards her brother.

'You're always on about your bloody illnesses,' snorted Soames, bulging eyes visible above the top of the news-paper. 'God knows how much *I* suffer!'

'Soames has dyspepsia,' explained Millie.

Throwing down the paper, Soames gripped the front of his waistcoat. 'Dyspepsia, my arse! I have ulcers!'

'But they're *very* elusive when he has X-rays,' Millie said with an aside.

'I damn well have,' rasped Soames. 'Go on! You mock. But I don't know what you'll do when I'm dead!'

Millie smiled sweetly at us and then even more sweetly towards her brother.

'Well, there's one thing for sure, dear Soames,' she simpered. 'I shan't have you stuffed.'

'What did you think of it all?' I asked Beth, as we arrived back home at the cottage.

'The house? Big. But you could use the side part as a surgery. It's almost self-contained with that side door and path. We'd still have two rooms downstairs and lots of room upstairs.'

And the garden for Sarah would be ideal. The house was in a fairly poor state of repair. If it hadn't been we couldn't have afforded what it would undoubtedly have cost.

'I'll tell Harry we'll buy it then.'

'All right,' said Beth, 'but we'll have to sit on orange boxes for a while.'

'As long as we've got a bed.'

'That's all you think about.'

'Ridiculous . . . and untrue. What's for dinner? I'm starving.'

I thought that I'd better let Harry know that the house would be ideal for our purposes. I didn't get to see him until late in the afternoon. There had been three home visits. A tonsillitis, a mumps and a something. 'A virus' had satisfied both patient and myself. I pulled up on the gravel drive in front of the surgery and parked between the potholes. Beside Harry's Mini was an unfamiliar car.

Mary answered the door.

'Doctor James. Doctor Brinckley is around in the barn with the man from the tax office.'

As soon as I got near the half-open double doors I could hear raised voices. They stopped as I came in. Harry introduced me to a bald-headed man in a blue, pinstripe suit, dwarfed by the cabin cruiser towering above him.

'Neville. Mr Regis from the Inland Revenue. Doctor James.'

'Pleased to meet you.' A perfunctory handshake. Mr Regis wanted to get back to the attack.

'As I was saying, Doctor Brinckley.' Mr Regis consulted his clipboard. 'You appear to have claimed this . . . structure' – he pointed to a huge, stove-enamel turning machine – 'as a practice expense!'

It was Harry's pride and joy. He had bought it only a few months previously for a price far in excess of that of the Mini.

'Quite so,' said Harry, totally unabashed.

'I can't see how you can possibly . . .?'

'It's quite simple,' said Harry, picking up a small carborundum wheel, slipping it on the central spindle and setting it spinning with a flick of the power switch. 'I use it to sharpen my scalpels.'

Mr Regis sucked his teeth, took a deep breath and started to shuffle through his papers again. Harry gave me a sidelong glance with the slightest of winks.

'And this item, Doctor Brinckley, your television. You have claimed your television against tax!'

'Of course.' It was obvious that they had more business to settle.

'Excuse me, Mr . . . er, Regis. Harry. I'll leave you. We'll have a word later. I think the house was just right.'

'Great!'

As I walked away, I could hear Harry begin to explain and had to listen for a moment.

'I only watch medical programmes on it. "Your Life in their Hands", that kind of thing.'

Mr Regis was reaching the limits of exasperation. 'That's absolutely ridiculous! How can you possible prove you do that?'

There was a pause. 'How can you possibly prove that I don't?'

Touché.

Mary was waiting for me by the surgery door.

'Doctor James. You're still on call, aren't you? I've got a request for a visit to School Lane. Mrs Smith. A very elderly lady.' She handed me the record envelope. Date of birth 1871. 'Her granddaughter just called.'

The front door of 17 School Lane led straight into the large living room. Large but crowded. An old lady sat in a tall, upright chair surrounded by what I presumed were her children, grandchildren and great-grandchildren. A couple of toddlers were playing on the floor. A large table

93

showed the remains of a high tea. The family gathering had obviously been a bit too much.

'The doctor's here, Grandma,' a lady bellowed into her ear.

'Oh yes,' she said. She looked, unseeing, in my direction and smiled.

'She felt a little peculiar a little while ago, Doctor. We've given her some brandy.'

I took the pulse. It was very slow. About thirty. As I held on to the scrawny wrist, both pulse and breathing stopped.

'She's gone,' I said. The distress was apparent in all their faces. They expected me to do something. Ninety years old she might have been, but fit.

I struck her in the middle of the chest. Immediately, both heart and breathing restarted. After a few moments her eyelids flickered and she looked up. Her lips began to move. A message from beyond, perhaps? Had she not already crossed the bridge? I leant down towards her. Her voice was quite clear.

'Can I have another cup of tea?'

The family rushed to brew another pot and brought another cup to her. Alas, she had recrossed the bridge and was not to be recalled by another hefty knock on the sternum. We all sat around the old lady, who just looked to be in a deep peaceful sleep, and drank tea. The small children continued to play. They had had the best lesson that they were ever likely to receive.

Nobody said anything for some minutes and I thought it was time to leave. As I stood, an old man came over and shook my hand. I realized with something of a shock, that it must be the son, or son-in-law.

'Thank you, Doctor. You were very kind.'

'Not at all . . . I'll have the certificate ready for you in the morning.' Now the awkward question that had to be.

'Do you know whether she wanted to be buried or cremated? It's the certificate you see, I . . .'

'Oh buried, Doctor! They were very close. The place is ready for her beside Father.'

Wuthering Heights to the end.

Home for tea. Harry rang. I asked whether he was likely to be sent to prison.

'Oh, old Regis is all right. We have the same kind of trouble every year. He was a bit sticky about Albert, of course. We always have an argument about him.'

'Albert?'

'My watchdog. Dangerous drugs on the premises and that kind of thing. Leaving the house unguarded in the middle of the night. Regis settled for half the food bill.'

'But no reading material.'

Harry laughed. 'No, I'm afraid not . . . Now, is it all right for you to take the calls tonight? Beth doesn't mind?'

'Of course not.' I knew the thought terrified her.

'Right then. I'll transfer the calls through to you and I'll see you tomorrow. Don't forget the lecture at the church hall. Seven thirty. They're on the phone. Amblesham 5320. Don't worry about it, they're nearly all beginners.' The night would be more daunting for Beth than for me.

'You're sure you'll be all right, darling?'

She smiled. 'I've got to learn sometime.'

What a responsibility! No medical training – except for asking me endless questions for my MB finals. When I was out over three thousand people's lives could be in her hands. And not just tonight. One night in two. Indeed, every other afternoon, evening and night she would be expected to be by the telephone. A prisoner of the house. Just as I was leaving the phone began to ring. I let her answer it.

'Amblesham 4089. Doctor James's house . . . Yes, Doctor James. He works with Doctor Brinckley . . . Mr Alec

Cowell, 33 Maple Court . . .' Thank heaven it was on the direct route to the church hall. 'Yes . . . how long has he had the pain? . . . Has he been sick . . .? Just a moment, I think I can catch the doctor for you.'

A youth of eighteen years. Stomachache for forty-eight hours. Vomiting, constipated, a temperature of 100°F. Very tender in the lower right abdomen. The most classical acute appendicitis. To hospital straightaway.

'Ah yes, Doctor James,' the houseman said. 'You'll be pleased to know that Mr Godden is coming on very well.' And chafing to come out, apparently.

St Mark's church hall was a squat, bunker of a building erected to commemorate the young men of Amblesham who had given their lives for God and country in The War to end all Wars. There seemed no ambiguity in the fact that only a few hundred miles away, similar structures commemorated similar young men who had given their lives for another country but, presumably, the same God.

The commandant of Amblesham Red Cross waited for me in the doorway. By his uniform, badges and decorations, he must have been at least a brigadier general.

'Mr Pearce, Doctor.' We shook hands and entered the hall, our feet clattering on the woodblock floor. The audience turned round to inspect us. They were all female, sixteen to sixty, bar one young man sitting at the back holding hands with his girl friend. Most were initiates, in twinsets rather than uniform.

'I am happy to introduce Doctor James,' said the commandant, 'who will be with us this evening for the fourth in our series of introductory lectures. Doctor Brinckley has been called away on urgent business.' There was a buzz of conversation and a scraping of chairs. 'However, I am pleased to be able to tell Doctor James that he doesn't have to work very hard for our benefit tonight, but can sit back with the rest of us and be entertained ... and, of course, educated.'

He smiled at the audience and pointed to the back of the hall where I noticed, for the first time, an ancient 16mm projector primed for action.

'The local ambulance station have lent us their new training film on the treatment of emergencies. I am sure that after we have watched it Doctor James will be able to fill in any gaps and answer any questions.'

There was a murmur of assent and several of the ladies smiled at me. I thought I could already recognize several from those that I had seen at the evening surgeries spent with Harry. I followed Commandant Pearce to the back of the hall.

'You'll like this one, Doctor. I've already seen it,' he whispered with a grin. 'Lots of blood. I think it will sort out the wheat from the chaff. Practical approach. That's what I like. The practical approach.'

I thought I had better sit at the back. As the lights went down I felt the familiar sinking feeling in my stomach and took several deep breaths.

It looked, however, as though it wasn't going to be too bad. Faints, fits, heart attacks – nothing too harrowing. Electrocution. Remember to switch off the power before you do anything or else you'll go up with a flash and a bang. Drowning. Unpleasant. Film of the new mouth-to-mouth method of resuscitation.

'Say they've been sick?' I heard someone whisper to their neighbour.

I was feeling a lot better. I looked back at the projector. From the amount of film left on the spool this so-called gory epic would soon be at an end.

On to the screen flashed a picture of a large woodwork shop with electric circular saws. A man was cutting a piece of wood. The camera focused on the faulty saw-guard and then panned down to a piece of loose material hanging from the sleeve of the man's overalls. Oh God! To anybody who might have turned to look at me, I would have appeared to have been scratching my nose. In reality, I was concealing the fact that my eyes were closed tight.

'This is the bit, Doc.' An excited Mr Pearce had sat himself beside me. I took my hand from my face and tried to watch the screen with unfocused eyes. From the sound track, there was a ghastly scream matched with a gasp from the audience as the screen turned red. There was a close-up of what appeared to be a hand with very short fingers. The sweat prickled on my brow and there was a whistling in my ears.

I recovered consciousness almost immediately. But I had not heard the crash as I fell off my chair, sending the chairs around me skidding across the floor.

The commandant put on the lights straightaway and in a few seconds was staring down at me, his protégés crowded about. Through half-open lids I saw him bend down beside me, giving the slightest of smiles – of understanding, as it were.

'Now,' he asked the assembled first-aiders, 'what do you think has happened to Doctor James?'

'He's fainted.'

'He's had a fit.'

'A heart attack?'

'What do I always tell you is the most likely cause of collapse in a healthy young person?'

'A faint?'

'A faint!' he said, with satisfaction.

I was feeling a lot better but I thought I'd better stay where I was.

'And what do we do for that?'

'Sit him up and give him some brandy,' said a middle-aged lady, bedecked with badges, who should have known better.

'We do *not*, Mrs Hutchley,' said Mr Pearce with a withering glare. 'We do *not* sit up the unconscious patient. Neither do we give him anything to drink!'

'Loosen his tie?'

'Yes . . .'

'Smelling salts?'

'If you have any, Miss Frazier-Gibbs.'

'Keep him flat and lift up his legs so that the blood can run back to his head,' said the young man.

'Very good, Adrian, well done!' The young man blushed and his girl friend gazed at him in mute admiration.

The back of my head was somewhat sore where I had hit it on a chair, but otherwise I didn't feel too bad. I propped myself up on my elbow and smiled broadly.

'Well done, ladies . . . and gentlemen. That was excellent!'

The commandant leant to help me up. 'Well done, yourself, Doctor. A novel tactic. Practical! That kept everybody on their toes.'

Excusing myself to go to the lavatory, I took several gulps of fresh air from the window and then sat on the loo seat for a few minutes to allow my blood pressure to reassert itself. When I returned to the hall I was able to say that the film had been so good that it needed no enlargement by me. They all clapped in appreciation.

I turned as I reached the door at the back of the hall.

'If you ask me again, I'll try and do an epileptic fit for you – or it might be a heart attack!'

They all laughed. Especially Mr Pearce. But I still wasn't quite sure how comprehending the understanding smile had been.

Chapter Six

'Like a what?' the woman asked.

'Like a seal. You know.' I made a barking noise down the phone.

'That's right, Doctor. That's exactly what it sounds like.'

Doing animal impressions at two o'clock in the morning was not my idea of fun, but it might have saved a visit. I'd only just got back to sleep after a call to an old lady with asthma. She'd needed an intravenous injection and I'd had to wait about to make sure that her spasm was easing.

'Have you put saucepans of water on the stove and got a good steam up?'

'Yes, Doctor Brinckley told us that last time.'

'And your little boy is still no better?'

'No. I don't think so.'

As if to confirm what she was saying, I heard a child crying in the background. The crying was interspersed by the unmistakable sound of croup.

My first night on after the Red Cross lecture had been blissful. The phone hadn't rung once. Tonight, my second duty, it hadn't stopped.

I was sure it *would* be a simple croup. But the nagging worry remained. There was always the outside chance that it *could* be acute laryngo-tracheo-bronchitis. And that could be very nasty.

'If you're not sure what to do about a child,' I could hear Harry saying, 'just imagine what you'd want done if it were yours.'

I slid my feet out from under the bedclothes. It was cold.

'All right, I'll come and have a look,' I said.

Beth stirred beside me, made a soft snuffling noise, but did not waken.

I got out of bed with enough fuss and noise to rouse her. I wanted her to *know* how hard I was working.

'Whassat?'

'I'm sorry, love. I didn't mean to wake you. It's another call.'

'Oh.' She pulled the bedclothes over her head again. I had always supposed that doctors called out of their beds were met on their return by bright-eyed wives ready with tea and biscuits.

I pulled on a pair of trousers and an enormous sweater. Purple and orange, it had been knitted for me by a hypomanic but somewhat myopic maiden aunt.

'I'll be going then.'

'Emmmmm.' The bedclothes did not move.

Early October and autumn was announcing its arrival in the cold, damp air. I cleaned the condensation from the Riley's windscreen with my sleeve. The wipers were still disconnected. With a noise like a dustbin falling off a high wall, the engine clattered into life at the first pull on the starter. Lights appeared in the bedroom windows of two of the neighbouring houses. On the dashboard the needles of the dials vibrated into a meaningless blur.

'He started getting better the moment I put the phone down, Doctor,' the lady said as soon as I arrived. 'I am sorry.'

I wasn't. Much nicer not to have to do anything. Next time she'd probably wait a little longer before phoning. I was back in bed asleep within half an hour.

'Would you like another cup of tea, President Kennedy?'

Her Majesty leant forward and proffered the silver Georgian teapot. How elegant it was on the lawn of

101

Buckingham Palace. The handsome, youthful American smiled his thanks.

'And you, Doctor James?'

'Yes please, Ma'am.'

This had to be the high point of my life. I was not quite sure why I had been invited to this intimate tea party. Something to do with saving the life of the American ambassador. Strangely, I couldn't remember exactly what I had done.

'Ma'am . . . I . . .?' A bell interrupted what I wanted to ask. 'Ma'am, I can't quite . . .'

The bell clanged insistently in my ear. Everything went black. I turned towards the bedside table and groped for the telephone once again.

'Doctor James speaking.'

'You've got to come and see my husband. Everything is going through him.'

'Who's that speaking?'

'Mrs Broxwood.'

'Mrs Broxwood . . . of what address?'

'Of 46 Dunkirk Road,' she said, in a voice that suggested I should have known. 'You'll have to come straightaway, Doctor. He's done it all over the bedroom floor and all over his pyjamas . . . and all over his new slippers. And he's got awful stomachache.'

'I see. Perhaps you could . . .' There was a click and a dialling tone as the phone was put down at the other end. Blast! That was the third time out of bed tonight. I looked at the luminous dial of the clock. Three thirty a.m.

Dunkirk Road. Part of an estate of prefabricated houses named by some wag at the Highways Department after notable British military successes. Dunkirk Road, Singapore Crescent and Tobruk Terrace. I crept along, revving the Riley's engine to produce some usable light from the headlamps, but I could see no house numbers. I stopped the car, walked up to a prefab and shone my auriscope at the door. There was no obvious indication of where I might be but I noticed a deficiency in the paint on the door shaped like a 28. I returned to the car and drove slowly along, counting. Thirty, 32 . . . 44, 46. Once more clearly visible on the green of the door, in unpainted undercoat, was a number. Forty-six. I rang the bell. I rang it again and banged the knocker. A light went on and a head swathed in curlers poked out of the window.

'Piss off! You're not bloody well coming back in here drunk again!'

'I'm sorry, Mrs Broxwood. It's the doctor.'

'Mrs who?'

'I'm sorry. Isn't this number 46?'

'No, it isn't. Waking people up in the middle of the night!' She slammed the window.

As soon as I turned the next corner I saw a prefab wreathed in light. A woman in blue overalls stood outside.

'Are you the doctor?' she called.

'Yes.'

'Ah. Good.' She disappeared inside. I got out and walked up to the front door. It was clearly marked 25. The woman was smiling a welcome. A young man in the same blue overalls was sitting in the corner smoking and reading *Reveille*.

' This is 46 Dunkirk Road? You are Mrs Broxwood?'

'That's right.'

'But it says 25 on the door!'

'Oh yes. It would.'

'The Council changed the numbers,' said the young man. 'Something to do with the drains. They haven't brought the new ones round yet.'

'Oh . . . I see.' I didn't . . . 'I understand you haven't been well.'

The woman cackled with laughter. 'No. That's my son,

103

that is. It's the old man who's been poorly. He's in the bedroom.'

I followed her in through the door. Mr Broxwood lay on the bed in his dressing gown, busy with his football pools. Beside him on the chair was a set of overalls similar to those of his wife and son. He smiled when he saw me and stubbed out his cigarette. There was a smell of Dettol in the room and a wet patch on the carpet bore witness to his recent accident.

'Thank you for coming, Doc. I'm all right now, I think. Had a good clean out. Must have been that corned beef sandwich I ate earlier this evening. Tasted a bit manky.'

I examined him but there was nothing to find. Mrs Broxwood hovered around, smiling and bobbing her head.

'We've only just got back from work you see, Doctor. Night shift at Atkinsons . . . in Westhaven. We thought we would call you. Save troubling you at the surgery tomorrow morning.'

I crawled into bed at 4.15. I knew I wouldn't go back to sleep again and I waited for a further, inevitable, phone call. It didn't come.

'Did you have to get up again after the lady with the asthma?' asked Beth, without looking up from the paper.

I buttered my toast with some venom. 'Of course I did. Twice.'

'Oooohh. Gosh. I *am* sorry. I've been sleeping very heavily recently. It must be my hormones.'

It was amazing. I felt very hard done by. Why shouldn't she have suffered a little bit as well? And she'd got the paper first.

'It's dreadful,' she said, without looking up.

'What?' I snapped.

'The Berlin Wall. Poor devils are still trying to get over it. I shouldn't think it will be up very long. The world isn't a very safe place.' She turned over the page and as she leant over to pick up her coffee she looked up at me and smiled.

'I meant to tell you, darling. I met a man who knows you. Mr Pearce. In the butcher's. He works there. He said that he was in charge of the local Red Cross.'

'Oh yes?'

'They were all very impressed when you pretended to faint.'

'Oh . . . good.' It was time to go. Obviously I wasn't going to get a look at the paper even though Beth would have *all* day to read it.

'I'd better be going.'

'Right ho, love,' she said with a smile. Sarah sat on the floor in the corner, putting octagonal plastic bricks into octagonal plastic holes.

'See you later, then.' She seemed engrossed in some advertisements.

'Eh? Oh yes, darling. I'm sorry.'

She got up and came to the door with me. I kissed her cheek and walked down towards the Riley. Reaching the gate I turned.

'What did you mean about your hormones?'

'I'm pregnant.'

'You're what?'

'Pregnant. With child.'

'You didn't tell me.'

'You didn't ask.'

'How long?'

'I'm three weeks late at least.'

'I hadn't noticed.'

'You weren't complaining,' said Beth. 'Neither was I, if it comes to that. I'm sure I am but you can take a sample if you like.' She went out to the kitchen and returned with a neatly labelled specimen.

105

'But you haven't been sick.' She had been wretched the first time.

'No! And I haven't needed to take any sleeping tablets for a few weeks.'

That was unusual. She often needed to take something at night. Most recently she had been taking a relatively new hypnotic. Safe and non-toxic, it was said – thalidomide. As my Grandad used to say, 'The advertisements speak very highly of it.'

I put my arms around her. 'I do love you ... even though you don't get up in the night and make me a cup of tea when I've been called out.'

As I drove to work I thought that I would let the Bufo Bufo toad confirm Beth's change of status before saying anything to Harry. I was half happy, half apprehensive. Beth had had a really bad time with Sarah. In common with so many doctors' wives and nurses, everything had gone wrong. She'd had a prolonged labour and an exquisitely painful delivery.

In a woman of Beth's nature, of wit, intelligence and a great ability to cope, the resultant postnatal depression that plunged her into the abyss of black despair was as cruel as it was unforeseen. The months that followed were desperate. Apparently happy one minute, she would plummet the next into a state in which life became meaningless and pointless. I had often held Sarah in my arms as Beth lay immobilized by despair.

As the illness had gradually begun to pass away, so we were left with a feeling of mutual interdependence stronger than any that had existed before.

Harry had already started surgery when I arrived.

'Had a good night, old son?' he asked. I told him. 'That's a bit rough ... all justified.' I described my excursion to Dunkirk Road.

'Oh dear,' he chuckled. 'The Broxwoods. Remarkable

106

family. Strangest of lifestyles. They're all employed by the same factory in Westhaven, you know. Worked nights as long as I've known them. A peculiar shift. They finish at three in the morning, then the son goes out and helps with the local milk delivery. They have breakfast-cum-supper at eight and then they all go to bed. I've heard it said that they keep the same hours holidays and weekends. It must be like living on another planet . . . That was a bit rough, though. I'm sure they didn't mean to be so thoughtless, but if I were you . . .'

It was a very sensible idea and made me feel much better.

Harry gave me the visiting list. 'Mainly kids. And Alf Hawkins. Pop in to see that he's behaving himself . . . and here's a letter for you.' Postmarked Westhaven and dated the previous Monday. I opened it.

Dear Neville,
Winston told me he had seen you at the cricket match and what had happened and that you were working with Doctor Brinkly in Amblesham. I got the adress from the telephone book. Daves back and we are all very well. I'm writing to tell you that I did what you said and went and saw my doctor and he was very interested in what you said and did the same thing with the tuning fork. He says he is going to send me to a specilist to look at my ears. He looked at the letter I had from the army hospital that said nothing could be done for my ears and said it just shows you shouldnt always beleive what they tell you in hospital. I am very thankful to you and hope to see you again one day. My best regards to your wife and your little girl, Sarah isnt it.
Yours faithfully,
Walter (Jessop)

I showed the letter to Harry.

'He could be a friend for life, Neville. We work in a very privileged profession. Sometimes so little effort to get so much gratitude.' He smiled as he returned to it.

'Ah . . . and one more visit to put down, Harry. A woman phoned a few minutes before I left home. She asked me whether we could visit her father this morning and get him put in somewhere. Very irate she was. She said he was in an appalling state and that something ought to be done . . . hang on a minute. Yes, here we are.' I pulled a piece of paper from my jacket and handed it to Harry. 'She said the place was absolutely filthy and that he should be put somewhere he could be looked after properly.'

Harry thought for a moment. 'Of course. Old Charlie. It's time for his daughter's visit. Every time she comes she gets agitated about him. He lives by himself. Right out in the country. Perhaps you'll go and have a look at him.'

It was a bright windy day as I drove along the narrow road towards the Downs. In the distance I could see the huge figure of the Old Man of Wilmington etched in white on the green turf.

Charlie, Harry had admitted, was not the tidiest of men. He lived alone except for his old dog, Jake.

'He won't have the home help,' Harry had said. ' "Interfering busybodies," he says. Nor meals on wheels. "I could spit more'n they gives you." But he does eat well enough. I don't think he ever takes his clothes off, so he's unlikely to get hypothermia. He's a bit niffy but healthy enough in his way. For eighty-six, anyway. You see what you make of him.'

I found Charlie's home easily enough but was surprised to discover not the flint-faced cottage common to the area, but an old wooden bungalow in a state of obvious decrepitude. From the planking walls, the vestigial curling flakes of grey paint suggested that, once, it might have been painted white. I made my way through the tall grass and nettles and knocked on the front door. There was no reply. It didn't look as though it had been opened for a decade.

I walked round to the back. There was a loud crunch as I trod through an old frame hidden in the long grass. The porch outside the back door was stacked high with papers and piles of magazines – *Lilliputs* and *London Opinions* dating from the war, yellowed with age and weather. There were cardboard boxes full of precious rubbish which had never quite made it to the dustbin. Grimy, burnt-out electric light bulbs, saucepans and kettles with no handles or bottoms, tin cans, empty bottles with antique labels, bits of metal and wood, a shoe tree, two tennis racquets without strings.

The back door led directly into a large kitchen. An old man sat with his back to me. He was poring over a copy of the *Daily Mirror* with the aid of an enormous magnifying glass. The smoke coming from an ancient stove in the corner was matched by that from the massive pipe clamped between the old man's jaws. Beside him, on the floor, a large dog of mixed parentage snored loudly, head between paws. The atmosphere of the room suggested that neither Charlie nor his dog were entirely continent.

I cleared my throat. He turned with a start. 'Gor blimey! You made I jump!'

'I'm terribly sorry. I'm Doctor James from Doctor Brinckley's surgery.'

He brought his spectacles down from his forehead and inspected me closely.

'What are you doing here, then?'

The dog woke, yawned, and appeared to go back to sleep again.

'Your daughter phoned and . . .'

The old man clicked his tongue and shook his head in irritation. 'Daft ha'porth. You don't want to take no notice of her. I'm all right.'

He certainly looked healthy enough. But the kitchen, like the porch, was completely filled with rubbish – including the largest part of three veteran bicycles – and almost every available surface was covered with dirty crockery, food packets and opened cans. On the stove stood three or four saucepans half filled with unidentifiable substances of dubious age. About two feet in front of the old man's chair a large television stood on a packing case, the twin antennae of the indoor aerial making the whole contraption look like one of the new Russian satellites.

'Oh well. As you're here,' he said, pulling himself to his feet, 'you'd better have a cup of tea. Though I don't want anything from you.'

He cleared a space among the mouldering debris on the kitchen table and brought a brown china teapot over from the stove.

'It's good and hot,' and sweet and strong, I thought, as he poured the black liquid on to the generous blob of condensed milk waiting in the cup.

'It was just that your daughter . . .' he shook his head again, '. . . wondered whether you could do with a bit of help. Tidying up. You know.'

'No fear. I had that done afore. Couldn't find a dang thing afterwards.'

He sat down again in the chair with a sigh of relief, took a long noisy sip from a large mug and wiped his mouth on the sleeve of his cardigan.

'People put too much store by being tidy. When I was at Wipers – in the Great War you understand – there was these young fellers, just come up from the rear. Replacements. And weren't there some mud! By God, I could tell you! Horses disappeared into it. Wagons and all. Anyway, these lads started on about their uniforms getting spoiled. The sergeant, old Smithy that was, he said, "You don't want to worry about getting mucky. You'll be dead tomorrow!" And they were too.'

He laughed heartily, his pipe giving out great puffs of smoke. Then he was silent for a few moments, bending down to scratch the old dog's neck. Suddenly he looked up.

'There is one thing you *can* do for me, now I come to think of it. Doctor Brinckley give me some ointment for my 'emmeroids, my piles, you understand. It weren't no good for me at all but I used some on Jake here and do you know what . . .?'

Back to Amblesham. Harry had asked me to drop in and see Alf Hawkins, the newsagent. He had had no more pain since the coronary.

'When can I go back to work then, Doc?'

'Not for six weeks at least, I'm afraid.'

'Six weeks! Jesus Christ!'

'We'll manage all right, Alf,' said his wife. 'Did the specialist say anything to you, Doctor?'

Apparently, Alf's ECG had shown a typical anterior myocardial infarct. There was no treatment but rest.

'There *was* a definite heart attack, Mrs Hawkins. We've got to let it heal properly.'

Alf sighed and took a packet of Players from his bedside table.

'I suppose I *can* smoke, can't I?'

'I don't see why not, Alf,' I said, 'though some people are beginning to wonder whether smoking is good for your heart ... I wouldn't worry too much about it. The time to stop smoking is when you see doctors giving it up.'

'Not much chance of that by the looks of the ones

round about these parts,' laughed Mrs Hawkins. 'Look at Doctor Brinckley. What does he do with all that tobacco he buys? Eat it?' I didn't tell her that she was nearly right.

'There is one thing, though, Alf. If you don't mind me saying. You seem to have a good business. Do you have to live over the shop? Couldn't you live away from it, put in a manager some of the time?'

He thought for a moment. 'I suppose I could. We've often thought of getting a bungalow on the edge of town – but I'd be twiddling my thumbs if I didn't have enough to do.'

'You could take up . . . gardening.'

'There you are, Alf,' said Mrs Hawkins. 'That's what I'm always saying. You could get a greenhouse. You've always wanted one.'

'Emmmm.' Alf Hawkins lay back on his pillow and watched the smoke drift from the end of his cigarette.

'But mind you, Alf,' I said, 'I should expect to have the first cucumber.'

It was just coming up to 11 a.m., the time Harry had suggested, when I pulled up, once again, outside 46 Dunkirk Road. I banged on the door. There was no reply. I rang the bell and then kept my finger on it. Eventually, I heard a voice within.

'All right! I'm coming.'

The door opened a little and an extremely bleary Mr Broxwood Junior peered through the gap.

'What do you want?' he mumbled. It was the middle of the Broxwoods' night.

'Doctor James, Mr Broxwood,' I said brightly. 'I thought I'd better drop in to make sure your father was all right.'

'Oh. It's you, Doctor. You'd better come in . . . Mum!' he shouted. 'Mum! It's the doctor!'

Mrs Broxwood came out of the bedroom door tying

the belt around her dressing gown. She smiled wearily.

'Hallo, Mrs Broxwood. I thought I'd better drop by and see your husband to make sure that he had recovered completely. Is he better?'

'Oh much. Thank you, Doctor.'

'Still, I'd better make sure.'

I brushed past her into the bedroom. 'Good morning, Mr Broxwood,' I boomed. 'I'd like to have a look at you.'

He winced as I swept the curtains aside and let the sunlight pour into the room. It was a very thorough examination with much prodding and listening. By the time I had finished he was well and truly awake.

'Would you like a cup of tea, Doctor?'

I turned. It was Mrs Broxwood with a tray.

'Funny thing,' said Mr Broxwood, 'I was coming up to the surgery on Saturday for some physiotherapy Doctor Brinckley fixed up. He says I don't have enough exercise. I'm sure he's right. All I do at work is sit about.'

Home for lunch. Beef stew and dumplings, tinned peaches and rice pudding. I sank down into the ancient armchair in a gorged torpor. Half day. No more work until tomorrow morning. My previous night's calls on the Broxwoods and others were catching up with me.

I listened, half awake, while Beth told me about her morning. Phone calls to the estate agent, the local solicitor and the insurance broker for the mortgage. The house purchase should be through in double-quick time. We should be able to move into Sangster Road in two weeks. Harry had suggested that we use Ron as an accountant as soon as he was fit for work.

'And Sylvia's going to babysit for us tonight.'

I woke up. 'What?'

'Have a sleep this afternoon, then this evening you can take me to the pictures.'

'It's not bloodthirsty, is it?'

'I don't think so. *West Side Story* — You'll like that.'

There was a tiny cinema in Amblesham, the Movie-drome, that still opened its doors to minute audiences. It was said that Bingo would soon replace Bardot.

'That's nice of her — Sylvia.'

'She's seeing Ron every afternoon at the hospital. She likes to come round here. Not having any children of her own, I suppose. Any excuse to play with Sarah.'

I put my hand to my mouth. 'Pardon!'

'Are you all right?'

'I've eaten too much.'

'You'd better sleep it off.'

I put my feet up and looked at the paper. A quick survey of the world affairs before I dropped off again. Mainly about the Berlin Wall. On the sports page, 'Will Spurs do it again?' The League and Cup double. A small item about some fervent rock-and-roll fans in Liverpool, of all places. An article about the new contraceptive tablets of which there was much talk, how soon they would be generally available, when . . .

'Beth?'

'Yes,' from the kitchen.

'I was reading something in the paper and there's a damn great hole in it.'

'I expect that was Sarah. I got her some children's scissors at the shop this morning.'

It wasn't. The square was neat and symmetrical. It didn't matter anyway. I dozed off. I heard the telephone ring just before Beth picked it up.

'He's asleep at the moment. He is off duty actually. Oh . . . it's you, Mary . . . Yes . . . Yes . . . I'll get him.'

Mary was terribly sorry. Harry was at a confinement and couldn't be reached. There had been a call from the police. They wanted a doctor straightaway at an address on the outskirts of Amblesham.

'There must be a pig farm nearby,' I thought, as I approached the cottage at the end of the track. I knew I must be at the right place. Two police cars were parked outside. There was a strong smell of . . . putrefaction, I realized with horror.

As I stopped the car and got out, a young policeman appeared at the front door, his face white and shining with sweat. He vomited on the step. Griff Thomas appeared and steadied him with a hand on the shoulder.

'Neville . . . glad you could come. Unpleasant business, I'm afraid. I have to get you to confirm a death. Miss Thompson. She's a bit of a recluse and hasn't been seen for a week or two.' He wiped his nose with his handkerchief. Even here, outside, the smell was overpowering and nauseating. 'Insurance man who comes once a month found her. She must have felt the cold or something. She was in the kitchen with two electric fires full on. Big ones. Three bars each. It must have been 120°F in there and you can imagine . . .' He didn't have to say any more. He led me past two more ashen-faced policemen into the kitchen.

As soon as I had driven around the bend in the track and was out of view of the cottage, I stopped the car and opened the door. Just in time. Beth's lunch deserved better. I wiped my mouth with my handkerchief and took a few great breaths of fresh air.

Only the general shape and the stained clothes had borne any resemblance to a human being. There had been an awfulness on the floor under the chair. The abdomen, apparently, had ruptured when the young copper I had seen at the door had tried to move the body.

Griff had sent to the station for a body bag. He and the senior sergeant would package the remains.

'Can't expect the lads to do it,' he had said.

115

Leading from the front. Griff, the opening bat.

I was glad we were going out that evening. There was a little sweet shop near the cinema exactly like those I remember from my childhood. The window was filled with all manner of sweets, boxes of chocolate, pipes, lighters and small toys.

'We'll get some sweets,' I said.

A bell tinkled above the door as we pushed it open. A pleasant grey-haired lady smiled at us from behind the counter.

There were row upon row of sweetjars and boxes of all kinds of candy, fudge, chocolate brazils, nut brittle. Nut brittle!

'Nut brittle. Could we have some of that?'

'And Murray Mints, please,' added Beth, 'a quarter of each.'

The lady tipped the mints into the scales. They measured well over the quarter pound but she didn't take any notice.

'You're Doctor Neville James, aren't you?'

'Yes, that's right.'

'I thought so,' she smiled. 'I've seen you about the place. I think you know my son.'

'Oh yes?' I said with no obvious enthusiasm. I wasn't going to be drawn into any more problems that day.

'He told me that he thought it must be you.'

'Oh yes.' I was anxious to go. The film was due to start any minute. 'I've seen him at the surgery, have I . . .?'

'Oh no,' she laughed. 'He's a doctor. He wasn't at your medical school but he used to live in the same university residence as you. About five rooms away, he said. I'm sure you'd remember him . . .'

'What a nice lady,' said Beth, as we fumbled our way through the darkness to find our seats. 'It certainly is a small world!'

'It certainly is,' I mumbled through a mouthful of peanut

brittle. Long before anyone met a girl called Maria I was fast asleep.

'There's a phone call for you, Doctor,' said Mary, as soon as I arrived at the surgery the next morning. '. . . Inspector Thomas, I think.' It was about the old lady. Further investigation of the cottage had revealed a cupboard full of tablets. Bottle upon bottle. All exactly the same.

'Thyroid extract. That's what the chemist says they are, Neville.'

Griff went on to explain. It transpired that Miss Thompson apparently had had a private doctor in Westhaven. He sent her a prescription every month but she discouraged him from visiting her.

'Apparently she always got the pills, but never took them. Funny that.'

Of course! Myxoedema! The old lady had suffered from a failing thyroid gland. Her whole system would have slowed up. No doubt, if she hadn't taken her pills, she would have had the dry skin, the coarse hair, the constipation, the increasing mental confusion that accompanies thyroid deficiency. And the feeling of always being cold. That would have explained the electric fires.

'Does anybody know why she didn't take them, Griff? She'd have been as well as you or I if she had.'

'Oh. Some religious sect or something a friend had persuaded her to join. Said that medicines were evil. Against the will of God.'

There was a dearth of patients that morning but one I would have good cause to remember. I had never met the man before but as soon as he entered the consulting room, hands clutching his doffed flat hat, bowing and exuding the most obsequious of smiles, I had a feeling who it might be.

'Doctor James. I'm Mr Littlebone, Doctor. It's such a pleasure to meet you.' He offered me a limp hand, but his

117

piercing blue eyes, tiny behind thick bottle-bottom lenses, were unblinking. I looked at his medical card: 'Plantagenet Peregrine Littlebone.'

'Sit down, please, Mr Littlebone.'

'Thank you, Doctor. But I'd rather stand. The knees you know.' He lifted his leg stiffly and winced.

Placing his cap on the desk he consulted a list he had in his hand. 'I don't like to trouble you, Doctor, but I'd be most grateful if you could let me have my sustificate, one hundred sleeping tablets for me, six crepe bandages, two hundred codeine for Mrs Littlebone, some bowel medicine for the baby and a very large bottle of cough medicine – our last doctor always gave us three. You can leave out the sustificate for me in future. I'll just send one of my boys to pick it up . . . thank you, Doctor.'

That was it. Immediately all my senses went into action. The pulse quickened. I wasn't going to have any of this . . .

'Mr Littlebone, I . . .'

'Just two more little things. I want a letter for the Welfare. Extra eggs. They was prescribed. I get a special allowance. And a new . . . support. I don't think the old one works like it used to.'

I leant forward. 'I think I'd better look at your . . . your . . . rupture, Mr Littlebone.'

There was some delay as Mr Littlebone undid first his large leather belt and then his braces. The truss, I discovered, appeared to be ex-army surplus from the Crimean War, projecting outwards in such a way as to make no contact whatsoever with the hernial orifices. Neither did it need to. There was no sign of any herniae.

'There must be,' he protested. 'The army doctor said I was ruptured. Failed me on my call-up medical. Heartbroken, I was.'

Nor was there anything in his notes about them. Perhaps the medical officer at the conscription board had decided that the Allied cause might be better served if Private Littlebone did not join the crusade against Fascism. He had attended many doctors since, all well intentioned. But the thick wadge of letters, cards and notes showed that every time an attempt had been made to get him back to work he had lost the job on the first day, or not turned up, or broken the shop window with a ladder, or driven the delivery van into a ditch. Whatever, he was always sacked within an hour or two. It had been found easier for all concerned to designate him as 'unemployable'. As far as he was concerned there was no way in which he would earn as much money as the State would pay him for not working.

' "Arfritis of the knees" my old doctor used to put,' he said, as he saw me pause at that part of the certificate that noted the causes of incapacity. 'Can't bend them an inch. They're all seized up.'

I made the certificate out for a week, determined that I'd get him back to work. I also wrote a note stating. 'This man has been advised that he needs more eggs'. I couldn't yet afford to reglaze the waiting room. In all fairness, if he insisted on wearing a truss, he could do with a new one. As he walked, stiff-legged, out of the surgery, his trousers projected like a man with two erections.

I looked down. He had left his cap on the desk. I ran to the waiting-room door. Too late. He had gone. I could see him in the distance pedalling vigorously up the hill on his bicycle.

Though I wasn't on duty, I thought I should go up to Harry's surgery to see how he ran his physiotherapy session.

As soon as I turned into the forecourt I found the 'class'

hard at it. About fifteen men, including Mr Broxwood and the lugubrious Arthur of the multiple pains, were attacking the drive with pick and shovel, breaking up the loose surface and filling in the holes.

'That's the way, Arthur,' encouraged Harry. 'Put your shoulders into it. Exercise. That's what you need. Good healthy exercise. Builds up the muscles.'

He saw me and grinned.

'Ah, Neville. What do you think of it? With a little luck we'll get it all done this morning. The vicar should be here with Agnes any moment.'

While I was still trying to picture some unimaginably muscle-bound, female parishioner, there was a loud squeaking and rumbling from the front gate. Albert and the geese retreated to a respectable distance as the Reverend Smarte came into view. Beside him, coat shining like ebony, harness decorated with gleaming horse brasses, a magnificent black shire pulled a large roller with no apparent effort.

'Agnes!' said Harry, with admiration. 'Isn't she a beauty, Neville? We wouldn't have got the roller up from the cricket field without her . . .'

'Bill,' he called, 'thank you so much. Let me introduce you to Neville James.'

The roller was unhitched and manhandled into position by Harry's physiotherapy class who began to flatten down their handiwork. Agnes clopped off into the orchard to crop the grass and have a well-earned rest.

'Has Agnes won much this year, Bill?'

'Not really, Harry. Haven't had much time.'

'Our vicar,' explained Harry, 'is probably the best ploughman hereabouts. It is said that not a small number of his flock have a few bob on him when there is a ploughing competition locally.'

'Only for the church funds,' grinned the Reverend.

Mid-morning, a lorry arrived with a load of tarmac. The driver, a swarthy man, supervised his two assistants – wife and mother-in-law, apparently – as they helped spread it on the ground with large rakes.

By 1.30 p.m. Harry had a new drive. Physiotherapy was over.

'Now for your medicine, gentlemen.'

As the sweating back-sufferers handed in their tools, each was presented with a large bottle of Newcastle Brown ale.

'Doctor James?' I turned. It was Mr Broxwood. 'I'm glad you were here. I've got a little something for you. Just a minute.'

He went over to a bicycle propped up against the surgery wall and took a packet out of the saddle bag.

'I hope you and Mrs James like them. They're Mrs Broxwood's favourite chocolates. In appreciation for all your concern, Doctor – coming to see me again like that the next day. We thought that was very nice of you. Mrs Broxwood said that was really caring, that was.'

They stuck in my throat – and it served me right.

Chapter Seven

'Congratulations, my dear,' said Harry. 'When's the happy event?'

'Early May.'

'That's splendid! I think we should all raise our glasses.' The mother-to-be beamed with pleasure.

'To Helen . . . and her happiness in the future.'

'To Helen,' we echoed.

The sadness in Beth's eyes did not betray her smile as she turned and chatted to Helen's husband, Jim Grastick, our rota partner and fellow dinner guest at Harry's table. Beth had miscarried three weeks before – two days after the laying of Harry's drive and the same morning on which the postman brought the letter from the pathology lab. confirming her pregnancy. In the event, Harry had never been told. Beth appeared to shrug it off.

'Nothing more than a heavy period,' she said. 'Not worth making a fuss about.' But when I came back home that evening her eyes were red.

As it happened there was not too much time to dwell on it. Within a week we heard from our newly acquired solicitor that we could move into Sangster Road. The vendors were happy for us to take possession even before the paperwork was finalized. We bought an old bed and wardrobe for seven pounds through an ad. in a shop window. We blew the bulk of our remaining capital in a Westhaven department store on a square of green Wilton carpet, especially designed to show up everything a toddler might spill on it, and a hideous three-piece suite, all uncut moquette and spindly legs, which I had persuaded Beth, against her better judgement, was the height of fashion.

We arranged to move in the next Thursday afternoon. I had surgery at Harry's in the morning, while Beth went round to the estate agent's to get the keys, open up, and check that the gas, electricity and telephone were all connected.

As we chugged into the drive Millie appeared from next door carrying a large package.

'Welcome, my dears.' She kissed us both. 'A little housewarming present for you. Unfortunately we didn't have room for it any more.' She smiled invitingly. 'You can open it now if you like.' She went to the car, opened the back door and made cooing noises at Sarah.

'It's only got one eye,' whispered Beth, as we stared down at the stuffed head, dust drifting down on to our shoes like dandruff. Millie appeared again.

'A particularly fine specimen of leopard. Great Uncle Walter shot it in Kenya. There's an eye missing, of course. Soames did try putting a marble in the socket but it didn't look quite right. I'm sure that the next time you happen to be passing a taxidermist he would be able to accommodate you.'

Beth examined the mangy relic with admiration. 'It's beautiful, Millie. We've never owned anything like this before.'

A tooth fell out of the open jaws and landed on the gravel drive. Millie tutted and picked it up.

'It's the thought that counts,' she said. 'I know he's gone to a good home.' Apologizing that she had to attend to Soames's toenails, she disappeared from view.

'You go straight through to the kitchen, love,' said Beth. 'There's a kettle there. Make us a cup of tea. I'll bring in Sarah.'

I thought I was dreaming. Above the hiss of the kettle I could hear a treble voice singing 'Once in Royal David's

123

City'. It was getting louder and was coming from the lounge. Beth was waiting for me as I came in. So were the rest of King's College, Cambridge, choir.

'Happy Birthday, darling.'

A stereo hi-fi! No little boy had yearned for a train set more. Two huge speakers stood on the bare floorboards on either side of the fireplace. Against the far wall a transcription turntable rotated silently. Expensively.

'How . . . where did you . . .?' Stereos were the latest thing. This must be one of the new special records. 'We can't afford it. There are so many things we need. You need. The kitchen. All kinds of things.'

'You can get those for me later. When you're rich and famous.'

I went and fiddled with the knobs. The whole room reverberated to the college organ.

'Where on earth did you get it?'

'A shop in Westhaven. A special offer. I saw an advert in the local paper.'

'And Sarah cut it out for you in a very neat square.'

'That's right. She's a very clever girl.'

'You're very quiet, Neville.' Harry had the bottle of claret poised above my glass.

I looked up. Beth and Helen had left the table. To help in the kitchen presumably. 'Oh, yes. Thank you, Harry . . . I'm sorry, I was deep in thought.'

Harry filled the glass to the brim. 'Jim was asking whether you had seen any more of your friend recently?'

'Mr Littlebone,' explained Jim Grastick. 'He was allocated to me a year or two back. Left my list because I wouldn't recommend him for an invalid car. Been to two or three other practices since then.'

I was able to tell them that he had been my very first patient on my first day's morning surgery at Sangster Road.

News travelled fast. He headed a queue of a dozen or so people stretching down the path when I opened the door.

'Nice place you've got here, Doctor,' he said. It was. What had been a granny flat for the previous occupant's housekeeper had been turned into a waiting room and office, the organ room was now my consulting room.

'Yes it is, isn't it. I'm glad you like it.'

Mr Littlebone plunged his mittened hand into the capacious pocket of his duffle coat and produced a large printed form.

'I want a letter from you to get me one of these,' he said, smoothing the piece of paper on my desk. It was an application for a free bus pass — for disabled war veterans. How on earth? 'Because,' he pointed to the relevant paragraph, 'it says in this section here that if you were on active service, and you're still ill from it now, you are entitled to free local travel.'

'But you weren't called up,' I protested.

'I was in the Home Guard.'

'But you weren't disabled in the war. Your knees. That trouble only came on a couple of months ago, didn't it?' ... Following a threatening letter from the Labour Exchange, I could have added. I knew his notes like the back of my hand.

He thought for a moment.

'I got a weak chest from all that standing in the rain. Guarding things. Bronickal!' He thumped the middle of his chest, a blow muffled by half a dozen assorted vests. A great rolling cough started somewhere in the region of his navel. 'Bronickal!'

'That's only because you smoke so much,' I protested. 'It's nothing to do with the war.'

'If you say so, Doctor. If you say so.' His eyes gleamed menacingly behind the thick lenses. 'But we shall have to see!' So saying, he swept out.

A second or two later his face appeared around the door. Smiling politely. 'I believe you've got my hat.'

'Have you heard any more about it?' asked Jim.

'Last week. A letter from one of the local councillors. "Dear Doctor James," it says. "I am very disturbed to hear that you feel unable to help an old soldier who has done his bit for his country . . ." It goes on about patriotism and not being aware of the debt that we all owe our nation's heroes.'

'An auspicious start,' said Harry.

'And that wasn't the end of it,' I added. 'The next person in was Mrs Anderson. Does the flowers at St Mark's Church.'

'Old man's a director of the big coal merchants in Westhaven,' said Harry. 'Rotarian. A bit up market.'

'That's the one. She was telling me about something or other when all of a sudden she went sort of . . . glazed.'

'She had a coronary,' said Jim, 'and you gave her immediate resuscitation. You saved her life and you're going to get a free lifetime's supply of nutty slack.'

'Not exactly. She was staring over my shoulder at something. I turned around. It was Sarah. She was just outside the French windows.'

'Looking in?' asked Helen, sitting down again.

'She was. Yes. She was obviously very interested in what was going on. Unfortunately she'd brought her pot with her and she was busy performing. Apparently Beth had left her in the kitchen.'

'And I suppose Sarah had decided to look for a more interesting setting.'

'Or sitting,' chuckled Jim. 'Beats taking the *Telegraph* crossword in with you.'

A delightful man, Jim. Thirty-four – ten years older than me. A boyish face, always smiling. But very shrewd. And a

126

great raconteur. He rekindled his cigar in the candle flame.

'I had a funny experience last week,' he said. 'This man came in to see me. "Doctor," he said, "I've got a problem. You see, I have the crabs." '

'Oh Jim,' said Helen. 'You can't tell that one, it's disgusting ... It's a joke,' she explained. 'This patient of Jim's. Every time he comes in he tells him a new one.'

Jim did tell it, however. It was very crude. And very funny.

We sat laughing and talking around the circular table, the candlelight sparkling off the cut glass and the silver coffeepot. Beth helped Mary clear the table.

'We'll have to be going, Harry,' I apologized. 'Babysitter ... can't keep Sylvia up too late. Ron comes back from the convalescent home tomorrow.'

'I hear he's bursting to get back to work again.'

'Can be a dangerous game. Cricket.' said Jim. 'Mind you, Ron Godden could have sustained the same kind of injury falling over in the garden. But it's not unknown to get a fractured skull. It's a hard ball.'

Helen shook her head. 'I can't understand why cricketers don't wear more protection. Particularly on their heads. Like motorcyclists. Some kind of helmet.'

Harry sucked in his breath. 'Oooh. They'll never do that. Not manly.'

He looked at us all.

'. . . But can't you stay a little longer? It's early.'

Helen touched his arm. 'I'm afraid we'll have to go as well, Harry . . . but before we do, how about a tune?'

Harry beamed with pleasure and went over to the piano and picked up his descant recorder.

'Just a little something then. A new Irish jig I've just learnt. And a dance. Thomas Arne.'

I had forgotten all about his musicianship. He bobbed and weaved and the sweet noise filled the room. Not a wrong note. The melody was crisp and clear. He finished with a flourish.

'Bravo,' we called. He smiled. Face flushed, he leant over and took Beth's arm.

'Now come on, Beth, a song from you.'

Beth looked flustered. 'No, honestly, Harry.'

'I insist,' said Harry. 'I know that you *can* sing, Neville told me.'

Beth glared at me. He was right, she could sing, but he didn't know how well. Harry stood Beth beside the piano and sat down to play.

'What's it to be?' he said, opening a songbook.

'Oh, I don't know, Harry. You choose.'

The book seemed to fall open at a familiar page. Harry hesitated a moment.

'This one. I'd rather like you to sing this one.'

I have heard Beth sing 'My Love is Like a Red, Red Rose' many times over the past thirty years but never with the beauty and poignancy that she did that evening. As she reached 'and I will come again my luve tho' it were ten thousand mile', Harry turned and looked at her with eyes misty from some memory that time had never diminished. He was silent for a moment when she finished, then he cleared his throat.

'Beth, my dear,' he said, 'you shouldn't do things like that to an old man.'

The new patient sat silent as I filled in the medical card.

'And you've just moved into the area?'

'Yes, sir. That's right.' A softer, West Country accent.

A young man with a mop of black hair, he was built like an ox. His bulging neck threatened to burst open his starched white collar and send the stud screaming past my ear like a piece of shrapnel.

'What can I do for you?'

'Well, sir. I . . .' He blushed deeply and his hands nervously patted the tops of his thighs. 'Well, sir, I . . . you see . . .'

The phone rang. 'Have you finished surgery yet, Neville?' It was Harry.

'Seeing the last patient now, Harry.' I smiled apologetically at my new patient. He shook his head vigorously.

'Hang on, Harry.'

'There are two more ladies,' whispered the young man, pointing to the waiting room.

'Nearly finished, Harry. A couple more.' Morning surgery had gone on longer than expected. 'Super dinner party last night. Beth and I really enjoyed ourselves.'

'Glad you did. Mary did us proud. By the way – you haven't forgotten about tomorrow night? You can cover me for an hour or so? I've got to go and pick her up from Brighton after her family visit.'

'That will be fine, Harry.'

'Anything exciting this morning, Neville?'

'Nothing at all. All coughs and colds. Very ordinary.'

'That's not always a bad thing,' said Harry. 'Anyway, why I really called – all the visits seem to have come in at this end today. Can you take two or three?'

'Of course.'

'There's one in Sangster Road, so you can certainly do that. One hundred and three. Mrs Portridge. Nasty chest, she says. I expect she has. Nice lady, but she smokes like a chimney. And a family called Russell at 32 Tobruk Terrace. All the kids have measles by the sound of it. And one more. You'd better do that first. New patient – at Greenways. Pretty little Georgian house nearly next door to the cricket pavilion.'

'I know it.'

'Better be on your best behaviour . . . it's another doctor.'

'A GP?'

'No. A medical missionary. Recently retired. Doctor Felicity Basingstoke. Her companion called. Seemed a bit upset. Says the good lady's a diabetic and could someone go round fairly soon. I'm a bit tied up at the moment with some insurance medicals . . .'

'Sure. I'll go round there in a few minutes. See you later, Harry.'

I picked up the medical card again. 'I'm so sorry, Mr . . . er . . . You were saying.'

'I've got a pain my ovary, Doctor,' he blurted out.

'I can't quite . . . you've what?'

His courage had almost deserted him. 'A pain in the ovary. The left one.' He pointed gingerly at his flies as though that which was behind them was about to explode.

He had got a tender swelling in the left side of his scrotum involving the testicle and the surrounding tissues. A typical epididymo-orchitis. I looked at his face – there was no sign of mumps.

'You've got an infection.'

'God almighty! My mother'll kill me! I haven't done nothing wrong.'

'No. no. Not anything like that. This kind of infection you can just . . . get. You don't have to catch it from anybody.'

He relaxed visibly.

'I've always had a weakness that side, Doctor. It always hangs kind of funny, like. Heavier. Lower down than the other one.'

'It does in everybody . . . Well, in men, anyway.' Clutching his prescription for tetracycline, painkillers and a scrotal suspensory bandage, he ushered in the people who had been waiting. A middle-aged woman with a child in a pushchair. And a younger woman.

'I'm sorry we're late, Doctor. I'm Mrs Farmer. I think

130

you know my son Alan. He opens the bowling for the cricket team.' I remembered the two lanky youths but not one in particular. 'And this is my daughter Christine – Christine Woods – and her little boy . . .' She smiled down at the chubby toddler in the pushchair '. . . Richard. Christine and Richard live with us for the time being.'

I smiled a welcome. 'Please sit down.'

Mrs Farmer offered the chair to her daughter who appeared to accept it gratefully. I fetched another seat from the waiting room.

'Christine is the patient, Doctor. She hasn't been at all well. I've made her come up to see you.'

A beautiful fawn like creature with high cheekbones and startling blue eyes. But terribly pale. I knew I had seen her before.

'I think we must have met at some time.' I said. 'I'm sure I recognize you.'

'No. I don't think we have,' replied the young woman.

'I expect you saw her on the front of last week's local paper, Doctor. A lovely big picture.'

'Of course.' I remembered the story. She had won a national art competition. Her husband was in the navy. The merchant navy, that was it. She'd taken up painting. Very successfully. 'You're an artist, Christine.'

'Not really.' She looked slightly embarrassed. 'Only as a hobby.'

'She's wonderful,' said her mother. 'But she's been doing too much of it, I think, Doctor. She's got over-tired.'

The young woman sucked her teeth with irritation. 'I haven't, Mum.'

'Her husband comes home on leave the week after next. She wants to be well then. I wonder whether she could have a tonic or something?'

She certainly didn't look at all well.

'Anything wrong in particular, Christine? Pain anywhere? Cough? Trouble with your waterworks?'

'Not really. But I feel so tired . . . lethargic. And I seem to be coming out in a lot of bruises.' She confirmed this by rolling up the sleeves of her cardigan. I indicated towards the examination couch, still catalogue new. She hesitated a moment. 'And I've noticed that my mouth and tongue are a bit sore.'

'Open wide.' I shone my torch. There were haemorrhagic spots on her tongue and palate. I had never seen anything quite like it before but it felt as though a cold draught had suddenly come into the room. Above her open mouth her eyes scanned my face for some kind of reaction. I remained impassive. She had obviously seen the lesions herself.

'Hhhmmm. We'll check your tummy and your chest.'

There was nothing to find. No enlargement of the liver, or spleen. No glands. But I still had a feeling of foreboding. She took her place again by her mother.

'Christine. I'd like you to have some blood tests. I'll give you a note for the pathology lab. at Westhaven General. You'll have to get them done there.'

I turned to her mother. 'Have you got any transport, Mrs Farmer?'

She bit her lip. 'My husband has. He's at work, but I'm sure he'd come home straightaway if I rang him.'

I could see that she was twisting the cotton gloves she held in her hand. Working up to it. 'Please don't ask me,' I thought, 'because I won't know what to say.' But inevitably, she did.

'It's nothing serious, is it, Doctor?'

I smiled broadly, reassuringly. Christine was watching my eyes.

'Oh. I'm sure . . . well, er . . . like you say, we must have Christine sorted out for when her husband . . .' I hesitated.

132

'David.'

'When David comes home.'

Suitably unreassured, the nice lady and her lovely, gifted daughter left the surgery. I picked up the phone to ring the path. lab.

'Would you like a cup of coffee, darling?' Beth poked her head through the French windows.

'I'm sorry, love. I've got to go straight out on a visit. A diabetic. I'll see you later.'

'Oh ... all right. Take care.' As she disappeared I could tell she was disappointed. She had been very quiet when we got home from the dinner party. Come to that, she had not had much to say for several days. I would have liked to have spent a few minutes with her, but if I had learnt anything about general practice it was that one's family had to come a very poor second.

As I pulled up outside Greenways a worried-looking, grey-haired little lady was waiting on the pavement.

'Are you the doctor?' she asked anxiously.

'Yes ... Mrs ...?'

'Miss Rutherford. I'm Doctor Basingstoke's companion.'

'Right.' I strode towards the front door.

'You can't get in the front door,' she said. I changed direction and made for the back. She puffed after me. 'Doctor!'

I tried the back door. That, too, was bolted.

'I was trying to tell you, Doctor. She's locked me out.'

From within the house I could hear the sound of crashing and breaking glass. Miss Rutherford wrung her hands.

'There is no way I can get in. She says she'll kill me if I try!' The poor lady burst into tears and I took her by the arm and sat her on a low wall. 'You'll have to do something, Doctor. We nearly lost her the last time this happened.'

She explained. Dr Basingstoke was, indeed, a diabetic.

Though regular and meticulous with her insulin injections, she tended to be rather forgetful about eating. Engaged as she was in writing her memoirs, she often missed a meal altogether, and consequently her blood sugar fell to dangerously low levels.

Sometimes, what followed was even more unfortunate. In most people this state of low blood sugar, hypoglycaemia, makes them feel unwell, sweaty, anxious, shaky and can progress into a coma, even death, unless someone gives them sugar by mouth. Or, if they have become unconscious, by intravenous injection. Once the sugar is taken, recovery is rapid. In a few unlucky patients, however, the hypoglycaemic state can see the emergence of a Mr . . . or Mrs, Hyde character. Unmanageable, hostile, violent.

Dr Basingstoke was, obviously, one of these. I had to get some sugar into her. Persuade her to eat some before she fell into a coma. In the circumstances an intravenous injection of glucose was out of the question. What was needed was a vet with a tranquillizer gun, but it was unlikely that any animal practitioner in Amblesham had dealt with an angry rhinoceros.

I went to the back door again. There was a small letterbox. I pushed it open and knelt beside it.

'Doctor Basingstoke,' I shouted through the opening. 'Doctor Basingstoke? I wondered if I might have a word with you. Miss Rutherford says . . .'

There was a crash of breaking glass and a hand holding a saucepan appeared through the shattered window beside me. I hopped back. Through the broken glass I could see a pale, sweating face staring at me, eyes black with hatred.

'Excuse me, I . . .'

'Bugger off. Leave me alone – or I'll bloody kill you!' The face disappeared.

'You must eat some sugar!' I shouted through the letter-box again, but retreated when I heard crockery breaking against the inside of the door.

I could have let her go into a coma and then rushed in to give her an injection, had Miss Rutherford not said that the last time things were allowed to go that far Dr Basingstoke developed a cardiac irregularity and nearly perished.

I remembered the advice given by a lecturer at medical school. 'There is nobody in the world so disturbed that they cannot be calmed down with a syringe full of an appropriate sedative — as long as you have eight large ambulancemen, two to each limb, to hold them down.'

I looked at Miss Rutherford. 'I'll have to get the police to break down the door. And the ambulance. And, I suppose . . .' I didn't know the niceties of the law. 'I suppose I ought to get the Duly Authorized Officer. To certify her, if necessary.'

'Oh no,' said Miss Rutherford. 'You can't do that. She's not mental!'

'She is at the moment! Well, she's certainly not a voluntary patient, anyway.'

I used the phone next door. The police were the first to arrive. Then the ambulance. The DAO turned up in her yellow Triumph Herald. She had been visiting a problem family in the middle of Amblesham and had only been a few minutes away.

'Don't be ridiculous! I can't certify a diabetic like that. She's not insane.'

We ducked as a potted palm came crashing through the front window. I marshalled my little task force. We moved towards the front of the house. The police were poised, ready to kick down the front door, when suddenly it swung open.

Magnificent in her twin set and pearls, her mighty bosom heaving with emotion, the medical missionary stood on the threshold. Her eyes bored into us with loathing and contempt.

'Right . . . you *bastards*!' she spat out and delved into the pocket of her tweed skirt. We all took several steps back.

'RIGHT!' She pulled out a handful of sugar lumps, stuffed them into her mouth and munched ferociously.

Within the next half hour, we were all sitting in the elegant, though somewhat disorganized, drawing room, sipping tea from a motley collection of cups, survivors of the assault on the crockery. A short while before, one would not have recognized the quiet, gentle, polite professional lady who now sat beside me. She looked nine inches shorter and half as wide.

'It seems that I have been a little difficult. I do apologize.'

I noticed a text on the wall. 'Blessed are the meek: for they shall inherit the earth.'

The other two calls were not quite in the same league of drama. Back for lunch. I bounded into the house full of myself.

'Beth! Beth!' I called. 'I've had the most extraordinary morning, I . . . really, I didn't know what to do, I . . .'

She came down the stairs.

'The path. lab. rang.'

Oh God! Christine Woods. I'd forgotten all about her.

'What did they say?'

'They just said it was urgent and could you ring as soon as possible.'

When I put the phone down, Beth came and sat beside me.

'Bad news?'

'It doesn't sound at all good. It was about a young woman I saw this morning. The lab. says she's very low on all her blood cells. A pancytopenia. They think she's got aplastic anaemia. They'll have to do more tests. Look

136

at the bone marrow. It's a pretty rare condition. And very nasty.' I gestured hopelessly.

'Oh dear. I am sorry. What on earth can have caused that?'

'Probably nobody will ever know. Chemicals, poisons, medicines even. They can do it. But as often as not there's no known cause that anybody can find. It just comes out of the blue.'

'What can they do for her then?'

'Not a great deal. It can develop very rapidly. The bone marrow stops working, and nobody can live without their bone marrow. They'll just try and catch up with it – transfusions, drugs, steroids, that kind of thing – and then hold on. Hoping that it will resolve itself. It does sometimes.'

'And if it doesn't? What will happen to her?'

'She'll die . . . It's so unfair. She's a talented girl.'

Beth looked up. 'I don't suppose her family would love her any the less if she wasn't.'

'I shall have to go and tell them. The hospital want her in this afternoon. They're afraid she might have some kind of bleed. They said that they'll arrange to contact the husband. He's away at sea.'

'Are you going to have a bit of lunch first? It's ready.'

'No, I couldn't. I'm sorry.'

The Farmers, with Christine, her husband and Richard lived in a neat little detached house, bright with fresh paint and fronted by a tidy geometric garden. Mrs Farmer had heard the Riley stop outside and was waiting on the front doorstep.

'Hallo, Doctor James.' The moment she saw my face she knew that something was desperately wrong.

'Hallo, Mrs Farmer.'

Mrs Farmer stayed on the doorstep. 'Before you come in, Doctor, tell me. Is it anything serious?'

'Well, yes . . . er, I'm afraid . . . quite likely . . . very serious. Christine has to go into hospital this afternoon.'

She took one long sobbing breath, squeezed her eyes shut and put her hand across them. Almost immediately she had recovered.

'You'd better come in, Doctor. She's down the garden. I'll call her.'

I sat down by the tiled fireplace in which a newly laid fire hissed and crackled behind a large, child-proof guard. Richard played on the floor surrounded by plastic cars and lorries. There was a picture of him as a baby on the mantelpiece. And a wedding photograph of Christine and her sailor husband. Between the two gilt frames stood a black-and-white snapshot of a soldier, in army battledress with sergeant's stripes, smiling at a young Mrs Farmer, hair piled high on her head. In her arms she held her little daughter.

But most striking of all were the extraordinarily delicate watercolours that decorated the walls. A young girl walking through a field of barley. Two small children picking poppies. A boy sitting on a beach throwing pebbles into the water. All signed 'C. Woods'.

'Christine,' I heard Mrs Farmer call. 'Doctor James has come to see you.'

She knew. I could tell as soon as she came into the room. Her mother smiled at her. 'The doctor says that it would be better if you went into hospital for a few days. To have some more tests. To get you properly well.'

She was very composed. 'Really? When?'

'This afternoon,' I said.

'Yes. This afternoon,' said Mrs Farmer. 'We want to get things cleared up as soon as possible, don't we? I'll look after Richard. Don't you worry.'

The young woman turned towards me. 'Thank you for coming round to let me know, Doctor. You must be very busy ... Do they ... do they have any idea

138

what it might be?' Her mother was watching me closely.

'That's what the tests are for,' I said cheerfully. 'They'll decide when they've done some more tests. They'll soon sort you out.' I had funked it completely.

'Don't worry, dear,' said her mother, smiling. 'You could do with a nice rest. Couldn't she, Doctor?' I nodded my head. 'We'll have a cup of tea, and then I'll phone up your Dad's work and get him to run you into hospital.'

As I drove away I knew that it had all been a charade. A charade in which they had both participated to spare me the pain of breaking bad news.

'Be with you in a minute, Neville,' said Harry. 'We're nearly finished, aren't we, old son?'

The little boy was just holding back the tears as Harry put in another stitch. The point of the curved needle disappeared into the skin on one side of the wound and reappeared out of the other. The child did not flinch.

'Good boy.' Harry had obviously used plenty of local anaesthetic. Gently, he pulled through the skin the needle, and all but an inch or two of the fine black silk thread that followed it. The sides of the wound were brought together and, having tied a knot, Harry snipped the silk close to the skin.

'I like this, Neville. See – the silk is joined to the needle, flush. No eye. You can only use them once. They're pre-packed, sterilized. Cost us a few bob but you get a much better result . . . Just one more, Nicholas.'

He pushed in the needle once more.

'Last time, Nicholas. My goodness me! You *are* a brave little boy. Isn't he, Mummy?'

The pleasant young woman in the blood-spattered trench coat smiled proudly.

'There we are. That's it.' He turned to the woman again.

'We'll take out the stitches next Friday . . . that won't hurt at all,' he added for the benefit of the little boy who was getting down from his mother's lap. Harry turned to me.

'Did it down at the recreation ground by the swings. Dangerous blooming things.'

The young woman cleared her throat. 'Will there be a scar, Doctor?'

'Of course,' said Harry, 'you can't avoid it.' The neat row of stitches ran for about an inch or so just above the right eyebrow. 'Not a bad one, though, so don't worry. All the heroes in books seem to have a scar. That spy chap everybody's reading, Secret Service . . .?'

'James Bond,' I volunteered.

'That's the one. He's got a scar as I remember. Or so the book said. Doesn't seem to stop him doing . . . whatever it is he wants to be doing.'

The young woman smiled. Harry reached for the sweet-jar.

'Two, I think. Yes, two. That was definitely a two-sweet operation.' The little boy plunged his hand eagerly into the jar. 'And,' said Harry, reaching into his trouser pocket, 'because you have been quite the bravest young man I have seen this month . . .'

The little boy left the surgery clutching the bright new shilling as though it were the Victoria Cross.

We went into the lounge. Harry took his pipe from the mantelpiece and sat down. Albert padded in and stretched himself across his master's feet. Harry scratched the old dog's flanks absent-mindedly as I told him about Christine Woods.

'So?' he said, when I had finished.

'I don't understand, Harry,' I said. 'So what?'

'So, what did you do wrong?'

'I completely fudged the issue . . . well, I certainly wasn't very frank.'

140

'You were frank enough. Do you know for sure what the exact diagnosis is?'

'Well. Not yet. For sure.'

'And they're doing more tests?'

'Yes.'

'Fair enough, then. Does the mother not think it's anything serious?'

'On the contrary – though I didn't really have a chance to tell her exactly what they thought.'

'There you are then! They're good honest people, the Farmers. Salt of the earth. They know that everybody will do the best they possibly can. The hospital doctors will tell them, and Christine, when they're absolutely certain. A day or two will make no difference.'

'I suppose not.'

Harry turned as the door opened. 'Ah, thank you, Mary.' Mary put down the tray of tea between us.

'Doctor James has kindly said that he will take the calls tomorrow evening, Mary, so that I can pick you up from Brighton.'

The housekeeper smiled. 'Thank you, Doctor ... I'd better get on. Making some cakes for my daughter.'

Harry took a paper spill and lit his pipe from the fire.

'It's a terribly difficult thing to judge, Neville – candour. People must be able to trust you, but sometimes it's difficult to know what the truth really is. And remember, optimism must help one recover from any illness. We've all seen the opposite – the patient turning his face to the wall. Tell people they're dying, for sure, and they'll oblige you in double-quick time. And who knows? Perhaps there is a positive, medical aspect of hope, the spirit or whatever, that may work through the brain, via the pituitary gland, say, actually increasing bodily resistance.'

He picked up the poker and stirred the fire into life.

'Honesty about diagnosis, of course, that's only fair. Patients have the right to know. If a woman goes into hospital and has her breast off, it would be rather stupid to try and pretend she didn't have cancer. But the prognosis, what the patient's expectation might be, that's a different matter altogether. Who knows what's going to happen, anyway? I've got a dozen or more patients who ought to have been dead years ago – and probably would have been, had someone been sufficiently pessimistic at the time. Old Royston Ackroyd. You remember, he used to work for me before you came. He had a biopsy. Lymphosarcoma. All over the shop. His number was up, they said. That was fifteen years before I met him. It all resolved itself, *spontaneously*. Perhaps the diagnosis was wrong. Perhaps it wasn't wrong, and something . . . something wonderful happened. But it's not just that. Sometimes we as doctors can act in a positive way, influence the prognosis if you like . . . hang on a minute.'

He got up and rummaged in his bookcase. Along one entire wall of his sitting room were row upon row of bookshelves. Harry collected books from all the local jumble sales and junk shops. He maintained that in his collection were a not inconsiderable number of, as yet, unauthenticated rare volumes.

'Ah, here it is.' He passed a book to me.

Bridge Under Fire by Colonel Peter Dorset. There was an inscription inside the front cover. 'To Harry. Best wishes. Peter.' In the back of the book was a photograph of an attractive middle-aged couple. Harry leant forward and indicated with the stem of his pipe.

'Peter Dorset and his wife, Marion. Lovely people. Peter was in the Royal Engineers during the war. The book's about the advance through Italy. Not much fun attempting to put a bridge together when the other side's trying to blow you out of the water.

142

'Anyway.' He took his seat again. 'Peter. Smashing chap. Afraid of nothing.'

'I suppose it was about six years ago. He went to one of those mobile mass radiography units that visit the area from time to time. His chest X-ray showed up a smallish carcinoma of the bronchus. The chest clinic called him up to see them. They told him that, although a large number of such cases were not operable, his might be and they thought it would be worth him seeing a thoracic surgeon. There was no sign of spread. Peter didn't believe them and was quite sure he was going to die. Two of his best friends had died of lung cancer, one only a few months after having surgery. So he took himself off home and wouldn't even talk about the possibility of any kind of operation.

'Marion rang. She was distraught. I called in on Peter. He was friendly, in a resigned, fatalistic kind of way. He didn't believe me any more than he did the chest clinic. I asked him if he would see somebody else. Not a doctor, I told him. "The parson?" he asked and added, "I suppose I'll be needing his services before long." '

Harry leant forward and lifted the teapot. 'Another?'

'Yes please.'

'I made a phone call to an old patient living in Westhaven. He said that he would be delighted to help. Peter had expected some kind of welfare worker and couldn't understand why I'd sent a clerk from the borough surveyor's office. Until the gentleman pulled up his shirt and showed him his thoracotomy scar. Through which he'd had his left lung removed. For lung cancer. Ten years previously.'

Harry smiled.

'Peter was off to see the chest surgeons before you could say "pneumonectomy". They operated on him and, although they couldn't promise anything, thought that he had a pretty fair chance. He moved to the Isle of Wight not long afterwards. He and Marion loved sailing. The last time he wrote to me, only three or four months ago, both he, and Marion, were in the best of health.'

Harry closed the book and put it back on the shelf.

'Though it must be said, Neville, you can't win every time. Sometimes tragedy has to be faced and shared with others. But never forget. A truthful diagnosis and an optimistic prognosis. That gives you the best combination of all. The trust of your patients and their reasonable hope for the future. Because there is no relationship without trust. And there is no life without hope.'

I called in at Sylvia and Ron's on the way home and then thought to pop into the police station to ask Griff to thank his men for their prompt service in the morning. There was plenty of police gossip and I left only a few minutes before surgery was due to start.

'Hallo, darling,' I shouted as I let myself in through the front door. There was no reply. I went into the living room. Sarah was playing on the floor with some saucepans. Beth sat in an armchair staring blankly into space.

'Sorry about being late.' She shrugged her shoulders. 'I feel much better now that I've had a chat with Harry.'

'Oh.'

'Can I get you anything? A cup of tea or something?'

'If you want.' Sarah banged a saucepan with a wooden spoon and laughed. Beth looked down at her with an expressionless face. An awful negativism.

'What have you been doing this afternoon, love?'

'Nothing much.'

'I saw Sylvia and Ron.'

'Oh yes.'

'They sent their love . . . and I dropped in at the police station. Griff Thomas sends his regards.'

Suddenly she looked angry. Bitterly angry.

'That's fairly typical.'

'What do you mean?'

'While I'm stuck here sitting with the phone, you're out wherever you like. I haven't been out of the house for more than an hour or two in the whole of the last week.'

'Except last night, of course. At Harry's.' It was the wrong thing to say. She turned away.

'I'm sorry,' I said. 'I didn't think.'

'You don't,' she said, without turning back. 'You never do . . . think.'

I tried to take her hand but she pulled it away.

'We'll go out tonight. I'll get a sitter. Harry will take the calls. I'll . . .'

'I don't want to go anywhere. I don't even want to be alive.'

I looked at her. Her lower lip began to tremble and her eyes filled with tears. I put my arm around her and she began to cry, the tears running down on to my shoulder. She put her arms around me and pulled herself close.

'It might have been a little boy,' she said. 'A little boy, for you.'

The next day, the sun shone. And so did we. Beth was radiant. Immersed in my work as I was, it was only in retrospect that I realized how unhappy she had been since the miscarriage. The cobbler's family is always the worst shod.

Harry took the calls in the afternoon. There was something we had to do. The Riley's condition was perilous. One of the front wheels was leaning out at an alarming angle. It took all of one's strength to hold it on a straight line. I'd told Harry about it that morning.

'Oh, all right,' he said. 'I'll get Ned to look at it. Needs some slight adjustment I expect.'

Ned Ridge owned a small local garage. He was the

secretary of the local Riley Owners' Club. His own 1.5 gleamed in showroom condition and he winced every time Harry's specimen rattled on to his forecourt.

'You'd better borrow the Mini today,' Harry said.

'That's very kind of you, Harry, but I think it's about time I got a car for myself.'

'What do you mean? You've got one!'

'I don't think I can presume on your generosity much longer.'

'Well. If you insist. Ned's always got some very nice second-hand cars he's done up. Anyway, as I said, you take the Mini today. I'd like a spin in the real car.'

Stopping off at the swings to give Sarah a ride, Beth and I walked through the park to the garage. Ned was in the workshop at the back. A bald-headed man with blue overalls, there was less oil on his hands than there was on the rag with which he was wiping them.

'He's not driving it, is he, Doctor?' he said. 'The Riley?'

'Yes, Ned.'

'It's a deathtrap. It's going to fall to pieces any day.' I had visions of a Disney-like car collapsed in the road, wheels out sideways, bumper turned into a sad clown mouth, and tears coming out of the headlamp eyes.

'Anyway,' he continued, 'I understand you're looking for a little motor for yourself. Got just the thing for you. Not very expensive. Belonged to Miss Tetley. She's gone to Australia to live with her nephew now she's retired.'

It was a typical schoolmistress's car. A black Standard 8, polished with love. Slow and solid, the large body pulled along by a puny engine. We drove around the block. It was ideal, and I hoped we'd get the bank to agree with us.

A happy day followed by a delightful evening. No visits. Sarah stayed up quite late but went to sleep as soon as she was put into bed. Beth snuggled up to me on the sofa.

'Let's go to bed,' she said. 'The phone might not ring and even if it does . . .'

It did. At eleven o'clock. It was the casualty department of a Brighton hospital. Dr Harry Brinckley and a Miss Mary Brewer had been involved in an accident.

It wasn't their fault. Nor the Riley's. A drunk had driven straight out of a pub car park and smashed into the side of them. Harry had sustained a compound fracture of the right tibia and fibula, and a broken right arm and several cracked ribs. Mary had a fractured left shoulder and possible internal injuries.

'Doctor Brinckley was most anxious that I should let you know,' said the casualty officer. 'Both he and Miss Brewer will be having surgery tonight.'

'How is he . . . in himself?'

'All right. Very upset though. His car's a write-off. It was some kind of special model, I understand. A valuable collector's item he told us.'

We were on our own.

Chapter Eight

I was very, very comfortable. The new fan heater wafted a gentle warm breeze around my feet. The chair was surprisingly soft. My eyelids began to droop. Soft. Warm and soft . . .

'And they shouldn't be, should they, Doctor? . . . Doctor?'

She was staring at me, the woman on the other side of the desk.

'I'm sorry, Mavis?'

'They shouldn't be like that. That's what I said to my husband and he said to go to the doctor.'

I had been up four nights in a row. Last night, 2.30 a.m. I couldn't believe it. Not another call. The young father had been waiting for me at the door.

'I hope I didn't get you out of bed, Doctor?' he said.

'Not at all,' I replied, as I trundled past into the hallway. 'I was down the garden digging my vegetable patch.'

I don't think he knew I was joking.

The problem that now faced me was to find out what shouldn't be what. Mavis was a very regular attender at surgery and even when I was at my most alert she still had a somewhat hypnotic effect. It was time to do some fishing.

'How long have you had this trouble, Mavis?'

'Like I said, Doctor. Ever since my operation. It was before you came, just after Arnold had had his veins seen to. And he's not been well. Perhaps it was the gas.'

Things were getting worse. It's bad enough to forget someone's name but you can always get off the hook by asking the person involved how they spell it. Unless, of course, they reply S.M.I.T.H. But not to listen to what somebody is saying to you, something of vital importance to them, is unforgivable. A clue was all I needed.

'Oh dear! That's most unfortunate ... when do you notice the ... er, problem most? Is it when you're in bed, or at the shops, or just sitting down watching the television?'

She flushed. 'Good heavens, Doctor. What on earth do you think I am?'

I was staggering. 'When then?'

'On the lavatory, of course. As I said to you before. Every time I go my ... motion, is very unpleasant. Odiferous.'

There at last.

'Ah, yes. Of course. Is there any blood, or mucus, or is it any different in appearance?'

'It looks the same.'

'Since your operation, you say.'

I looked through her notes. Six months before she had had a resection of her nasal septum and a cauterization of the swollen membranes of the inside of her nose. For chronic nasal blockage. Her sense of smell had dramatically improved as a result – and so had her awareness of her natural functions.

In any event I gave her a specimen pot. I would send off some stool to the lab. She could, conceivably, have some intestinal malabsorption giving rise to a condition of fatty, unpleasant faeces – steatorrhoea. It was said that a notable surgeon was once called 'Old Steatorrhoea' because the condition is described in medical dictionaries as 'pale, bulky and offensive'.

'Last one, Doctor!'

Lovely. Gwilliam Williams. Doctors should not have favourites. He was one of mine. A Welsh Father Christmas. A rotund octogenarian with ruddy cheeks, twinkling eyes and a mop of startling white hair. He held his shoulders in the hunched position common to most coal miners, the chest held in a constant state of inspiration. The stigma of 'the dust'. He sat down, his hands and paunch resting on his thighs.

'Tell me, Doctor, how's Doctor Brinckley and Mary?'

'Not too bad, thank you, Gwilliam. There was a bit of worry about Mary . . .'

'Some bleeding from the kidney, I heard from her niece.'

'That's right. But it all settled down.'

Gwilliam raised his formidable eyebrows. 'Not like Mr Godden, then?'

'No. He had to have an operation. Still, it was a part of his anatomy he could do without.'

'Yes, I understand,' said the old man with a grin. 'There's a bit of me like that. Still, we have to give the youngsters a chance, don't we! Will Doctor Brinckley be back soon?'

'No, I'm afraid not. He'll be at least another five or six weeks I should think. He's had an operation on his leg and he can't use his right arm. Useless, as a doctor. He wouldn't be able to write prescriptions.'

'You're all on your own, then, bach?'

'There you are, then, Gwilliam.' Two minutes of chat with him and the Welshisms of childhood summers came tumbling back into my speech.

'I shouldn't be troubling you then, Doctor, but it's the years. Waxed up again. I wondered if you could give them a blow through.' I went to the sink to fill a kidney dish with tepid water. 'By the way,' said Gwilliam, tucking the towel I had given him into his collar, 'did you see that your old Gran has been in the *Rhondda Fach Leader*?'

I had. My auntie had sent me a copy from Wales. Grandma James, my father's mother, still lived in a small village in South Wales, in a row of terraced, miners' houses built on the edge of a tributary of the River Taff. It had been headlines in the local paper. As a result of a miners' strike, the local collieries had stopped washing their coal in the river. Consequently, for the first time in generations, the water became clean. Not only that, but by some ecological miracle, it had filled with trout. People had been pulling them out with their bare hands.

A reporter from the local paper had come to see Grandma as she was, at ninety-five, the oldest resident of that part of the Rhondda Valley.

'Well, Mrs James,' said the young man, as she stood on her white scrubbed doorstep watching the goings on by the river. 'Have you ever seen anything like this before?'

'No, I have not,' she said, 'though I have lived here for sixty years.'

'You'll be having trout for your supper tonight, then?'

Horror filled her face. 'Indeed I will not. No doubt the fish in that river will all be suffering from pneumoconiosis!'

Gwilliam insisted on telling me all about it although he knew I had read the report myself. A Welsh tendency, this enjoyment of sharing amusing moments.

The syringe produced two plugs of black wax, each the size of a generous cigarette butt.

'How's that, Gwilliam?' He smiled at me. 'How's that, Gwilliam?' I repeated, louder. No reply. 'HOW'S THAT GWILLIAM?' I bawled.

'Much better, thank you, Doctor. Lovely.'

He dried his ears on the towel, picked up his cap and walked to the door. Turning round he smiled.

'I'll be back in by here next week. For my chest medicine.'

He could have had the prescription there and then but preferred to have the excuse to come back. For a chat. And I certainly wouldn't discourage him.

Finished. I looked at the list of visits I had collected. Ten new ones not counting the follow-ups. All to be done before the two evening surgeries. I couldn't close down Sangster

Road, not having just opened it. I was, therefore, having to work at both practice houses. Four surgeries a day. On call every night of the week bar one, the one that Jim Grastick covered, and as luck would have it I had been woken up in the early hours on almost every occasion. And Harry had been doing this for eight years!

I went through the French windows and walked round the back of the house to the kitchen door. The leaves on the flowering cherry were more gold than green. I could hear Beth singing to herself in the dining room.

The morning after Harry's accident she had come back from the shops loaded with groceries – and a dozen or more rolls of wallpaper. 'I might as well do it now as any other time,' she said. 'I'm not going to be able to get out much.'

'I am sorry, darling . . . you're sure you'll be all right?' I asked.

There was no word of protest against her enforced incarceration.

She came into the kitchen followed by her assistant. Sarah, covered in pieces of sticky wallpaper, had obviously been helping.

'You're sure you'll be all right?' I asked Beth as she sipped her coffee. 'I could try and get someone to come and answer the phone.'

'Who, for example?'

She was quite right. Most doctors did not have receptionists. They were a rare breed. The doctor's wife was expected to do all the work. She could see I was struggling.

'Don't fuss. I'll be fine . . . By the way, I did get one call in here. Jim Grastick. He wondered whether you'd like to go to the Medical Society meeting with him tomorrow night. He's presenting a case. I don't mind – I've got plenty to do here. I can phone you there if any visits come in.'

She passed me the biscuit tin. 'Did you see anything interesting this morning?'

'A girl with eosinophilia. Could have . . .'

'. . . allergy, asthma, aspergillosis, lymphadenoma, Loffler's syndrome, urticaria, polyarteritis . . . tapeworm? Has she been to Scandinavia recently? Eaten any raw fish?' Beth had gone through the lists of diagnoses so many times when I was doing my final examinations that they would, forever, be imprinted on her mind.

The phone rang. It was a woman from the Social Welfare department. Asking about old Charlie.

'He is your patient I believe?' The tone was mildly accusing.

'Yes. That's right.' I knew what was coming.

'His daughter is very concerned about him. She says that he is no longer capable of looking after himself and that he should be put in an old people's unit where he can be cared for properly. I understand that he's also somewhat mentally feeble.'

'Not at all,' I protested. 'And he's quite happy where he is.'

The voice became more irritated. 'That's not what his daughter says. I understand she requested that he had regular visits from the doctor but that nobody has been for some weeks.

'There's no need. He's perfectly fit. In any case, he doesn't want a doctor to visit and he certainly won't go into a home.'

'It might be necessary.' There was a hint of satisfaction.

'I can't see that you can *make* him leave.'

'Oh yes. It's quite possible. On health grounds. If our medical officer thinks that he is living in circumstances that are dangerous to his health.'

She'd get him out of there, the daughter. Put him in a private home. Comfortable. Charlie was not poor. Some years before he had applied for – and got – planning permission to demolish his bungalow and build eight houses on the site, but had decided to stay where he was. He would be well looked after, of course, and his daughter wouldn't have to think about it. Exchange a smelly independence for three meals a day and clean bed linen.

I put down the phone. Wheels had been set in motion that would be difficult to stop.

'You don't look very pleased,' said Beth.

'I'm not. It's poor old Charlie.'

'With Jake, the dog?'

'That's right. His daughter's trying to have him put away.'

'It seems so . . . Blast!'

The phone was ringing again. An urgent call.

'Hang on a moment.' I put my hand over the mouthpiece.

'It's Reginald, darling. He's just collapsed in Robson's stores. I'll have to go.'

'Oh,' said Beth. 'I hope he's all right.'

Reginald, a delightful old gentleman and a stalwart of the local Baptist chapel, always stopped to chat with Beth and make a fuss of Sarah when they met at the shops, where, it seemed, he spent most of his day. He had lived alone since his ancient parents, for whom he had cared most diligently, had died within two days of each other in 1956.

'I'll do that first. I don't know how long I'll be with this lot.' I brandished my visiting list.

'Never mind,' said Beth. 'It's cold lunch, anyway.'

Robson's Stores was the first of its kind in Amblesham. A self-service food shop. Customers no longer waited in a queue to have their orders made up but walked around the colourful displays of tins and packets, picking up from the shelves whatever they wanted, paying at a cash desk on their way out. A revolution indeed! One local gardener had been heard to say in a pub that he'd gone in to look around, had bought nothing, but had still been given 'a lovely wire basket, just right for my taters'.

I wasn't sure whether the idea would catch on. There seemed a lack of intimacy. After all, the grocery queue was a place of pleasurable gossip and an exchange of views.

A worried-looking lady in a blue overall took my arm as soon as I pushed my way through the swing doors.

'Doctor James? . . . Oh good. Can I have a word with you first in confidence?'

She took me to a relatively private place behind a mountain of soap powder packets.

'I'm afraid that the gentleman was . . . well, to put it bluntly, he was seen shoplifting.'

'Shoplifting? Reginald! I'm sure you must be mistaken. He's well over seventy, you know!'

'One of the girls saw him. He was seen putting the things into his shopping bag instead of the basket. He looked very furtive the girl said . . .'

'And?'

'We stopped him as he was going out. When we accused him he said that he hadn't got anything in the bag, but we insisted we look. Underneath a newspaper we found a packet of biscuits and a tin of pink salmon. We took him to the office and told him that we would have to phone the police. That's when it happened.'

'What?'

'He fainted. Went clean out. That's when we rang you.'

I started to make my way towards the back of the shop.

'I'd better see him straightaway.'

The lady hurried along beside me. 'He's all right now, Doctor, he's come round.'

Reginald sat on a chair in the back office. A frail little figure dressed in a black coat and Homburg hat . . . legacy

155

from a working lifetime as a solicitor's clerk. He was trembling. The manager stood beside him, his face a mixture of emotions, part injured, part concerned.

'Here's Doctor James,' said the lady in the blue overall.

'Oh, Doctor!' The elderly man gripped my hand and began to sob. 'They're accusing me of the most dreadful thing. They say that I've been ...' he produced a large white handkerchief and wiped his eyes, '... stealing!'

The manager shuffled his feet and looked awkward. 'You see, Doctor,' he said, 'I ...'

'I understand perfectly. Your assistant told me,' I replied, icily.

I knelt beside the old man and put my arm around his shoulders.

'Now don't you worry, old chap.'

He looked up at me. 'I don't remember taking anything that I shouldn't have, Doctor. I can't understand it. I don't know what can have happened. I had my shopping list and plenty of money ...' With a pathetic gesture he fumbled in his pocket and produced a small leather purse. '... But it's this new kind of shopping. I get so confused. It might have been those new tablets you gave me.' He started to sob again. 'I'm sorry for all the trouble I've caused.'

I glared up at the manager accusingly. 'This gentleman is not in good health. He is on a large number of pills. Essential treatment. Any one of them could have affected him.'

The manager cleared his throat. 'Well ... in the circumstances, Doctor, perhaps we won't take any further action.'

'Perhaps you had better not,' I snapped. 'I don't think it would do your company's image any good at all ... Come on, old chap.'

Reginald winced with pain as I tried to move him. 'I think I've hurt my knee – the bad one. When I fell over.'

It was decided that he should stay in the shop for a little longer. The lady in blue overalls made him a cup of tea and the manager said he would run him home in his car.

Feeling like St George who had begun his day by killing a dragon, however small, I started on my list of visits. The first was to The Duck and Donkey in the High Street. I had learnt by now that any visit to a pub was always fraught with danger. A secret world lay beyond and above the gleaming woodwork and brass of the bar, the oak beams, the crackling fire and the polished bar chairs.

The publicans and their families, I had discovered, often seemed to live in what appeared to me to be a series of narrow passages hemmed in with empty crates, cartons of cigarettes and boxes of potato crisps. There was none of the glitter and cosiness that greeted the customers downstairs. But, cluttered as it was, this domain, with its hoards of spirits, tobacco and cash, was the best guarded in the kingdom. Not by locks and bolts, but by the most ferocious of animals.

They have a special breed of dogs on licensed premises. I had visited The Ram opposite a week or two before. As I picked my way through the empty crates and barrels to the back entrance, a huge slavering Alsatian crashed into the barred door. With much shouting the publican restrained the beast with what appeared to be an anchor chain from the *Queen Mary*.

As he let me in, he confided . . . 'Would've killed you if I hadn't been here.'

There was no reply as I rang the back-door bell of The Duck and Donkey. Cautiously, I let myself in.

'Is that you, Doctor?' a woman's voice called from upstairs. 'Come on up.' There followed a burst of coughing. I had nearly reached the top of the dark narrow stairs when I felt the hairs on my neck stand on end.

A shadow moved from behind some boxes and stood in front of me. A Doberman pinscher. On the top step. Facing me, about three feet away, eyeball to eyeball. He showed his yellow fangs and from his chest came a low threatening rumble. I stood rooted to the spot. His black eyes seemed to be fixed on my throat and I could see the muscles tightening in his lean flanks.

'Don't worry about the dog, dearie,' called the woman. 'He wouldn't hurt a fly. Soft old thing, aren't you, Ripper? Just push him out of the way, Doctor.'

Feeling anything but like St George, I fled from The Duck and Donkey, even declining a free drink from the owner. Luckily he had chosen the moment of my canine dilemma to come into the back of the pub to replenish his bar stock of Woodbines. The Doberman slunk off and lay down among the ashtrays on his mistress's bed. The lady was sure she had bronchitis. I was happy to agree. Without examining her.

A variety of tonsils and ears followed. Then three families with measles. A really nasty illness. The virus itself and the secondary infection of otitis media and bronchitis that so often accompanied it seemed to knock the kids down for weeks. The proposed new measles vaccine couldn't come soon enough as far as I was concerned. I phoned up Beth from a call box. I wouldn't be able to get back for lunch. There was one more call in – Charlie wanted to see me. I'd leave that visit until last.

'Mr Styles?'

'That's right, Doctor. Mrs Styles is upstairs in the bedroom.'

I'd never met this family before. Jill Styles's record envelope was very thin indeed.

'I'm really sorry to get you out, Doctor, but I just couldn't make it to the surgery.'

A pleasant lady. Brown eyes. Black curly hair. Her ankle

was badly sprained, the outer aspect blue and swollen. I turned the foot slightly.

'Golly, that hurts!' she said, sucking in her breath. 'I'm sorry, Doctor.'

'How did you do it?'

'She fell off a chair, Doctor. I tell her to be careful but she doesn't take any notice.'

'Oh don't make such a fuss, Jack . . . it was in the kitchen, Doctor. I wanted to get something off a high shelf. I stood on the chair and I had a dizzy turn – I do get them from time to time . . .'

'Ever since she had that virus, Doctor. A year or so ago. In her inner ear.' I looked at her record card. Nearly two years in fact. Harry had diagnosed labyrinthitis, an infection that disturbs the balance mechanism and causes acute vertigo.

'It doesn't happen very often, Doctor, and I'm not going to stop doing the things I want to do.' And what she wanted to do seemed fairly considerable, including looking after a huge garden and working as a dinner lady at the local school.

'When can I walk on it again? I've got to get all the shrubs and things tidy for the winter. No use leaving it for Jack to do. He's hopeless. He doesn't know the difference between a weed and a walnut tree!'

'Not for a few days, at least, Mrs Styles . . .' I was deliberately vague. It was certain that she would be out and about as soon as she could stand on it. '. . . But like your husband said, do be careful.'

I walked back to the car carrying three young chrysanthemum plants. It was always a bonus visiting a gardener.

'What am I going to do, Doctor? They'll take old Jake away from me, for sure.' The mug of tarry tea that Charlie had given me was more than welcome. I hadn't eaten since breakfast. 'They want me to sign this form. Something about Turneys. I don't know why the girl don't leave me alone.'

Charlie picked up his magnifying glass and inspected the pile of papers beside him. 'Thissun, here, I think,' he said, handing it to me. Power of attorney. 'She's always been a tidy little madam,' he said. 'That's what she wants to do with me. Tidy me up. Put me away in a home, more like.'

The form was made out to give financial control of his estate to his daughter.

'I don't mind. I've had a good life.' He leant down and patted the old dog's head. 'But old Jake. He wouldn't understand. Not if he had to leave here.'

Before going home I drove to Alfriston to call in at the butcher's. I never missed the opportunity when I came across to this part of the Downs. He did, indeed, make marvellous sausages. Peppery, spicy, delicious.

By the time the two evening surgeries were over, I was out on my feet. I couldn't go to bed. There were bound to be further calls. I sat on the sofa, Sarah on my lap. The remains of the sausages and chips on a small table beside me. Beth's favourite programme was on the television – 'Rawhide'. Every time Gil Favor appeared, covered in dust and sweat, waving his arm to 'Get 'em up, move 'em out', she was inclined to make a lascivious comment. She definitely had a thing about cowboys, much preferring Gil Favor to Rowdy Yates, played by a young actor called Clint Eastwood. A wave of nausea surged over me as the phone rang yet again.

The woman on the other end was far from happy that it was me.

'We've not met, Doctor . . .?'

'James.'

'Then you don't know my husband's case at all.'

'I'm afraid not, Mrs . . .?'

'Lucton. I must speak to Doctor Brinckley. We *are* private patients of his.'

I explained the position to her. Private patients or no, Harry wasn't about to be unhooked from his traction and brought along to her residence. Mr Lucton, apparently, had been very ill and was now in acute abdominal pain. Doctor Brinckley *did* know all about it. There was no way out, I would have to visit.

It was a big house on the Lewes road in an area favoured by the local gentry. As so often seemed to happen, I was not taken straight to the patient's bedroom but to the drawing room – a most elegant one – to be briefed.

'My husband,' said Mrs Lucton, a woman no longer young but still of considerable beauty, 'has cancer . . .' she offered me a cigarette from a gold cigarette case, '. . . of the back passage. The rectum. I don't know what can have happened. He only saw Mr Sandown this morning – at his rooms in Westhaven – and he was feeling quite well then. Mr Sandown is going to operate at the weekend. My husband has a private room booked at the General. But since this afternoon he's been in a terrible state. Dreadful pain.'

I knew what to expect as I climbed wearily up the stairs. Intestinal obstruction. The distended abdomen, tight as a drum. The bowel blocked off. I did not find it. Mr Lucton, a large balding man in striped pyjamas, lay grey with shock, his face racked with pain. His pulse was rapid and there were beads of sweat on his forehead. This was not intestinal obstruction. The abdomen was like a board and he winced at the slightest touch. He had peritonitis.

I would have to phone up the consulting surgeon, Mr Ian Sandown. A most distinguished man, I understood, though I had never met him. His wife answered: they were having a dinner party she told me. He came to the telephone.

'It can't be,' he said. 'I only saw him this morning

and he was perfectly all right then. You do *know* the diagnosis?'

'Yes sir,' I stammered. 'CA rectum. You're operating on him this weekend, I believe . . . sir.' My God! He did sound like a 'sir' too.

'Oh dear,' he said, 'I'd better come out and see him then . . . peritonitis. That's very strange. From where are you speaking?'

I gave him the address some ten miles or so from where, I imagined, he was just about to pour the Nuits-Saint-Georges.

Mr Sandown arrived within twenty minutes. Not only did he sound like a 'sir', he looked like one. The sleek Bristol car, the beautifully cut suit, the silver hair, the walk – more on oiled rollers than feet – and an air of total mastery of the situation. He swept into the bedroom where he and the patient, who, of course, by now was feeling much better, vigorously apologized to each other for the inconvenience caused.

As a gesture the sheet was pulled down and an elegant hand was placed on the abdomen.

'By George,' he said 'it *is* peritonitis!'

I waited for him to arrange the hospital bed. He turned and smiled.

'I'll have to do him tonight. Would you like to assist? . . . No? Never mind. I'll ask my registrar. We've seen plenty of each other today. I didn't finish my NHS list until 8.30 this evening. Two abdominoperineals for carcinoma of the rectum, would you believe, apart from the other stuff?'

I might be tired but Mr Lucton's life depended on this man being as fresh as he had been fourteen hours and several demanding operations ago.

I picked up Jim Grastick the next evening. There was little point in taking both cars into Westhaven for the Medical

Society meeting. He looked somewhat preoccupied. It was fair to assume that the easy and entertaining manner in which he spoke at medical meetings concealed the nervousness he felt as much as anybody else in the same position.

'Dermatitis herpetiformis. A woman I saw a few weeks back,' he told me when I asked what case he was presenting. He said that the patient, a woman of fifty, had had considerable investigation to find whether there was an underlying cause for her condition, an excruciatingly irritating skin condition characterized by blistery lesions on limbs and trunk.

The Medical Society meeting was well attended. A gathering of about sixty local GPs and consultants, all of whom seemed to know each other. The bar was crowded and the air was heavy with tobacco smoke.

'Ah! The opposition. We meet at last!'

I turned. A broad, jovial-looking man. Middle-aged, he seemed to me. About thirty-five.

'You're Neville James,' he said, extending his hand. 'Pleased to meet you. Paddy Kearson.'

The opposition indeed. It was extraordinary that we had not met before. I knew the name, of course; he was the junior partner of the other, the original, Amblesham practice. Paddy Kearson gestured towards the crush by the bar. A familiar figure.

'Ian pointed you out to me.'

Mr Ian Sandown smiled in our direction and glided over towards us. He beamed at me.

'Ah . . . Doctor James. Delighted to see you here. Mr Lucton is doing very well. Colostomy of course. But it's a good job they sent for you. Let me get you a drink.'

'Thank you. A small one. I'm on duty.'

Jim Grastick had another gin and tonic. I was on for him as well.

Paddy Kearson asked about Harry. There had obviously

been some tension when he had first put up his plate in Amblesham. In opposition he was, after all, taking bread from the mouths of the existing practice. Nevertheless, although they didn't have much to do with each other on a social level, the relationship was now fairly amicable. It seemed, from Paddy Kearson's manner, that being a second-generation 'squatter', as it were, I was innocent of any of the 'poaching' of my predecessor. Except . . .

'I understand you've pinched one of our patients from us.' This was an awkward moment. 'Arnold Morgan told me that if I was to bump into you I should tell you to watch out for flying tins of fruit.'

Of course. The Littlebones. It was Doctor Morgan, Paddy's senior partner, who had had them removed.

'Anyway,' said Paddy, 'you must be pretty pushed at the moment. If there's anything we can do to help . . .' I knew he meant it.

The meeting began, some short cases were presented. Then came a local consultant giving an outline of some of the medical and surgical advances of the last year. Interferon, perhaps the future answer to cancer. The significance of hard and soft fats, or saturated and unsaturated as they were now called, in relationship to heart disease. The first glimmer of hope in the treatment of leukaemia. The use of cell poisons, or cytotoxics, including the inoculation of one, methotrexate, directly into the spinal canal. The removal of the pituitary gland for breast cancer and the new technique by which actual X-rays could be made of the blood vessels to the heart, the coronary arteries. The blockages could be shown, but how long would it be before surgeons dared operate on such a dangerous area? The new drugs. Penbritin, a new penicillin from Beecham that everybody was using. A warning about the hypnotic, thalidomide. I had a personal stake in this. Beth should not take it again. It was, according to recent evidence, thought to cause in a few susceptible individuals rather nasty problems with the nervous system. It should, at least, be used with caution. He finished up by suggesting that, if we really wanted to keep up with modern discoveries, we should all watch the new programme that had started just a week before on television . . . 'Dr Kildare'.

Under the covering darkness of the slide projection time, Jim, knowing that he wasn't due to speak until the very end, slipped out several times for refreshment and fortification.

A gynaecologist gave a short talk on the oral contraceptive tablet or 'the pill', as it was coming to be known in some quarters. He also mentioned a Glasgow hospital where they had used a machine employing ultrasound to determine the position of a baby in a woman's womb.

A pathologist spoke about the greatest problem of the day. A problem that plagued us all one way and another. The continual infection of hospital patients with virulent, pathogenic staphylococci. Resistant to all antibiotics, they could cause anything from sticky eyes in the babies to fulminating abscesses and osteomyelitis, the bone infection that had caused so much dread in pre-antibiotic days. He also mentioned the new oral polio vaccine and the impending measles vaccine.

At 11 o'clock, Jim was called on to speak. Usually the epitome of moderation, he was very relaxed indeed. Having mounted the rostrum, he took out a pair of glasses and a piece of paper. It was a dry-cleaning receipt.

'Excuse me.' He rummaged about in his pockets until he found his notes. 'Before I present my case, I should like to tell you about a man I saw last week.'

He squinted in my general direction and grinned evilly.

'Doctor,' he said, 'I've got a problem.' My God! He wasn't going to tell that one! He continued. 'You see I have the crabs . . .' He was going to tell that one.

The story unfolded. The underpants were packed with crushed ice. I slipped further down into my seat. Suddenly, the punchline, with Jim thrashing his arms to show how the pediculoses pubis tried to keep warm, was greeted by a great roar of laughter and applause.

'To be serious,' he continued, 'I wish to present this evening a case of drematosis heripi . . . drematositis herrpit . . . a skin rash.' He then went on to give the results of the pathology investigation. 'The haemoglobin was 63 per cent, instead,' he added, pausing for dramatic effect, 'of the usual 100 per cent.' It was as though Winston Churchill had stated in a lecture on naval history that Nelson had one arm instead of the customary two.

'Best one all evening,' said my neighbour, as we joined in the applause at the end of the presentation.

We were just leaving the hotel when a clerk ran up. A message for me to phone Beth. It was Reginald. His knee was causing him agonizing pain. Unable to get out of bed, he had called a neighbour.

He had, in fact, sustained a haemarthrosis. The knee joint was full of blood. There was little I could do that night but give him some painkillers. He had a phone by his bed that he could use in an emergency.

As I walked back towards the front door I thought that it would be a good idea to ring Beth before I went home. There might be another call. I couldn't see a phone in the hallway and, not wanting to disturb my patient again, I decided I would look in the downstairs room. There was a door at the end of the passage. It was locked. A glint of metal on a shelf caught my eye. A key projecting from behind a potted plant. It opened the door.

It was not easy to get in. One wondered what the handyman who had installed them had been told all the shelves were needed for. Floor to ceiling. On all four walls. Stacked with goods of every conceivable nature. Tins,

166

packets, pullovers and cardigans still in their plastic bags, umbrellas, kettles, packets of nails, pots of paint, plastic footballs, a large woollen coat on a hanger, jigsaws, fruit cake – mostly mouldy – toys, socks, underpants, packets of washing powder. Each with a neatly printed label tied on with string. 'Home and Colonial, Hailsham, March 1957'; 'Co-operative, Westhaven, May 1960'; 'Green and Company, Amblesham, June 1956'. Unopened and unused, as they had been on the day on which they had been . . . obtained. He had not used any of them. That, after all, would have been dishonest.

Like the head that decorated Millie's hallway, these were the trophies of many an adventure. Not an adventure that carried the danger of attack by a big cat of the jungle or the charge of an angry water buffalo, but a far more exquisite peril. That of public exposure and humiliation.

One shelf was only half full. The two most recent items sat in glory. In all the fuss they had been overlooked and had once more been hidden underneath the newspaper. A tin of pink salmon and a packet of Huntley and Palmer biscuits. 'Robson's Stores, Amblesham, October 1961'.

Chapter Nine

'And so I'd like you to sign me back to work.'

'You'd what?' I could hardly believe my ears!

'From tomorrow. I start at Bowkers, working in the stores.'

Mr Littlebone indicated the National Health Service certificate on my desk. 'One of them I want. A final one.'

Of all the forms that I might have filled in that morning, this had to be the least expected. I'd already given up protesting against most of Mr Littlebone's demands. It was easier just to sign whatever piece of paper he chose to put in front of me and hope that someone else would sort it out. Perhaps, at last, he had realized the pleasure to be gained from being self-sufficient, of earning his own keep.

'It will be really nice to work again, Doctor, get myself back on my feet,' he added, as if to confirm my own feelings.

He crouched down on his haunches, then stood up again. 'The old knees are better. I'm sure I'll be able to do this job.'

'I'm sure you *will*, Mr Littlebone . . . I'm very pleased for you.'

I signed the certificate with a flourish and handed it to him. He leant across the desk and shook my hand.

'Thank you, Doctor, for all you have done.'

Perhaps I was getting the hang of general practice. Asserting my personality. Enabling those such as Mr Littlebone to gain strength from my reassurance. It was being single-handed, I suppose. Harry and Mary had now been in hospital for three weeks. My feet had hardly touched the ground.

Beth's decorating marathon had taken her out of the living room, into the dining room, up the stairs, around the corner and into the bathroom. I had chosen the colour scheme for the living room. Beth's taste in the dining room, I felt, with its soft browns and golds, had been rather conservative. This was the sixties. A touch of flamboyance was needed.

Nevertheless, now that it was done, I was not entirely convinced that the green wallpaper went with the pink paintwork quite as well as I had hoped. Even Sylvia and Ron, the least transparent of couples, when they had been round the previous evening were moved to call it 'unusual'.

Perhaps it would look better, I thought after they had gone, with more subtle lighting. In fact I had said as much over breakfast.

'I don't think it's that bad, love.'

'What did you say?'

'I don't think it's that bad. The living room.'

Beth poked her head round the doorway from the kitchen. 'You'll have to speak up. I can't hear you. I told you last week my ears were all blocked up. You said you'd syringe them. Three times at least.' She was quite right. But something kept on cropping up. I promised once again, that I would do them as soon as I had a spare moment.

Ron had now fully recovered and was back at work, busier than ever. He had decided to take on an articled clerk to train as an accountant. It had turned out to be the happiest of choices. I had become accustomed to living in a twilight world of chronic sleep deprivation. Every time the phone rang at night I got out of bed to visit, as yet too inexperienced to be able to tell which request really justified a call. It was like having a perpetual hangover. The mouth dry, the head aching.

I had discussed with Jim Grastick the possibility of our covering each other's night duty on a more rational basis.

The main stumbling block, however, was our manually operated local telephone exchange. It was difficult enough sometimes to get through in the day. In the middle of the night things could be particularly bad. The operator always seemed to be answering a call of nature, or be at the crucial part of a romantic novel or negotiating the most difficult part of a knitting pattern. Whatever the cause, if a transfer of call was also involved, the patients might well be dead before the doctor's phone rang.

But this was my half day. Jim would cover the calls from lunchtime onwards. Once morning surgery and visits were over, I was off duty until midnight. We were going to Brighton. Beth would take Sarah to the seafront. I would drop into the hospital to visit Harry.

My success with Mr Littlebone had acted on me like a tonic. The headache had disappeared. The morning surgery flew past, one case following another with no real problems. Gwilliam Williams had come in, ostensibly to collect a prescription for cramp tablets but, in reality, to discuss the Welsh rugby football fifteen. Millie had dropped by to ask for some dyspepsia mixture for Soames – and then beguiled me with a scandalous story that concerned a brush with royalty in the twenties. I was generous with the sweetjar and open-handed with advice and opinion.

A morning on which one realized that there was no comparable branch of medicine which held as much joy and job satisfaction as general practice. Yes, and humour. I was still smiling at my last encounter, and was about to close the surgery door, when I saw a couple walking slowly up the path. Mr and Mrs Farmer had come to tell me that Christine had just died.

'This morning, Doctor. Peacefully in her sleep.'

It was with sick horror that I realized that I had had no communication with the Farmers since Christine had been admitted. I had been notified by the medical registrar that the bone marrow test had confirmed aplastic anaemia and that she and her parents had been informed of the diagnosis. Christine's husband had been flown home on compassionate leave. I had intended to go and visit them but, immersed in my new responsibilities, I had completely forgotten.

'It was all very quick in the end,' said Mr Farmer. 'They think she had some kind of internal haemorrhage. She seemed to feel better yesterday. A lot better. David took Richard to see her and . . .' He was unable to continue. His wife clasped his hand.

'We thought we'd come and let you know. Straightaway, Doctor,' said Mrs Farmer. 'Because you were so good and concerned. And for getting Christine in like that. So quickly. We were most grateful.' She took her husband's arm and led him outside.

'Concerned!' I said bitterly to Beth as we drove away from Sangster Road. 'I'd pushed it right to the back of my mind.'

'You had too many other things to think about. It is a tragedy. It is terrible. But there wasn't anything you could do about it.'

I knew she was right. I found it impossible to distance myself from the people I was looking after. I could not come to terms with a patient's death, however inevitable. I regarded it as a sign of failure on my part. There was no more half-day feeling.

There was one more visit. I had left it until last. It was on the route to Brighton.

'If it isn't too urgent,' Beth asked, 'can we go to the market for a few minutes first? Sarah loves to see the chicks.'

The cattle market, though smaller than the ones at Lewes and Hailsham, was the high point of the week in Amblesham. It thronged with people. The air was full of the sound of broad, rural Sussex accents. Of the cut-glass voices of gentleman farmers. Of talk about the state of the winter barley, or the prices of sheep. Of the smell of cow dung.

'Hallo, Doctor.'

I didn't recognize Vic Wheeler for a moment. Last time we met he had been wearing his cricket flannels.

'Hallo, Vic. Down here on business?'

'Yes, her ladyship wants us to put in a few hundred more daffodil bulbs this year. I was seeing if there was any going cheap. She doesn't like spending money.'

Lady Westhaven did, indeed, have a reputation for thrift.

'Anyway, I'll be coming to see you soon. I've got a funny noise in my ear.'

I was just about to warn him that there is rarely anything a doctor can do about tinnitus when he added, 'I hope you can do something about it. It keeps Amy awake.' He looked past my shoulder. Keeps Amy awake? 'Ah, there's old Fred. I'll have to go, otherwise they'll all be gone.'

He made his way off through the jostling crowd towards a man pushing a barrow loaded with baskets of bulbs.

I walked with Beth and Sarah around the large hut with its trestle tables loaded with scores of tweeting cardboard boxes. Each contained dozens of chicks, bright yellow balls of fluff. I didn't enjoy the market much, particularly the sight of the farmworkers prodding and poking their terrified cattle in and out of the trucks – out for the auction ring, in for the slaughterhouse. Most disturbing of all, the calves. Bambi like, muzzles raised in pathetic cries. But I know that I would have forgotten them before next I sat down to eat a veal and ham pie. There wasn't much room for sentimentality in farming – or in medicine, it seemed.

'I don't think that I'll be many minutes,' I said as I got out of the car for my remaining visit. Sarah was already asleep. Unusual for her. She was always full of bounce in the mornings. Archie and Bertha's house stood beside the half dozen dingy greenhouses that constituted their market garden. Before I went through the front gate, I looked once more at Archie's medical record envelope. It revealed a bizarre situation.

I remembered first meeting Bertha, a gentle, rather ingenuous lady of sixty-seven at one of Harry's evening surgeries. Vitamin pills. 'To keep me going,' she said. She had come to visit me at Sangster Road the day after I opened. On that occasion she had been accompanied by a wizened little man with jet black hair and white eyebrows whom I assumed to be an elder relative.

'Archie, my husband,' she introduced him. He smiled toothlessly. Bertha continued her explanation. 'You see, Doctor, Archie hasn't been too well recently. Tired all the time he seems. He can hardly do anything, put a fork in the garden, let alone dig. I have to do all that. A few hours potting out in the greenhouse is about all he's capable of. It's getting all too much for you, isn't it dear?'

Archie smiled again and nodded his head. He was no great conversationalist. 'We got married rather late in life, Doctor,' continued Bertha. 'In 1945. At the end of the war when we were both fifty. A whirlwind romance I suppose you'd call it. I'd been working as a cleaner at some government offices – always been in service before that – and Archie had worked in a munitions factory. They were bombed and everything.'

'I got a certificate for it,' he said.

'He did indeed, Doctor.' She turned and smiled at him. 'That's quite right. Anyway, I came down here from London to get a job as a chambermaid in a Westhaven hotel. I met Archie at a social . . .'

'A dance,' interjected Archie.

'That's right, dear, a dance . . . beautiful dancer he was too, Doctor, and very soon after we got wed. He had

173

a little market garden. Lettuces, tomatoes and cucumbers. Chrysanthemums in the winter. It was all right at first but over the last few years Archie has slowed right up. It's worse recently. I don't know what's wrong with him. I wondered whether it could be his glands?'

Perhaps it could. I remembered the awful day of the dead lady. It was just possible he had myxoedema. Not as common in men and the more easily missed for all that. The lack of energy, the wrinkled skin, the premature ageing, the slow mental state.

'I think we may be able to help you, Archie,' I said with a smile. 'Excuse me a moment. Let me get out your medical card.' I flipped through the files. . . . 'Here we are, 274 Brighton Road.'

'That's right, Doctor,' said Bertha. I scanned the front of the card. I stopped as I noticed the date of birth. Eighteen seventy-seven! Fourteenth of September, 1877!

'Er . . . what, actually, was your date of birth, Archie?'

The old man pursed his lips, in thought. 'September, I think . . . the fourteenth, isn't it dear?'

'That's right,' said Bertha, and added, 'Eighteen ninety-five. Same as me.'

There were a couple of ancient letters in the record envelope. One regarded the removal of Archie's appendix in 1938. The discharge note from the hospital gave the patient's age as sixty-one. I thought I'd better check there'd been no mistake.

'You used to live in Westhaven, Archie? St Mary's Road?'

'That's right. A long time ago. In lodgings.'

Not sixty-seven then, as his wife imagined. Archie was eighty-four – and a fairly ancient eighty-four at that. I said I would do some blood tests.

They turned out to be normal, of course. No pill had yet been invented that would revitalize the aged Archie. I had said nothing to Bertha. It was going to be difficult if today's visit turned out to be for the same reason.

Bertha answered the door.

'Archie's got a bad chest. I thought I'd better call you. And he's just as tired.' She continued, her voice laced more with disappointment than criticism, 'I don't think anybody's got to the bottom of it.'

As we went through the tiny front room, Bertha picked something off the mantelshelf to show me. 'That's it,' she said, 'Archie's certificate.'

A framed picture of St George and the Dragon. 'With grateful thanks to . . .', Archie's name had been written in, 'whose contribution helped pave the way to victory.'

'You go on up. I'm making a hot drink for him.'

Archie sat up in bed like a little gnome. He hadn't bothered to dye his hair for some while and the white roots made a startling contrast with the black hair. The stethoscope was hardly necessary to detect the wheeze and crackles of his bronchitis.

'Archie,' I said, as I wrote the prescription, 'there seems to be some confusion about your date of birth. It's the . . .?'

He thought for a moment. 'The fourteenth of September.'

'Eighteen . . .?'

'Eighteen ninety-something. I forget.'

'It's not eighteen seventy-something?'

'No, I shouldn't think so,' he said with a grin.

'I'll let myself out,' I said as Bertha came into the room with a steaming mug of cocoa. 'Get this prescription for Archie at the chemist's this afternoon. Some antibiotic tablets and some cough medicine. Let me know if it doesn't work soon. He should be a lot better in a couple of days.'

As I passed the mantelshelf again, I had a closer look at Archie's certificate. It was most attractive and ornate. Around the rim of St George's shield, barely visible amongst the tracery, I could just make out some roman numerals. I doubted whether they meant much to Bertha. They represented the year in which Archie had ceased making guns for soldiers to use at the front. In the Great War. 1918.

'What did you do then, about poor old Reginald . . .?' asked Harry, propping himself up on his good arm. With his leg in traction and his plastered right arm held high in the air like a child asking to go to the lavatory, he made a comical sight. '. . . Send him in? . . . By Christ, this does itch.' In an impotent gesture, he scraped his nails vigorously against the plaster.

'No, not that night of course.' I took another one of his grapes. 'I went round to see him the next morning. The knee was still very painful. I told him that I'd have to get him down to the casualty department to get it X-rayed.'

'Then you phoned up the duty psychiatrist to get him to look at the old boy at the same time.'

Harry knew I had learned that ploy from him.

'Exactly . . . Here, let me give you a hand.' I pulled off a few of the remaining grapes for him and put them in a saucer. 'They've taken him into hospital for a bit. We've had all kinds of different people involved. The Welfare. The DAO. Some of the stuff has been taken back. The rest he's paid for. There isn't much call for a fifteen-year-old fruit cake. None of the shops has preferred charges. He says that he'll never do it again. But we'll have to keep an eye on him, though.'

Harry leaned back on to the pillows. 'And how's Albert? Does he miss me?'

I assured him that the old dog was in the best of health. Sylvia was spoiling him badly. A great deal to eat, little exercise and no vocabulary lessons.

'Ron was here a day or two ago,' said Harry, 'telling me about his new assistant. You know him I believe?'

'Smashing bloke.'

Harry groaned, and scratched again.

'It must be getting better,' I said. He laughed. 'Aren't you getting pretty bored, though, Harry?'

'I doze off a lot of the time. Been getting up to date with my medical reading. The houseman's been letting me have a look at his *BMJs*. Have you read any recently?' I had to admit that my copies of the *British Medical Journal* had not even been taken out of their wrappings for the last four weeks.

'Very interesting, some of the stuff,' said Harry. 'Do you remember that little kid with the nettle rash? William something . . . with ginger hair?'

'Aspell.'

'That's right. William Aspell. His mother swore blind that he got it after eating ice lollies.'

'I remember.'

'Couldn't believe it when I read it in the *Journal*. Loads of letters. All about kids getting urticaria after eating ice lollies. One of the dyes apparently . . . and another thing there's been a lot about. Thalidomide.'

'Yes – we were talking about that at the Medical Society meeting.'

'People getting side effects. Some kind of neuropathy they think . . . go on, you have it.' I ate the last grape.

'An odd illness, they said at the meeting, Harry. Doesn't happen very often but quite nasty when it does. Weakness, loss of sensation. They're saying we should be pretty careful about using it.'

'Damn shame, really,' said Harry. 'Much safer drug than the barbiturates. No reports of any cases of overdose, I believe. Perhaps it'll just be used on people who need a sleeping pill now and then. In the short term. Or anxiety state . . . Talking about which, how have you been keeping?'

I had to tell him that, most of the time, I lived in a

state bordering on terror. Always desperately afraid that I was going to make a mistake, miss something, give the wrong drugs.

'Do you know, Harry, when I go into a house, perhaps when there's been a collapse or something, I can see all the relatives looking at me, thinking, "Thank goodness, the doctor's here!" I want to look over my shoulder to see where he is.'

Harry chuckled. 'Don't worry, old chap. I still feel like that now. You think you're expected to be a cross between Albert Schweitzer and the seventh cavalry. You're not really . . . Hang on a minute,' he added in a conspiratorial whisper. 'Have a look at this.'

'Coming for a walk, then?' I turned. A large, gormless-looking man was staring down at us.

'Not today, thank you,' replied Harry tartly. The man grinned and shuffled away. Harry sucked his teeth.

'He says that to me every morning and every afternoon . . . Did you notice his pyjama trousers?'

It would have been difficult not to. Had he been in the street he would have been arrested for indecent exposure. But what he exposed was, nevertheless, spectacular.

'I sometimes think,' said Harry philosophically, 'that like the shrub whose branches have been removed to increase the size and strength of the roots, so there is a certain association between cerebral poverty and pubic splendour.'

He wanted to know about everything that was happening at the practice. I told him about Jill Styles. And Jim Grastick's lecture. And that I had seen the sad lady who had put a stop to his visit to see *El Cid* at the cinema.

She was now quite well into her pregnancy and happy enough in a resigned sort of way. I had written an arm-twisting letter to the local gynaecologist to ask him to sterilize her after this confinement. He was most reluctant.

'You can't help feeling sorry for women, Neville,' said Harry. 'They don't seem to have any say in their own future. Unless they're wealthy, of course. A law for the rich and a law for the poor. Those with the money won't find it difficult to get their tubes tied . . . or have their pregnancy terminated if it comes to that. . . . Not around here. Up in London,' he added. 'Unfair life is sometimes. Perhaps this birth pill they're on about will make things easier.'

His eyes brightened suddenly. 'Something else to tell you . . . You know the Riley? The accident assessors have seen it. Complete write-off. Tragedy really. But,' he tapped the end of his nose with his finger, 'did pretty well with the insurance company. I'm getting forty pounds for it – and I knocked them up from thirty-five.'

I picked up Beth and Sarah from outside the Palace pier. Sarah had been sick.

'She's very hot,' said Beth. She was. Burning.

As we arrived home there was an unfamiliar car parked in the drive. Seeing us pull up, an ample lady in a large fur coat opened the door and extricated herself from behind the steering wheel.

'Doctor James?'

'Yes.'

'I've been waiting for you.' She looked as though she was about to hit me, and, with little ceremony, introduced herself. She was Charlie's daughter.

'Ah. Yes, of course. Hang on a moment, I'll go round and open the waiting-room door for you.'

Beth looked at me enquiringly as soon as we got in the house. I screwed up my face in anticipation of the pain to come.

'I'll tell you about it later.'

179

As soon as I opened the surgery door the lady swept past me into the consulting room. She seemed even larger and more threatening when she sat down.

'I have been to my solicitor and we are considering taking you to court for . . .' she grasped for the words – '. . . alienation of affection.'

'I'm sorry . . . I don't understand.'

'I think you do.'

She reached into a large handbag that had once been the more attractive part of a crocodile and pulled out a letter. She thrust it into my hand.

'There!'

'Bingle, Bingle and Dodds. Solicitors.'

I read it. Well well! Old Charlie had done it. He had talked about the idea. I told him to contact his solicitor. But now it was signed and settled. Thank God I hadn't witnessed the document when he had changed his will or I might have been in real trouble. I read the relevant paragraph once more.

> . . . and a copy of the correspondence we have received from them. It appears that your father had altered his will, or rather, the conditions that apply to it. You, as his only child, remain sole beneficiary but with one proviso. If, at the time of his death, he has not resided at his permanent address (see paragraph III) within the previous three months, then the entire estate will be divided, equally, between the Royal Society for the Prevention of Cruelty to Animals and Battersea Dogs' Home. Your father has arranged to review the conditions of this will on a yearly basis with his solicitors, Messrs Fernley and Archibald, should his own circumstances change in the meantime.

'Slammed the door. Nearly came off its hinges,' I said to Beth. 'She could have killed me . . . These are good!'

Fish and chips. In the newspaper. Delicious. I looked at the news under my piece of cod. 'CHRISTINE DOES IT AGAIN' proclaimed the headline on the sports page. Christine Truman, the English rose of tennis, was doing well in the United States. Playing against a seventeen-year-old youngster, Billie Jean Moffatt. Always producing some new wonder kid or other, the Americans. But no doubt she'd disappear as quickly as the rest.

'I've put Sarah to bed with some junior aspirin,' said Beth. 'She's not at all well.'

'I'll have a look at her in a minute,' I mumbled through a mouthful of chips.

'What?' Beth grimaced and poked her little finger into her ear. 'I keep on asking. Couldn't you syringe them for me? I'm really deaf.'

'Of course. I'll do it in a minute when I've finished my . . .'

The phone rang. It shouldn't have done. It was the midwife. Our patient Mrs Barclay had just gone into the second stage of labour. She had started in the afternoon when I was out. The midwife had thought she had better let me know.

'Yes. Of course,' I looked at Beth in resignation. 'I'll be along straightaway.'

Mary Barclay, like so many of the women in our area, was to have her baby at home under the care of the midwife and her own GP, me. I had had my fill of obstetrics in my last hospital job. Even in the best of circumstances, childbirth was the most nerve-racking form of medical experience I had encountered. However normal the pregnancy or labour might have seemed, you could never be sure what would happen until the very last moment. In my view, all women should have their babies in hospital where the equipment was always at hand to deal with any unexpected emergency.

Harry and I only booked for home confinement women who had no chance of getting a hospital bed. Those women expecting their second, third or fourth babies who had had no previous obstetric complications. Some doctors still seemed to thrive on domestic midwifery and could, with some justification, claim that home was a safer and more natural place to have a baby, particularly in view of the staphylococcal infections endemic to most maternity units.

'There shouldn't be any trouble at all, Doctor,' said the midwife. 'She hasn't had any problem with the previous three. Very easy labours. I'll be quite happy to deal with it myself.'

'No, no. I'll come.' That's what we were paid for. Twelve pounds for the antenatal consultations, attending the confinement, postnatal visiting and a full postnatal examination. It compared favourably with the thirty shillings which was our total remuneration for looking after an NHS patient for a year, twenty-four hours a day. We always attended the delivery of our own patients – that was why Jim Grastick made sure I was notified.

'I'll probably only be a few minutes,' I told Beth. The midwife usually called at the beginning of the second stage of labour when the cervix was fully dilated and the baby was ready to be pushed out. Mrs Barclay wouldn't be long doing that.

I could see the midwife's bicycle propped up against the hedge as I approached the Barclays' house. Mr Barclay, an officer with the local fire brigade, was looking anxiously down the lane.

'There's some trouble I think, sir!'

I hurried past him to the front door.

'Is that the doctor, Mr Barclay?' a woman's voice shouted from upstairs. 'Tell him to come straight up.'

182

Mrs Barclay was lying on her back, smiling down at the screaming baby she held in her arms. She beamed at me as I came in.

'Another little boy,' she said.

Her legs were opened wide and between them was a pool of bright red blood. The midwife, blue uniform sleeves rolled up above the elbows, was rubbing the slack, newly flattened abdomen with an urgent vigour.

'It's a PPH, Doctor. She's had some ergometrine, but it won't stop.'

My stomach fell. A post partum haemorrhage. Just about the nastiest thing that could happen. Exsanguination and collapse could take place in minutes. The uterus still contained the afterbirth and was unable to squeeze down upon itself and stop the flow of blood. Mrs Barclay lifted her eyes from the baby for another moment.

'Everything's all right, isn't it, Doctor?'

'Yes, yes. Don't you worry.'

I took off my jacket, slipped on a face mask and hurriedly drew up another dose of ergometrine. I'd have to give it intravenously.

'Just let me have your arm a moment.'

She was a well-covered lady. Not a vein to be seen! I squeezed past the midwife to the other side of the bed . . . to the other arm. Nothing to be seen again but I could feel a vein under the skin.

'Please let me get in first time,' I prayed. Blood poured back into the syringe as I withdrew the plunger. I shot in the ergometrine.

'Blood pressure's ninety/fifty,' said the midwife. A bit low. But almost immediately she gave a cry of delight.

'Here it is, Doctor!' With a soft, squelching noise, the blue, glistening frying pan of a placenta slithered into view. The ergometrine had done its job, encouraging the muscles of the uterus to push out the now unwanted afterbirth.

Gently, the midwife lifted it clear, taking care not to leave behind any of the transparent membranes. If fragments were to be left they could prolong the bleeding.

'That's better,' she said with evident satisfaction and relief as she felt the abdomen once more. The uterus, now empty, had tightened down on itself like a clenched fist.

The midwife moved the rubber sheet under Mrs Barclay so that she could clear up the scarlet pool of blood clot. As she did so the space between the legs began to fill up again. The bleeding hadn't stopped. I heard the midwife gasp 'Oh, God!' She whispered to me, 'I'll call the flying squad, Doctor.'

We had an obstetric emergency service, which was run from a Westhaven hospital, that would come to such a catastrophe with doctor, nurse and, most important, blood for transfusion. Sometimes they could take an age to arrive, time that Mrs Barclay did not have.

'Yes. All right ... no, hang on, though, just a few seconds.'

I took a large handful of gauze swabs and tried to get a better look at the perineum, swollen and congested from the recent passage of a nine-and-a-half-pound baby.

'Open your legs a bit wider, Mrs Barclay.'

A fine jet of bright red blood splattered over my face and shirt front. That was it. The blood wasn't coming from the womb at all! I used some more swabs and another fine jet of blood went over my shoulder and hit the bedroom wall. Arterial bleeding. At that pressure it could be nothing else. There was a ruptured blood vessel somewhere in the lady's tail end.

'Spencer Wells, quick!'

The midwife fumbled in her bag and produced a pair of the toothed forceps. I swabbed again, and clamped where I thought the jets of blood were coming from. The forceps clicked shut. Another scarlet spray. Another swab. The forceps unlocked and locked again. Swabbed again. The perineum was dry. The bleeding had stopped.

'He's a beautiful boy, isn't he, Doctor?' said Mrs Barclay. I looked up. The mother was smiling down at me blissfully unaware of the drama that had taken place thirty inches from her nose.

'Getting on for thirty ounces,' said the midwife, estimating the blood loss. Mrs Barclay looked very well. Her blood pressure was normal. A woman in labour can lose quite a lot of blood without much upset, particularly one like the buxom Mrs Barclay.

'It was really lovely,' she said. 'It's so much nicer having a baby at home.'

Beth held the thermometer under the bedside lamp.

'One hundred and five point two,' she said. I had a look as well. There was no doubt.

Sarah was a sorry sight. She lay back on the pillows of our bed, limp and pale. Very poorly. Her cough was getting worse all the time. There was no evidence of pneumonia to be found when I examined her chest but I felt it could not be far off. No infection in her ears. Her throat was a little red and I'd already started her on penicillin. She had become more ill on each of the five days since we had taken the trip to Brighton and now seemed to be getting worse by the hour.

'She was very twitchy when you were in the surgery,' said Beth. 'I did try and cool her down. You don't think she'll have a convulsion do you?'

'Oh Sarah,' I said, leaning forward to stroke her hair. 'We'll have to sponge her down again, Beth.' Gently I put my arm under Sarah to lift her out of bed. As I brought her head forward she winced and began to cry.

'What is it?' said Beth anxiously.

'She's got a stiff neck.'

The significance was not lost on her.

'Meningitis?'

'Well, meningism, anyway . . . she's certainly got some irritation in her neck. It could be meningitis. I'm going to get a paediatrician to see her.'

I put Sarah back down again and went to the phone. Before I could pick it up, it rang.

'Doctor James.'

'Doctor James.' A woman's voice. 'I would be most grateful if you could come round and see me. I am a private patient of Doctor Brinckley. He always visits when I ask him.' I took down the name and address.

'What can I do for you?'

'A check-up, Doctor, I like to have a check-up — a full medical examination — once a year and I see from my diary that it's well overdue. I shall be leaving for Scotland tomorrow to stay with my sister until the New Year. I would like it done before I go.'

'I'm terribly sorry but I can't come at the moment. My little girl's ill and I . . .'

'Oh, dear. I *am* sorry. Later this morning, then.'

'I'm afraid not. I have several visits to do, all rather urgent.' I looked at the visiting list in my diary. 'I could come this afternoon, before evening surgery.'

There was the suggestion of an irritated snort at the other end of the line.

'That's out of the question. I have some last-minute shopping to do in Westhaven. I don't bother the doctor very often. I'm sure that Doctor Brinckley, were he available, would tell you that himself. I would be most grateful if you *could* come this morning. Otherwise I shall have to make other arrangements.'

'I'm sorry. I just can't. I . . .' The phone was put down.

'Why,' asked Beth, 'don't you get Jim Grastick to see her?'

How had she known?

'Who? That woman?'

'No! Sarah!'

He was still doing surgery. 'Of course. Delighted to, Neville. In about half an hour or so. I've got a couple of things to do here first, then I'll come straight over.'

I had time to do a couple of visits close by and then returned to Sangster Road. Jim pulled up at the same time.

'Let's have a look at you, Sarah.'

She was unprotesting as Jim examined her until he came to lift her head. Once more she winced and grizzled. Jim was very thorough. He left examining her throat until last. Many children hate having their throat examined. Sarah was no exception and would run half a mile if she saw a doctor approach with a tongue depressor. Today she made little fuss.

'Hmmmm,' said Jim as he stood up.

'Shall we get her into Westhaven General, Jim? I've already checked. They have got beds on the paediatric ward.'

Jim put his instruments back into his bag.

'Not unless you want to give all the rest of the kids measles,' he said with a grin.

'Measles!'

'Open wide, Sarah.' Jim shone his torch into her mouth. 'There they are.'

There they were indeed. On the inside of the cheeks. Tiny white spots, like particles of silver sand. Koplik spots. The diagnostic fingerprints of measles. Sarah had seemed so frail, I hadn't looked hard enough.

'She'll be smothered in spots tomorrow, I should think,' said Jim. 'Always the worst day, the one before the rash comes out. I'm sure you must have seen dozens of kids like this over the past few weeks. I know I have. Mostly with spots, of course. The mothers usually wait a bit longer than we tend to.'

Of course I had. But none seemed as ill as Sarah. I said as much to Jim.

'That's only because you haven't been this close to it. Involved. The kids are really quite sick.'

I wondered how many mothers I had reassured in the most patronizing fashion that their child had 'only got measles'.

'Keep up with the penicillin, though. It helps to keep down the secondary infection – otitis media, bronchitis.'

Jim stayed for a cup of coffee.

'How's Harry . . . and Mary?'

We told him that Mary was expected to be discharged in the next week and would be going to convalesce at her sister's. Harry might, with luck, be out just in time for Christmas.

'And my old friend, Mr Littlebone?'

I told him about our recent encounter.

'Fantastic! What kind of magic power do you have over him? Back to work. Unbelievable!'

I had to tell him the rest of the story.

The day after Mr Littlebone had been given his final certificate he came to see me again. At evening surgery. He looked as though he had been hit by a tram. Right arm in a sling, head held rigid by a large, white, padded surgical collar. He groaned with pain as he slumped into the chair in front of me.

'Mr Littlebone . . .?'

'I've just come from the hospital, Doctor. Did my neck and shoulder at Bowkers this afternoon. Lifting.' He was seized with a spasm of pain. 'Oh! Oh! That's agony! . . . It was too much for me. They told me to lift these heavy boxes on to a shelf. I tried. I tried. It was too high. Dangerous. Something just went.

'Oh God!' He groaned and tried to straighten his back. 'You'll have to sign me off again.'

188

It had, at least, been worth a try. Bad luck, I supposed. I started to write out a National Health certificate. Mr Littlebone turned stiffly and pointed with his finger.

'Not there. There. That part of the form. Industrial injury. I did it at work, didn't I? After all, I was fit before I went, otherwise you wouldn't have signed me back, would you?'

'No. Of course not.'

I handed him the piece of paper. He thanked me once again and with some difficulty let himself out of the door.

Yes. Bad luck. Back on the sick again. Bad luck? A possibility suddenly came to me. Industrial injury! Paid at a higher rate than either sickness benefit or the dole: one or the other of which was Mr Littlebone's habitual source of income.

'I was fit before I went, otherwise you wouldn't have signed me back, would you?' Surely not! I felt the colour rise to my face.

'Next!' I shouted angrily, scratching my findings into Mr Littlebone's notes.

'Yes. What can I do for you?' I said, without looking up as the next patient came in from the waiting room, a patient who would have waited for a long time. I was running very late. The voice was gentle, appealing – and familiar.

'Doctor. I wonder whether you could syringe my ears for me?'

It belonged to Beth.

Chapter Ten

'Is that any better, Gwilliam?' I asked anxiously.

The old Welshman took several gulps of air and managed a smile.

'Aye. I think so, Doctor. But the breathing,' he rested for a few moments, '. . . is a bit like . . .' I waited again. '. . . Blowing up a balloon with a hole in it.'

In spite of having worked a lifetime down the pits, his pneumoconiosis was not *that* bad. It was the chest infection that had tipped the balance. That in turn had followed the 'flu and, as he had told me when he caught it, there was a lot of it about.

Gwilliam's daughter had waited nearly all night before calling me. He had insisted that I should not be got out of bed. By six o'clock in the morning, however, she could wait no longer. The antibiotics I had given the day before had not yet had time to work. His bronchial tubes, narrowed and irritated by silica and countless Woodbines, had gone into spasm.

He sat propped against the pillows, shoulders hunched, as his chest tried to grasp every available scrap of air, watching the colourless liquid that was being injected, very slowly, into his arm.

I never much liked using aminophylline. For a start, it has to be given intravenously and it isn't always easy to find a vein. Doctors in the movies never seem to have any trouble in that direction, just sticking the hypodermic into the arm to the instant relief of the patient and the admiration of the relatives. 'Thank God you were in time, Doctor!'

Gwilliam had already received one injection, a mercurial

diuretic into the muscles of his backside. It was not just the bronchitis that was making him fight for breath. His heart, under strain, had begun to fail. The tell-tale crackling noises at the base of the lungs indicated a build-up of fluid. The diuretic would get rid of that, and increase the urine output, but it would all take time. The bronchospasm was the more immediate concern. Fortunately, Gwilliam's massive arms, shaped by fifty years of swinging a pick at a coalface, were all muscle – muscle across which snaked veins as large and as prominent as gas pipes.

There was another problem, though. The aminophylline had to be given very, very slowly. If it were not, it was possible that the patient, instead of benefiting from the relief that the drug invariably gave, would go into a state of collapse.

I looked at my watch on the bedspread. Seven minutes so far. The syringe was two thirds empty. I looked up at Gwilliam, he smiled again.

'That's much better, thank you.'

It was beginning to work. The improvement when it came was sudden and dramatic.

'What you really need, Gwilliam, is two weeks in the south of France being looked after by some of those ladies you see in the newspapers.'

His eyes twinkled. 'Have you seen the pictures of them, Doctor? Some of the girls don't wear anything except their knickers. I'd most likely have a heart attack!'

As he broke into a wheezing laugh I watched anxiously lest the needle be dislodged from the vein.

'In any case, you have to be careful with holidays. There's a story about . . .' He took a chestful of air. 'An old lady in the Rhondda, Mrs Llewellyn, her husband Alwyn died. She had him in a coffin in the front room – you know how they do that.'

I did indeed. The Welsh front room is the starting point

for the three most important occasions in life; baptism, marriage and funeral.

'Well, Mrs Evans came in from next door to have a look. "My goodness," she said, "there's a lovely tan your Alwyn has got, Mrs Llewellyn." "Yes," said Mrs Llewellyn, "we'd only just come back from a fortnight by the sea at Porthcawl when he was taken." "He looks lovely though," said Mrs Evans, "there's no doubt . . ." '

Gwilliam stopped. Exhausted, he took several more deep breaths. I waited for the familiar punchline. He must have told me this joke on at least a dozen previous occasions.

'. . ."No doubt," said Mrs Evans, "the holiday did him a lot of good." '

I couldn't help laughing. I did every time. Gwilliam chortled and wheezed and then began to cough. The syringe was empty and I took the needle out of the vein. The coughing became more violent. Great fruity, racking coughs. He leant over the side of the bed and spat a huge lump of black-flecked, yellow phlegm into a flowered chamberpot.

'Oh Dieu,' he said. 'That's good. I'll be much better now!'

I returned home to the smell of cooking bacon.

'I didn't think you'd want to go back to bed,' said Beth, 'and I expect you're hungry.'

I was. Sarah sat opposite me spooning porridge on to the top of her head. She was a lot better, but, even though the measles had come and gone two weeks before, she was still hacking at night.

We had shown her a few small fireworks through the window on the fifth of November but hadn't taken her out into the cold air. I never did like fireworks much in any case. Not since 1943 when a Junkers 88 had dropped a large banger fifty yards from our front door.

'It's a Jerry!' I had shrieked with excitement. It was. Very low. Great big black crosses on the wings. All over in a second, it looked like a dustbin falling out of its belly. I knew what to do; I had seen the men doing it at the pictures. I threw myself on the floor and was instantly projected a couple of feet into the air to meet the ceiling coming down. Not all of it, as it turned out. Nevertheless, it was a very big bang.

'Was it anything in particular?' asked Beth.

'I'm sorry, darling. I wasn't listening. What did you say?'

'The other call in the night. Did it turn out to be anything important?'

'Oh yes. Definitely. Renal colic. Commander Dymock. You know him – anyway, he knows you.'

A delightful man. Ex-Royal Navy who, encouraged by government spending cuts on defence, had taken early retirement. He and his wife ran the bookshop in Amblesham. Having no children of their own, they remembered other people's with particular clarity. Beth had taken Sarah to the shop on several occasions to buy picture books.

'Nice man. Is he all right?'

'He wasn't when I got there.' He had been in real agony. Renal colic, the pain that arises when the kidney tries to push out a stone, is said to be one of the most acute that can be suffered. Commander Dymock had been writhing on the bed, clutching his back and vomiting into a towel. I gave him a large shot of pethidine and was happy to see him improve. If he hadn't have done, I would have had to have sent him into hospital, there and then. I hoped that the stone, if not too large, would pass through, down into the bladder.

Harry had told me that of all the acutely painful conditions that got him out of bed for a visit, he had found renal colic to be the most common.

'Particularly when it's hot. Dehydration. And always get them to pee into a metal bucket or something for a day or two afterwards. They'll hear a "ping" as the stone comes out. Otherwise you'll lose it down the lavatory.'

A rattle from the front door announced the arrival of the post. Beth picked up the scattered envelopes. Mainly drug advertisements. They all went into the dustbin without being opened.

'There's one to you *and* me,' said Beth.

'You open it,' I replied, generously.

She scanned the contents.

'We've arrived at last. Celebrity status. It's from St Anthony's infant school. They're having an autumn bazaar next Saturday, and it's going to be opened by Lady West-haven. There's to be a fancy dress competition and we're invited to be judges!'

I thought I might as well open surgery. It felt halfway through the day already. There was one man waiting. Vic Wheeler.

'Come in, Vic.'

'Hallo, Doctor.' He took off his cap and sat down. 'I was a bit longer getting round to see you than I thought I would be. But it's been murder on the estate. There's talk of it going up for sale.'

There was little of importance on his medical card. The Wheelers were not ones for going to the doctor.

'Vic, you said something to me at the market about noises in your ears.'

'That's right, Doctor. This one.' He indicated with his right hand. 'Amy told me to tell you. It keeps her awake.'

I sighed. 'I have to tell you, Vic, that tinnitus, the noise that you get in your ear, isn't generally something we can do anything about. I'm sorry about Amy. The noise makes you very restless, I suppose. Twisting and turning. Fidgety.'

He nodded his head. 'It does that, of course. It's very annoying. But that's not what she means. She says that it's the noise coming out of my ear that keeps her awake.

194

She can't get off to sleep with it. Mind you, she's got very sharp hearing.'

I looked at his ear. Nothing abnormal to see at all. I picked up my stethoscope and put the bell to Vic's ear. There it was! Not true tinnitus at all, audible only to the sufferer. But quite loud. A whooshing sound coming out of Vic's head, his ear amplifying it much in the same way as an old-fashioned gramophone horn. It was loud enough, indeed, to hear without the stethoscope.

The still of the night in our part of East Sussex was fairly undisturbed. In the Wheeler's cottage, situated in the middle of Lady Westhaven's estate, the silence was total. The slightest noise would sound like thunder. Sleeping next to Vic's ear would have had the urban equivalent of living next to an iron foundry.

But that was not all. The implication of the noise was quite possibly serious. I smiled weakly.

'Oh yes! I can hear it.'

Vic was pleased that he hadn't been making a fuss.

'What do you think it could be, Doctor?'

It could, amongst other things, be a dilated artery within his skull, an aneurysm, possibly threatening to burst.

'I think it's a blood vessel in your ear or somewhere that's making all that noise. We'll have to get it attended to – Amy must get her sleep.' I paused for a moment not sure how he would react. 'There is one thing. I might want to send you up to London. I think that would be the best place to get you sorted out. You'll need some special X-rays.'

He was delighted. 'Cor! I love London. Haven't been up for years. St Paul's, I love that. And Kew Gardens. I might have a chance to go there . . .' The tempting list unfolded in his mind. I told him that I would ring him at Lady Westhaven's as soon as I had fixed up an appointment.

I had seen the next patient, a pleasant friendly lady, on several occasions.

'I understand you'll be coming to the Autumn Fayre on Saturday, Doctor.'

'That's quick, Joan. We only had the invitation this morning.'

'I know. My neighbour sent it. He's on the parents' committee. He felt sure you and Mrs James would help out.'

'Very kind of him.' I wrote out a prescription for her tablets. 'How are you, Sally?'

The pretty little girl sitting on her mother's lap giggled and coyly turned her face away, her long, blonde hair falling in a golden stream over her shoulders.

'Very well, Doctor. She won a prize at school for art. And for her writing.'

Sally's face reappeared, smiling. Her mother took the prescription and put it into a shopping bag which seemed half filled with . . . silver paper? She stood to leave.

'We'll see you on Saturday, then, Doctor . . . Come on slow coach.'

The little girl hobbled purposefully towards the door, her tiny wasted legs supported by large metal calipers. She had been born too soon. Another couple of years and polio immunization would have protected her against the tragic effects of infantile paralysis.

I wondered in what guise she would appear for the fancy dress. One thing was for sure, her mother would come up with something original.

As soon as surgery had finished I phoned up the neurological department of a London teaching hospital. They would be delighted to admit Vic in a day or two. I knew they would. Every student in the place would be shown his ear. They would then spend the rest of their professional careers listening to every ear with 'a noise in it' hoping to find another such one.

Vic wouldn't mind. It was the price to be paid for

going somewhere special. He knew that Harley Street was in London, therefore London must be the centre of the medical world. He would need a number of investigations, particularly a carotid angiogram, in which radio-opaque dye would be injected into his carotid artery to show up the blood vessels in his head. Perhaps one day it would be possible to investigate the inside of the skull without such intrusions. But it was difficult to imagine how.

There was a tapping on the French windows. I turned. It was Beth. I waved her in.

'Coffee, darling. And there's a new patient who's come to join your list. He's in the living room.'

I clicked my tongue with irritation. 'Oh dear. I'm so sorry.'

I hated it when patients came to the front door. Home was home. It was bad enough living on top of your place of work, without patients invading the house. I followed Beth into the living room.

Ron Godden's new assistant accountant had come to join my list. He stood as I entered, his face wreathed in smiles, and extended his hand. A massive, black hand.

'Neville!'

'Winston. How are you?'

Winston was to say many times subsequently that to introduce oneself to a prospective employer by putting him into hospital was probably unprecedented in industrial relations. Nevertheless, on the occasions after the accident that Winston had visited Ron in hospital a great attachment had developed between them. It soon occurred to Ron, who had for some time been looking for someone to help him, that he was unlikely to find a better articled clerk than a demon fast bowler who shared his love of cricket – and who had a degree in mathematics.

'And you've moved to Amblesham itself, Winston?'

'Yes. To a flat. Over Hawkins, the newsagents. You know them, I'm sure.'

'Of course.'

'The flat went with the job. Chrissie's taken over as manager. Mr Hawkins wants a bit more time off, apparently.'

I was puzzled. 'You mean Chrissie's given up nursing?'

'Yes. In the circumstances she had to.'

He hesitated for a moment and reached to an inside pocket to produce some medical cards.

'Here we are.' There were three. Winston Franklin Jenkins, Christianne Ruth Jenkins . . . and Michael Everton Richards?

'That's why I'm here, Neville, about Michael.' He suddenly became very serious. 'He's Chrissie's nephew. Her sister Ella's son. She lived with her husband in Bolton. He worked for British Rail up there, in the ticket office. They were both killed in a road accident a little while ago. We took Michael.' Winston opened his hands in a gesture of helplessness. 'There wasn't anybody else.'

'I am sorry, Winston. Of course I'll be delighted to look after all three of you. But you said that it was about Michael you wanted to see me. Is he not well?'

Winston explained that when they had collected Michael they had been shocked at his condition. Unfortunately, Chrissie's sister and her husband did not believe in doctors, but had been trying various herbal remedies. The little boy was lifeless, not eating, complaining of pains all over his body and he was getting worse all the time. I said I would go around and see him that morning.

Visits were light. Before going to see Winston's nephew I dropped in at the chemist to get some more cough medicine for Sarah.

Joe Baker, the pharmacist, a pleasant red-headed man in

his late fifties, was sorting through some ancient cardboard boxes in his dispensary.

'Hallo, Joe. New stock?'

He grinned. 'Neville. You don't fancy these, do you?' He reached down into one of the boxes and pulled out an ancient pair of pince-nez. 'They'd give you a certain ... presence. An air of authority. Or this ...?' He dangled a monocle on a red silk cord in front of my face. 'I've been clearing out the optical room. This stuff's been there for donkey's years. Since before I came. Belonged to old Chalky Unstead.'

As well as being our local chemist, Joe was also the optician, a practice he had taken over from the venerable Obadiah Unstead.

'And look at these.' He lifted on to his work bench a small chest of many drawers. The type of cabinet in which the butterfly collector keeps his specimens. He pulled out a tray.

'All colours,' he said. 'Look at them. Old as the hills.'

He went to put the box down again.

'Hang on a second, Joe.' I looked in the other trays. 'Can I have this one?'

'As many as you like, old son. I've got no use for them.' I slipped the prize into my pocket.

'And that?'

'That too, if it's any good to you.'

I was just going into Hawkins newsagents when, across the other side of the road, I saw the entire Littlebone family for the first time. Walking in file, Mrs Littlebone, head brilliant with coloured plastic rollers, dragged a toddler along with one hand and pushed a massive, battered pram piled high with shopping with the other, while children of various sizes trailed along behind. At the head of the column was Mr Littlebone. He was carrying an enormous television set with no apparent difficulty. I was about to call over when a furniture van came between us. When it moved on, the Littlebone clan had disappeared from view. There would be another time.

Mr Hawkins was behind the counter of his shop. He looked fully recovered from his coronary.

'Hallo, Doc. You see I did what you told me. Nice people,' he said, as he led me through the shop to the stairs beyond.

Chrissie opened the door. There was a strained smile on her face. She took me towards the back bedroom.

'Winston's had to go back to work,' she apologized. 'Michael! Here's the doctor to see you. He's come to make you better.'

He was a poor little thing. Tiny. Chrissie said he was nearly five, though he was smaller than the average two-year-old. She helped him off with his pyjamas. He looked like one of the new Oxfam advertisements. His arms and legs were like matchsticks, his eyes huge in the bony face, his teeth looked too big for his mouth and I could count all his ribs. Disproportionately, his abdomen was large, distended. A small umbilical hernia made his navel stand out like a little nose. I was reminded of the man I had met on my first day in Amblesham. The man dying of stomach cancer. This child was really ill.

'Let's have a look at you, Michael.'

I placed a hand gently on his abdomen. It was not distended with gas as I had hoped. Both liver and spleen were huge. I pulled down his lower eyelid to look at the colour of the mucous membrane. Almost white. The whites of his eyes themselves were yellow. There were enlarged glands in the neck.

It was most likely something awful. A childhood cancer, perhaps. Or, leukaemia. It occurred to me that if he hadn't been black the pallor would have been much more noticeable. As it was . . .

Black! Of course! There was an alternative diagnosis. Still serious, but not fatal.

'Chrissie. You can see Michael's very poorly. We'll have to get him into hospital. But I'd like to take him there myself, to get a blood test done. I'm not that pushed for time.'

We drove to Westhaven hospital and went straight down to the laboratory. Jim Slater, the pathologist, deftly pricked the end of Michael's finger and smeared the drop of blood on to a glass slide. Taking the slide through a series of reagents until the film was stained, he examined it under a binocular microscope.

'Hhhmmm . . . yes. There we are, Neville.' He moved to one side. 'Have a look.'

I adjusted the focus. There were the familiar round, red blood corpuscles. But between them were the other, strange, distorted cells.

In the mists of time and by the process of natural selection, Michael's forefathers, in the fever zones of Africa, had become different from their brothers. They had developed in their blood a special form of haemoglobin that gave them a slight advantage over nature. This molecular change in the red cells had made them just a little more resistant to their greatest enemy, falciparum malaria – the malarial parasite.

This trait had been passed down through the centuries, sometimes hidden, but sometimes, by genetic accident, taking an acute self-destructive form. Now it had manifested itself in someone who had never been nearer the fever coast than Bolton, Lancashire. The blood cells under the microscope were twisting and destroying themselves. Sickle cell anaemia.

'How bad is it, then?' Beth asked later. I had to tell her that it was bad enough. The sudden haemolytic crises in which the blood cells disintegrated could cause death from acute worsening of the anaemia. In the wild, as it were, those afflicted would not live beyond childhood. But with modern medicine, the availability of blood transfusion, of antibiotics to counter the infections that frequently developed in the weakened state, it was not uncommon for those with sickle cell anaemia to live to a reasonable age.

Michael was admitted to Westhaven paediatric ward immediately. He would probably be there for two or three weeks. Chrissie remembered later that, as a teenager, her sister had had several strange episodes of shivering attacks and near collapse. That no medical conclusion about them had been reached apart from 'nerves' had in no small part contributed to her future attitude towards orthodox medicine, an attitude that had nearly cost Michael his life. In retrospect, it was almost certain that the 'attacks' had been symptoms of her sickle cell trait, the genetic potential to carry the condition, to suffer from it in a very mild form without the full blown anaemia that her son was to develop.

I put on my interview suit for St Anthony's Autumn Fayre. That, and my black shoes. There were large holes in both soles but our bank overdraft would not allow a trip to the cobblers. I effected an emergency repair. Beth had made herself a new dress using the ancient hand-cranked sewing machine her mother had recently given her. I looked forward to future prosperity, doubting that my hernial orifices would stand a lifetime of lugging it up and down stairs.

As we entered the school of St Anthony's, we made, I felt, a most elegant couple. No heads were raised, however, from the frantic rummaging of the jumble of second-hand clothes. Cardigans, trousers, coats, jumpers, jackets were being purchased at twopence and threepence a go. Great armfuls of clothes could be bought for half a crown. I saw several jumpers that I could have fancied but Beth steered me through the crowd towards the dais.

The headmistress, Miss Finch, a large lady with threatening bosoms, looked at us blankly. I recognized her from her picture in the local paper. St Anthony's was always in the press.

'Are you from the *Gazette*?' she said. 'Lady Westhaven is expected any moment.'

'No, I . . .'

'Then you must be from the rag company. I'm afraid you're far too early. You can clear the residue at the end of the afternoon.' She stood on tiptoe to see if her distinguished guest had arrived.

'No. I'm Doctor James. This is my wife. We were . . . invited.' She looked mildly surprised.

'Oh, yes. I remember hearing something about it. Thank you for coming, I . . .' She was staring over my shoulder. Suddenly her face broke into a smile. 'Excuse me.' She hurried past us towards the door.

'Lady Westhaven!' she cooed. 'How gracious of you to come.' A severe-looking lady, thin as a rake and at least six foot two inches tall, stood in the doorway. She was dressed from head to foot in duck-egg blue. An iceberg. Beside her, a good nine inches shorter, stood her grey-liveried chauffeur.

'She used to be a model,' whispered Beth.

It wasn't easy to imagine what for.

The headmistress took Lady Westhaven's hand and gave a slight curtsey. None of the rummagers bothered to look up from their search. The guest of honour was led through the bustling crowd to the dais.

'Lady Westhaven,' said Miss Finch, 'I would like to introduce you to Doctor and Mrs . . .?'

'James.'

'Yes. Doctor and Mrs James.'

The tall lady stared down her elongated nose at me. She extended her gloved hand with appropriate *noblesse oblige*.

'Ah, Doctor James,' she said. 'One of my daily women speaks very highly of you.'

She ignored Beth completely. It was a good job she did. My wife would have shamed me by laughing out loud.

We sat through Lady Westhaven's address, a homily on the benefits of free state education, laced with the theme that people should, nevertheless, know their place and not rock the boat of our ordered society.

Getting rather stiff, I crossed one leg over the other. Lady Westhaven looked down in horror. She, and the audience, could see the large strips of Sellotape that were holding the soles of my shoes together.

By the time she had finished most of the jumble, the potted plants, the jars of chutney and marmalade had been sold. It was time for the fancy dress parade. The usual contemporary figures were there. Sooty, Henry Cooper, Dixon of Dock Green, Perry Mason, Elvis Presley, Yuri Gargarin. One extraordinarily large ten-year-old was dressed as 'Cheyenne'. He definitely needed an X-ray of his skull.

'Pituitary gigantism,' I whispered to Beth.

The contestants walked around in a large circle. All of a sudden I saw Sally. Not walking, but being pushed along on an old pram by her elder brother. The lower half of her body was encased in hundreds, thousands, of the milk-bottle tops her mother had been collecting with such energy.

Except that, now, the old pram was a carriage, painted the blue and white and green of sea foam, her brother was King Neptune complete with silver crown and trident, and Sally herself was a mermaid, the light shimmering on the silver and gold scales of the fish tail that her mother had so painstakingly made.

The cavalcade marched three times around the hall. Lady Westhaven whispered something to the headmistress, who, in turn, whispered to us.

'Lady Westhaven thinks the mermaid is best.' We agreed immediately.

Sally was called up and accepted her prize. The cardigans and blouses flew through the air as the rummagers dived into the piles of clothes for one last time to make sure that no treasures had been left undiscovered. The headmistress and Lady Westhaven drifted away to another part of the building and we were left alone. Our impact upon society had been less than shattering.

As we walked out of the door, Beth smiled at me, sweetly. 'Don't worry, love. Her daily woman speaks very highly of you.'

Before we reached the car a short, dumpy lady in her early sixties puffed up to me and took hold of my hand.

'Doctor James?' I didn't recognize her.

'Doctor, I wonder if you can help me? You saw my son Harold yesterday – at evening surgery. He's . . .' she hesitated, 'in the army.'

Of course I remembered. A most striking young man, very tall, with a shock of red hair. We'd had a long chat. He had done very well for himself. He had been brought up in a tiny cottage, the only child of elderly parents he told me. His mother was now a widow. His uniform had been immaculate, the khaki battledress looking as though it had been cut by a Savile Row tailor, and the webbing blancoed to the consistency of velvet. The army boots shone like polished jet. He was about to go to an officers' training unit, it appeared, and it had been suggested that he might be commissioned into one of the crack infantry regiments of the British Army. With all the excitement he had had a little insomnia and had requested a few sleeping tablets.

'A very fine boy, Harold. You must be very proud of him.'

I used the word 'boy' easily. He must have been at least six years younger than me.

'Yes, Doctor . . . I suppose I am. But did you think there was anything wrong with him?'

I smiled at her reassuringly. 'Not at all. Fit as a flea. I'm sure he'll do really well.'

The next day was one of the most irritating kind. After morning surgery one call followed another, but always allowing sufficient time in between for me to get home first. On each occasion I came through the door, Beth had a fresh visit. I was sitting down to a very belated lunch when the phone rang again. I swore loudly. Beth hid behind a newspaper.

'I'll be at the Rigfords'. It's way out in the sticks. Miles from anywhere,' I moaned. 'She's not progressing with her labour. Christ knows how long I'll be. I'll ring you when I get there in case anything else comes in . . . and I expect it will,' I added bitterly.

Mr Rigford let me in through the back door of the bungalow. The front was blocked by an overgrown blackthorn hedge.

'I'll just use your phone, if I may, to ring my wife,' I said.

'Don't work,' he said. 'Hasn't done for a week or more. Can't get them out to fix it. The nurse had to go into town to phone you.'

I trudged into the bedroom which Mrs Rigford shared with her son's motorcycle. Fortunately my appearance had a dramatic effect on the uterus. Mrs Rigford's contractions suddenly got stronger. Within half an hour the cervix was fully dilated, and, fifteen minutes after that, a third Rigford daughter was nuzzling at her mother's breast.

Beth was waiting anxiously when I arrived home.

'I tried to get hold of you,' she said, 'but there was something wrong with the Rigfords' phone.'

'What's the matter, then?'

'It's Mr Styles. He says his wife has fallen out of a tree or something.'

'Oh God! What have you done?'

'I phoned up the ambulance on 999 ... and, I hope you don't mind, but I gave Jim Grastick a ring as well.'

'How long ago?'

'About fifteen minutes.'

By the time I arrived at the Styles's, both Jim Grastick and the ambulance were already there. Jim was kneeling beside Jill Styles, who lay flat on her back among the rose bushes under the bedroom window. The ambulancemen were sorting out what appeared to be a collection of metal tubes.

'I'm so sorry, Jim. I'm sure Beth told you. She couldn't reach me.'

'Not at all, Neville. Thank you for coming.'

Jill Styles looked up from the ground. She appeared perfectly well.

'Hallo, Doctor. Sorry to have caused you all so much bother. I'm sure I'll be able to get up now.' She moved slightly.

'Stay perfectly still,' said Jim sharply. 'Absolutely still!'

Mrs Styles almost came to attention. Jim looked at me.

'Have you dealt with this kind of neck injury before?' he asked quietly. I had to confess that I hadn't. 'One rule. You have to assume the worst possible until you can get an X-ray.'

Mr Styles was at my elbow. 'She was up a ladder, Doctor. Pruning the wisteria of all things. High up there, under the eaves. She had another of those dizzy turns. Fell right on her head.'

'You saw it?'

'I was just coming up the garden path from work when it happened!'

I looked down at Jill Styles. 'How do you feel Jill?'

She shivered a little. 'I'm getting a bit chilly. Perhaps if I got up . . .'

'Don't move an inch,' snapped Jim.

The ambulancemen arranged the tubes under the patient, fixing them together so that she was on a stretcher without having been lifted. Very gently she was moved into the ambulance. I heard her apologise again for 'all the trouble' she had caused and Jim tell the driver not to exceed twenty-five miles an hour.

The next morning the phone rang while I was eating breakfast. It was the casualty officer from Westhaven hospital about my patient Mrs Styles. He thought I might be interested to know that Jill had sustained a fracture of the odontoid peg.

A hangman's fracture. The odontoid is the bone by which the skull rotates on the neck. It is also the bone that is snapped as the hangman's noose crashes into the base of the skull severing the spinal cord. The ultimate in broken necks. She had, the casualty officer continued, no signs of any spinal cord injury and was expected to make a full recovery. If Jim Grastick had let her move an inch, she would have died instantly or, more likely, been paralysed from the neck down for the rest of her life.

I went into the hallway where Beth was picking up the mail and told her what had happened.

'I'm glad I called Jim, then' she said.

'You probably saved Jill Styles' life. She was bound to have tried to get up if I'd been a long time getting there. Thank you . . . but you haven't noticed, have you?'

She looked perplexed. I pointed up with my finger.

'Uncle Walter!' Beth looked up at the mouldering leopard's head high on the wall. 'He's got two eyes!'

'I picked one up at Joe's. He had a whole boxful.'

'You could have got one to match.'

'Absolutely. A perfect match I expect, if I'd wanted. He'd got all the colours of the rainbow. But there's something dashing about one blue and one brown.'

'The monocle's going a bit over the top though, isn't it?'

I had to agree. 'Perhaps you're right.'

I shivered slightly. 'God, it's cold this morning.'

'Is it?' said Beth. 'I hadn't noticed. Seems a bit warmer if anything.'

She was right. I was getting 'flu. There was a lot of it about.

And in his bedroom under the eaves of a tiny cottage, Harold, the immaculate soldier, was, for the hundredth time, examining his prized possession.

Chapter Eleven

'Mrs Rowbuck wants some more Librium. I've written her out for thirty. And Mr Rowbuck. I've given him thirty as well. Not the green and black ones he said, but the green and yellow ones. They're five milligrammes, aren't they?' I nodded weakly. Beth looked at her notes.

'And Mrs Croker came in. She said that she had been feeling tired for some while and now she's got some red lumps on her legs. She insisted on showing me. They were quite big and tender.' Beth hesitated for a moment. 'I don't know, of course, but I think they might have been erythema nodosum. I remembered from a picture in one of your books. I told her to come back at three o'clock to see Jim.'

I lifted my head from the pillow but it hurt too much and I let it flop back again.

'She'll need a chest X-ray,' I croaked.

'In case of sarcoidosis,' said Beth. 'Sarcoidosis. Streptococcal infection. Sulphonamide. Primary TB,' she added, repeating the litany of differential diagnoses she had asked and repeated countless times.

'She did say that she had a very bad sore throat four weeks ago.'

That was it then. It would be streptococcal. With my little remaining strength I scratched out my signature on the prescriptions.

'Beth?'

'Yes, darling?'

'I think I'm going delirious,' I said weakly.

'Why, love?'

'Just now. I could have sworn you said someone wanted a tetracycline tablet for their goldfish.'

'I did. Mr Thatcham from two doors away. He said Harry gives him one every November to put in his fish tank. Says it keeps the goldfish healthy through the winter. I found one in your bag for him.' I'd never thought of a fish having bronchitis.

'I'll see another three then I'll be back up,' said Beth, before she disappeared downstairs.

I had been confined to bed for three days, confined by the inability to get out of it. There is an old medical truism that 'if you think you're dying, you've got the 'flu'. Influenza can make you very ill. Nobody ever worked through the real thing, whatever they might say. Through a heavy cold, perhaps. Real influenza lays one flat – it did, after all, do that in a permanent fashion to million upon million in 1919.

The day after Jill Styles broke her neck, I went from slightly unwell at breakfast to being poleaxed with a temperature of 104° at teatime. My fever had remained at that level ever since. I had managed an awful evening surgery but had then begun to shake and vomit. Inevitably, the phone rang. One of my regular customers thought she had broken her wrist and wanted me to visit. No. She would not go to Westhaven casualty department. She wanted to see her own doctor, at home. If I did not come she intimated that she might complain to my employers, the Executive Council. She mentioned that she had passed the surgery earlier but it was too crowded for her to visit.

Beth drove me to the house. I almost fell through the front door but spent some minutes examining the lady so that I could breathe over her as many influenza viruses as possible. There was no sign of significant injury.

The single-handed GP is never more vulnerable than when he is ill. He remains responsible for all his patients,

211

even if he is lying unconscious on the floor. Were any patients to come to harm because he or another doctor was unable to attend them, he would be in severe trouble. The Health Service makes no provision for replacements. It is the individual doctor's responsibility.

There was no chance of getting a locum at such short notice. Fortunately, Harry did have an understanding with Jim Grastick about sickness which neither had ever used. It remained for me to phone Jim and tell him of my plight. It was arranged that he would do my visits, see any patient of mine who could get to his surgery and do a short consultation at our house, in the middle of the afternoon, for those who could not. The rest Beth would manage, with me signing the forms.

It had been a very revealing experience. Beth's ability to cope with almost an entire surgery without an atom of formal medical training made me feel entirely redundant. One or two patients insisted that they *must* see me. Urgently. I put on my institutional, brown furry dressing gown and staggered down to the living room.

One such was Miss Clementine Smith.

'I'm sorry you're feeling unwell,' – Unwell! I was dying! – 'but I knew you wouldn't mind seeing me.'

Her eyes quickly scanned the shelves and mantelpiece for the cross-eyed man. She couldn't see him.

'I wonder whether,' she lowered her voice lest anyone (who?) should hear her, '. . . I may have some more . . . pills.' I was starting to shiver. In a minute or two I'd have a proper rigor. '. . . Laxative pills,' she whispered.

I scrawled out a prescription for senna and crawled back upstairs to my bed. I'd meant to ask Beth about the cross-eyed man. I had visited Miss Clementine Smith on numerous occasions. On the last she had insisted that I should accept 'a little something' for being so kind –

a pottery figure with eyes like the silent film star, Ben Turpin, set in a hideous squint, with one arm held out at an extraordinary angle. It had, obviously, been knocked off at some time and had been stuck back on in totally the wrong alignment. In all, absolutely ghastly.

'Genuine Staffordshire,' said Miss Smith, and she should know, for she was an expert on such things. I told Beth as much when I took him home. We had no antiques and I suggested he should go in the middle of the mantelpiece. He was no longer there.

I looked at the thermometer again. 103.8°. I took my temperature every fifteen minutes. My sole amusement. I felt too ill to read, even to listen to the portable radio Beth had borrowed from Sylvia Godden. Sylvia was looking after Sarah during the day. I checked my pulse once more. God! It was fast! Perhaps I had myocarditis. The influenza virus rotting away my heart muscle.

Beth came up again.

'Mr Huster . . . his digoxin. 0.25 milligrammes a day and his headache pills. I can only see Panadol on the card. And his National Health certificate. Jimmy Greenfield has fallen off a wall and hurt his ankle. I've written a note for the casualty if you could sign it . . . and Harold something or other.' She clicked her tongue. 'I've left the card downstairs. You know, the one in the army.'

'Oh yes,' I said. 'Nice lad.'

'Do you think so?' said Beth. 'I don't know. Almost *too* nice . . . anyway, he says that you gave him a prescription for some sleeping tablets but he's lost it. Could he have another one?'

She looked at her piece of paper once more. 'And Mr Littlebone came to ask for a copy of all his medical records. His union have instructed a QC to represent him. He's suing Bowkers apparently. Something to do with the shelves.'

Jim Grastick came over in the afternoon. I was comforted when he listened to my chest, though I knew he wouldn't be able to hear the more sinister things that I feared could afflict me. There had only been three or four patients to see, ones that Beth had been unable to sort out and who could not get to Jim's surgery.

'That was very good. The erythema nodosum diagnosis, Beth. I'm sure you're right.'

Beth smiled. 'It just stuck in my mind.'

And so it did in mine. I remembered the very afternoon before finals on which she had tested my knowledge of the collagen diseases – rheumatic fever, rheumatoid arthritis and the like.

She was well into her pregnancy. I had come home early from medical school at lunchtime, intent on doing a heavy session of revision. Beth met me at the door, her face streaming with tears.

'What on earth's the matter?'

She broke into great shuddering sobs and I led her upstairs to our flat. I assumed something dreadful must have happened.

'I was sitting by the window,' she said, sniffing loudly, 'when this blind man came into the road.'

'Yes?'

'He was playing a piano accordion outside in the street. He was all in rags and he had an old cap on the ground to collect money and he was playing and smiling and he didn't know there was nobody in the street. Not a soul. Because he couldn't see. He was smiling at people who weren't there!' She began to sob again. 'It was so sad. It made me feel so miserable.'

I gave her my handkerchief.

'Did you go out and give him a couple of bob?'

'I wasn't *that* miserable.' We were pretty hard up at the time.

214

That night I felt a little better. Beth made me a large glass of whisky and hot lemon and I began to sweat. One of the physicians at our teaching hospital always said that if a case of influenza was admitted to a medical ward a hundred diagnoses would be made before the right one was achieved. He added that you could assure the patient that they were getting better when the steam began to rise. And it was. Great clouds of it. Everything was soaked. My temperature fell to a hundred and I felt as though I had melted. Any longer at 104° and I would have started playing with my bed covers like the dying typhoid victim.

'We'll have to start our Christmas shopping soon,' said Beth, beside me in bed, looking up from the *Telegraph* crossword. I had not anticipated living that long. Presents. Now was a good time to ask her.

'What happened to Ben Turpin? Clementine Smith was looking for him today.'

Beth became slightly flustered. 'Oh – I meant to tell you. A little accident, I'm afraid. I knocked him off the mantelpiece when I was dusting. I'm dreadfully sorry, love, really . . . "Sailor indisposed goes mad", five letters, first one "R".'

'Rabid.'

Beth screwed up her nose. She hadn't got it. 'Yes. Rabid. AB – able seaman, in disposed . . . in disposed . . . rid. Rabid!'

She might be able to run the practice without me but she needed my considerable intellect to finish the crossword.

The next day my fever was back to 102° but within another forty-eight hours I was, rather shakily, able to take surgery. I was as weak as a rat and Beth had to drive me on my visits. Jim Grastick insisted on doing all the night calls. I did not argue. If one good thing did come of my illness it was our determination in future to have a proper night rota.

While I was still in bed, Beth did have two more strange confrontations. Both on our front doorstep. On the first occasion a young man, squirming with embarrassment, asked to see her father – responsibility was making me age prematurely. On being told that her *husband* was in bed, ill, he asked her whether she could help him with his . . .

'Yes?' said Beth, waiting for him to compose himself. With his piles. This was a no-go area to my wife, one in which she had no experience, neither personally, nor in helping with my pre-MB studies. Haemorrhoids had been in the surgical finals paper the previous year and they were very unlikely to come up again for some time.

Nevertheless, she asked him if he was having any treatment. Doctor James had given him suppositories, he said, but he was finding them very uncomfortable to use. Scratchy. Using a process of deduction, she was able to improve matters by advising him to remove the silver paper before insertion.

The second incident occurred at lunchtime. The front door bell began to ring and did not stop. Beth found a large lady in the porch; a large, inebriated lady, leaning on the bell push to steady herself.

'Ah, Beth, my dear. Beth.' It was Dora. She and her sister, who lived together in legendary enmity, were frequent callers at the Tarrington-Bagfords'. Millie took great pleasure in introducing them to us.

'I think my sister, Dorothy . . .' She began to giggle and the shopping bag in her hand clicked with the sound of bottles. '. . . *Dorothy*, has taken all her pills . . . again.' Beth was aghast. How was she? When had it happened? Dora thought for a moment and then addressed herself to a point some inches from Beth's left ear.

'I'm not *absolutely* certain, not absolutely, you understand. I thought she might have done when she didn't wake up this morning. But I wasn't really sure. Sometimes she does sleep heavily. So I went out to friends for . . . coffee. When I got home she was still asleep and making funny noises. And all her pill bottles were empty. I suppose I should have noticed this morning.'

She began to laugh again. 'Silly woman. Just because I beat her at canasta last night. One of these days she'll really hurt herself.'

The ambulancemen were quick and after some days of struggle the staff of Westhaven hospital were able to save Dorothy's life. She regretted her action very much and swore to the doctors that she'd never do it again. Next time she'd put the pills in her sister's tea. On hearing the good news Dora somewhat reluctantly returned her new dress to Marks and Spencer's and got her money back. She did, after all, feel that black suited her.

When I started to walk about it felt as though the ground had turned to cotton wool. The surgeries were very light, however. Word has got out that I was ill, had had a nervous breakdown, tuberculosis, a heart attack. Nevertheless, there was a kind consideration that made people wait a little longer than usual before 'bothering the doctor'.

I visited Harry in hospital.

'Neville. You look really dreadful.' I had lost three quarters of a stone. 'Is your flu better? . . . Good!'

'I'm glad you came. There's something I want you to do for me. Something *very* important.' He paused for maximum effect. 'I want you to sell my library.'

He lifted his hand to silence the protestation that I was not about to make. 'I know it's a big step. But you could do it for me, couldn't you? Make an approach to the major London book merchants? Foyles, etc. Get them to arrange some kind of deal?'

His eyes shone with an almost maniacal fervour. At

the best times, when he had plenty to occupy him, Harry came up with new schemes almost every day. Now, unable to move, shackled by counterweights and harnesses, he had nothing to do but think. The more harebrained the scheme, the more attractive it seemed. He indicated the pink pages of the *Financial Times* spread across his bed cover.

'I'm thinking of going in for stocks and shares. There is money to be made. I can raise the capital to build a portfolio by selling my book collection.'

He leant over towards his bedside cabinet and picked up a piece of paper that was leaning up against his flower vase.

'Just put these few volumes to one side. Nothing particularly valuable, they're just the ones I want to keep. For sentimental reasons. They're mostly ones given to me by friends.' He was silent for a few moments but his face suggested a pleasurable anticipation. He would make his fortune, he had decided . . .

He shook himself back to reality. 'And the practice? You're doing splendidly, I'm sure.' He grinned broadly. 'I did have a get-well card from the Formbys.'

He showed it to me. A picture of a large teddy bear covered in spots. 'Hurry up and get better. We miss your skill' was written inside. 'Mr and Mrs Formby.'

'George' Formby was definitely one of my failures. I had been called to see him a couple of weeks previously.

'It's not Doctor Brinckley, then?' said the lady who opened the door. 'My husband always sees Doctor Brinckley.' 'George' Formby lay stretched out on a couch in the living room, beside him a brimming ashtray and a pile of newspapers.

'I'm very sorry,' I said, 'Doctor Brinckley's still in hospital.'

'Then it can't be helped,' said Mr Formby. A pale, rather sombre man, nobody could have been more different from the toothy, banjo-playing comic after whom he had been nicknamed.

I examined him. It was a classical presentation. He had an acute lumbar disc lesion – a slipped disc. 'Have you any idea how you did it?' I asked. He looked rather embarrassed.

'It's his own fault, Doctor,' his wife chipped in. 'He did it dancing. We go to the Old Time dancing club every week, and last Tuesday, at the end, the young man who plays the records put on this new thing . . .'

'The Twist,' said George sheepishly.

'And look what happened,' said his wife. 'He would try it.'

I gave him some analgesics, told him to lie flat on his back and assured him that he would be much better in five days. I gave him the same assurance five days after that, and five days after that, by which time he was unable to walk across the room.

Harry listened to the story with interest. 'I'm sorry about it, Harry. I've had to ask David Hasling to come and see him at home next Monday.'

David Hasling, one of the local orthopaedic surgeons, would probably put him in a plaster jacket.

'Don't worry. I'm sure you've got everything under control,' said Harry, in a tone that suggested our conversation was nearing its close. I heard a rattle and turned to see the supper trolley approaching. 'And remember, if you do have the time – and I don't expect it's too busy at the moment . . . doesn't tend to be before Christmas – see about the books for me.'

By Monday I felt that, at least, my life-support systems were working, though to walk fifty yards felt like running a marathon. Sensing my recovery, the patients appeared in large numbers, the most unexpected, beaming all over his face, being 'George' Formby. It was a miraculous recovery.

I said as much. The last time I'd seen him he'd been unable to get out of bed.

'Miraculous is exactly the right word, Doctor. Exactly.' He meant me to understand the deep significance of what he was saying. 'There will be no need for the surgeon to come and see me. I got it sorted out for myself.'

He'd been to an osteopath, that's what he'd done. Osteopaths always make people better, or so it seems, because the people who have paid their money and don't get better never tell anybody.

'You've been to an osteopath, haven't you, George? The one down opposite the station. He's very good I hear.'

'No, no. I've been to him before. Didn't do me any good. No. I went to someone ... Someone ...' but he was lost for a sufficiently splendid adjective.

Reaching into his breast pocket he produced a card. It was gold-edged and printed in gothic script. The gentleman named, at an address in Brighton, seemed to have about fifteen qualifications all of which, I must confess, were completely unfamiliar to me. Across the bottom of the card shone out the words 'POWER FROM THE COSMOS'.

'That's him, I took this article about him out of a magazine.'

He showed me a photograph of a very well-dressed young man with an American haircut and a smile that suggested expensive orthodontics.

'Amazing!' I shook my head in wonder. 'What kind of treatment did he give you?'

'It was so simple, Doctor. He had this box with all lights flashing on it and there was this great big kind of vibrating plastic thing coming out of it. He held it in my back and it was like a buzzing. "Cosmic force," he said. He did it for about twenty minutes. When he'd finished the pain had gone. As you said. Miraculous.'

Extremely impressed, I stood up to shake his hand as he

left. Quite astonishing. A man who hadn't been able to get out of bed until . . . until? I cleared my throat. Mr Formby was just going out of the door.

'Er, Mr Formby . . . George.' There was one thing that wasn't quite clear. 'Where did this . . . er . . . gentleman give you the treatment?'

'In Brighton. At his home.'

'You took a taxi, did you?'

'Good heavens, no! Couldn't afford that. I went on the motorbike.'

In the afternoon I phoned up two or three of the major London book dealers. One was particularly interested. The company would send down their chief buyer on Thursday afternoon for a preliminary survey of Harry's library. Had we got an inventory? Unfortunately we had not. Perhaps, he suggested, a direct sale could be arranged between Harry and a learned institution.

Within a day or two I found that I was reassuring people over the telephone that they had only got the 'flu, that it was nothing to worry about, that they didn't need a doctor and that there was a lot of it about. I knew, I reassured them, because I had had it myself. One call seemed exactly like the rest. Hot, shivering, ill, vomiting. Why I visited, I don't know. I just did. In the event the young man had acute appendicitis. There had been no mention of pain. After that I visited every call for 'flu that came in.

On Wednesday evening Harold's mother called. She sounded very distressed. Could I come and see her son? She was calling from a telephone box but rang off before I could get any more information.

There was only one small downstairs room in her cottage – that, and a tiny scullery. The stairs to the bedrooms were curtained off in a corner of the sitting room.

Harold was nowhere to be seen. His mother asked me

to sit down but I had to wait for a minute or two before she was able to start.

'Oh dear. Oh dear.' She wrung her hands, not knowing where to begin. 'You see, he's not really in the army, Doctor. Not any more. He's been discharged. Medically unfit.'

'You mean Harold? But I thought he . . .'

'He's still got the uniform. I expect he stole it. Or didn't hand it back in. But he got into a lot of trouble. Hit an officer. He was put in prison first, a military prison. Then they transferred him to a hospital.'

She stood up, went to the mantelpiece and took a buff envelope from behind the clock.

'I had this. From the army doctor.'

It was a very kind letter. The medical officer had been thoughtful enough to write, personally. Harold, he was sorry to say, was not suitable for service in the army. He was keen and might have had real potential. But he *did* have a personality disorder which made his behaviour both erratic and irresponsible. There was no known treatment that would help him, the doctor explained, but he advised that the family doctor be contacted when Harold came home. He was very sorry indeed, but added that there was some hope. Sometimes people with this kind of problem could mature, grow up, albeit late in the day, and become more acceptable members of society.

'And how is he now?'

She was very distressed. 'I'm so frightened for him, Doctor, that he'll harm himself. Or somebody else. He told me that he's been to Westhaven this afternoon and thrown a brick through a window of the Army Recruiting Office. He says that some people who knew who he was saw him do it. But he said he didn't mind.'

'I'd better see him.'

The stairs were almost as steep and as narrow as a ladder. At the top were two small doors, and from behind one came the sound of rock-and-roll music. I lifted the latch and entered.

It couldn't be Harold! He didn't notice when I came in but lay, eyes closed, on a small bed under the sloping wall. The room smelt of sweat, beer and cigarette smoke. A single, naked electric light bulb hung from the ceiling. The walls were covered with posters of tanks, guns, Second World War aeroplanes. Harold, dressed in jeans and a camouflage smock, looked filthy and unshaven.

His uniform, swathed in protective polythene, was placed carefully on a hanger. Buttons gleaming, knife-edged creases. His boots, black mirrors, stood on the floor beside a shoe-cleaning box.

'Harold?'

He opened his eyes and sat up with a jerk. 'Hallo Doc. Come on in. Sit down. Have a drink.' His speech was rather slurred. He picked up a flagon of beer. 'A beer . . . or whisky?' he added, picking up another bottle and turning it upside down. 'Sod it. All gone . . . Never mind.'

Pouring some beer into a china cup, he passed it to me. I sat down beside him on the bed. There was no chair.

'I expect the old lady called you, didn't she? She does go on.'

I told him what she had said about his trip to Westhaven. I didn't mention the hospital or the medical discharge.

'You should have seen it. Fantastic. Shattered. Do you like this?' He indicated the record player.

'Yes . . . Good. Little Richard, isn't it?'

'That's right.' He was impressed. He proceeded to talk about rock music and how he thought he might form a band.

I brought up the subject of window-breaking again.

'I'm going down to Brighton, tomorrow, to do the same thing there.'

'But you mustn't, Harold. The police are bound to find out. You'll get into a lot of trouble.'

He winked at me conspiratorially and put his hand inside his jacket.

'If the police come here, I've got a surprise for them.'

He must have stolen it from the army. A service revolver! He produced it from a large inside pocket and with one movement cocked back the hammer and pushed the end of the barrel into my umbilicus.

I assumed the shape of the letter 'C' but the deadly object followed my retreating navel. I attempted to continue my inane chatter trying desperately to keep my mouth open and my bowels closed at the same time. Harold told me that he had nothing against me personally. I was happy to be reassured but I hoped that no spasm would suddenly afflict his trigger finger. He was only demonstrating, he told me, what he would do if the police did try and interfere. It was not the time to get into an argument. It seemed an age. There was a tap on the door.

'Harold?' It was his mother. She sounded very nervous.

'Harold,' she called again. 'There's some gentlemen downstairs who would like to see you for a few minutes.'

I knew it was the police. Harold knew it was the police.

'All right, Mother. I'll be down in a minute.'

He smiled and squeezed the trigger. There was a loud . . . click.

'It's a replica,' he grinned, 'You know. A model. Good, though, isn't it? Really puts the shits up people.'

He stood and opened a bedroom window. 'Always went out this way when I was a kid,' he said, climbing up on the sill. 'You can jump down. Cheerio.'

I never saw Harold again.

The man from the bookdealers was most impressive. Three-litre Rover and pigskin briefcase. I met him at

Harry's as arranged. Sharp on 2.30. He was the kind of man who would always be on time.

'Doctor Brinckley,' he said, extending his hand.

'Doctor James, actually. I'm acting on behalf of Doctor Brinckley. He's in hospital, has been for several weeks.'

'Oh, I'm sorry. Nothing serious, I hope.'

I tried to imagine, for a moment, a condition that wasn't serious but would keep a man in hospital for several weeks.

'An accident. We hope he'll be out fairly soon.'

'I see . . . You do understand that this is a preliminary survey, to assess the most advantageous method of sale. The full valuation will come later.'

'Of course.' I opened the front door for him. 'If you'll excuse me, I have a visit to do. I'll be back at . . . a quarter to four.'

That would give him more than an hour for the initial browsing and finishing in time for me to get back to evening surgery.

I'd got one afternoon call to do. Fred Turner. Very odd. As far as I could see from his records he'd never had a medical visit in his life. He'd only attended surgery on two occasions in the last fifteen years, and one of those was a medical to confirm him fit for driving. 'Driving medical. Fee paid – one box of cabbage plants' Harry had written in the notes. In truth, Fred hadn't called this time. It had been his daughter.

'Please don't tell him I called you, Doctor James,' she said as she let me in. 'Just say you happened to be passing.'

This request, so frequently made, always struck me as extraordinary – 'Hallo, Fred. I just happened to be passing and I thought I'd drop in and see how you were' would hardly ring true for someone to whom the doctor was a complete stranger.

'We'll see, Elsie,' I said. She led me through the living room. I could see an old jacket hanging over a chair. Above the mantel a sepia picture of Fred's battery taken in 1916.

'He's upstairs,' said Elsie.

He was in the bedroom, but not in bed. Sitting on his haunches, he was curled up in a ball, his face turned to the wall, knees bent right up to his chest with arms clasped around them.

'Mr Turner?' He turned towards me. His eyes streaming with tears. 'Mr Turner! What's the matter?'

'It's the doctor,' explained Elsie beside me.

He sobbed, 'It's no use, I'm done. You'd be better off without me.'

'He says he's going to kill himself, Doctor. I didn't want to call you but I can't manage him any longer.'

The old man stared at the wall and did not speak any more. It was the most acute state of depression I think I had ever seen.

'He's been like this ever since he had the 'flu a week ago. He seemed to be over it and then suddenly he went – like he is now.'

I examined Fred. No sign of pneumonia. Nothing to cause a toxic confusional state. But, in all fairness, he was not confused. I had heard of this, but never witnessed it: acute post-influenzal depression.

I explained to Elsie that her father would have to take some antidepressant pills and that for a few days he should not, in any circumstances, be left alone. Giving her a prescription for some imipramine and high-dose vitamins, I asked her to ring me the next day. A few years earlier there would have been little alternative but to admit Fred to a mental hospital.

Thinking I'd go back home for a little while, I was turning the car around when I remembered that I had not told the bookdealer about the pile of volumes on the living-room table. The ones, not part of the transaction, that Harry had wanted to keep.

226

To my surprise I found him getting into his car. I'd been away for less than half an hour.

'Oh, Doctor.' He looked embarrassed. 'Oh . . . I left a note for you. In the letterbox.'

'I see. When will you be coming back?'

He didn't quite know what to say. 'I don't actually think there'll be any need.'

When the phone rang at the end of my evening surgery I was pretty sure who it would be.

'Neville? Harry. Has he been?'

'Yes, Harry. Yes.'

'What did he think?'

'He's prepared to make you an offer.'

'Already? Well . . . good.'

'Thirty shillings.'

'Thirty what?'

'Thirty shillings. One pound ten. But he says you'll have to arrange to get the books to the shop.'

'Oh . . . Oh . . . I see.' Disappointment did not have a place in Harry's view of things. 'Thirty shillings, you say.' I heard a rustle of paper. 'I could use it to buy two Hovis McDougal shares.'

November passed into December and was preceded by a series of sharp frosts. Strangely though, as Harry had predicted, the workload dropped from the impossible to the just manageable. People *did* seem more concerned about the forthcoming festive season than their own ailments.

A week after he started the imipramine, Fred Turner appeared downstairs, dressed.

'I've got to get my roses pruned.'

He was better. Shaky. A little morose. I had no doubt that he had been in mortal danger and that, given a reasonable opportunity, he would have killed himself. He would, however, go on to make a complete recovery.

Mr Lucton, for whom I had requested a domiciliary consultation with such trepidation, was recovering well. A mixed pathology was revealed at operation. The cancer of the rectum was localized as had been anticipated, the peritonitis being caused by another condition entirely – diverticulitis. The bowel, over many years, had become inflamed, thinned, covered by small pouches, the diverticuli, one of which had ruptured allowing the contents of the colon to pour into the peritoneal cavity.

Ian Sandown had done several domiciliaries for me since. He treated everyone with great courtesy and kindness, his impeccable bedside manner matched by his surgical skill. On such visits, he, and Peter Fairling, the cardiologist, a most astute physician, helped fill the considerable gaps in my basic knowledge.

One of my worst fears was dispelled when Vic Wheeler and his wife came to see me.

'It was a lovely place,' he said, 'that hospital in London. But the things they did. Hundreds of doctors came to see me and they took me into this enormous lecture room, rows and rows of seats going right up to the ceiling. They even put a tiny microphone in my ear so that everybody could hear the noise. But they were a bit disappointed in the end, I think.'

'Why was that then?'

'It's getting better,' said Amy. 'It's not nearly as loud as it was.'

It turned out that all Vic's tests had been negative including the carotid angiogram. There was no sign of any intercranial lesion, aneurysm, tumour or otherwise. The neurologists and neurosurgeons had come to the conclusion that a combination of slight hardening of the arteries and a trick of haemodynamics had produced an organ-pipe effect in one of the otherwise normal blood vessels.

'It's still there, a bit,' said Vic, 'but it's getting less every day.'

'Doesn't bother me none,' said Amy. 'I sleep like a baby, now.'

'She wears earplugs,' explained her husband.

If I'd have thought of that in the first place and known there was nothing seriously amiss, it would have saved the Health Service a great deal of money.

Beth was discovered. She didn't know what to say when I confronted her. I had found out the truth when, walking down Amblesham High Street, I happened to glance in Marlen's window. A pretty little shop. It had its usual display of pottery and old china.

There he was. Right in the middle of the window. There could be no other. The cross-eyed man.

'I didn't know what to do, Beth. He didn't look at all broken to me.'

Beth apologized. He hadn't *actually* been broken, she explained. She had, as it were, to tell the absolute truth, put him in the dustbin. Some enterprising, entrepreneurial dustman must have recovered the treasure and sold it to the shop.

I'd had to buy him, of course. There was no other way. Miss Clementine Smith was a frequent customer and would be bound to see him, even if she hadn't already. 'I only put him in the window half an hour ago, Doctor, so you're lucky to get something of a bargain,' said Mr Marlen.

I left the shop, Ben Turpin tucked under my arm, seven pounds poorer. Seven pounds! A whole week's house-keeping money. But, as Mr Marlen had said when he sold me the figure, it was a piece of genuine Staffordshire.

Chapter Twelve

'It's sore all over, Doctor. Goes right into my back!'

I would have expected to find a tender spot under the ribs on the right side. But it was clear, from the position of the pain, what was wrong with Henri Martin. Cholecystitis. An inflammation of the gall bladder. Not surprising in the circumstances.

'Does it hurt there?' I pressed again.

'It hurts everywhere.'

With great difficulty he fastened up his trousers. An occupational hazard for a cook I supposed, particularly one who was so keen on sampling his own creations. And they were worth sampling. He was, after all, as his French father had been before him, a chef in Seahaven's most prestigious hotel. Henri, apart from his name, was as Sussex as a trug.

'We'll get a cholecystogram done, Henri – an X-ray of your gall bladder. I expect you've got some stones.'

I handed him the appropriate form.

'And if it does show them? Stones?' The chair creaked as he sat down.

'You'll have to have your gall bladder out.' His face fell. 'But don't worry, it's not such a big operation. Not much more than an appendix . . . in the meantime,' I started to write out a prescription, 'I'll give you some antibiotics. A new kind. Ampicillin. You can take penicillin? . . . Good. And some Panadol for the pain, and indigestion mixture. There we are.'

He stood up to go.

'Now, you'll have to be careful what you eat for the

time being. No fat. No cream. No butter, nothing like that.'

'But, Doctor,' his face filled with dismay, 'it's Christmas next week!'

'I'm very sorry, Henri, but that's the way it is. You've got to give your biliary system a rest, otherwise you'll be in real trouble.'

He was, definitely, not a satisfied customer.

'Next please,' I shouted. Henri stuck his head back round the door again.

'I was the last one, Doctor, you can lock up now.'

There were two cards left on my desk. I had to fill in the records of the two domiciliary consultations done for me the previous morning.

David Hasling, the orthopaedic surgeon, *did* have to come and see George Formby in the end. George had celebrated his cure by laying a new garden path. Unfortunately, flagstones had overcome cosmic power and following his collapse with the most acute of prolapsed intervertebral discs, David had to take him into hospital and put him on traction. It seemed most likely that he would eventually come to surgery.

The other home consultation had been yet another by Ian Sandown: a very old lady in her nineties with vomiting and a lump in her groin. Were the two connected? Had she got a strangulated hernia and, if so, could she survive surgery? Ian thought she had, and would. And she did. He operated on her later that afternoon and today the hospital had said that she was in the best of health. Before going back to the hospital Ian came back round to Sangster Road for a cup of coffee, delighting us with his gentle, dry humour.

'What on earth are those things in the corner?' he asked.

'Speakers – part of my hi fi stereo.'

'Good heavens!' he said in amazement. 'You'd do just

as well with a record player. That's all I've got. Nothing as huge as that.'

I pointed out of our living room window at the splendid vehicle that half-filled our drive.

'And you could get around in something a deal smaller than *that*!'

He sniffed thoughtfully. 'That's not the point, Neville. Not the point at all. When I turn up outside somebody's house in my new car,' he paused, 'they think, "By God, he must be pretty good to afford one of those!" ' Smiling, he added, 'They're halfway cured already.'

There was a knock on the surgery door. Blast! I shouldn't have sat about musing. I had a lot to do. Harry was due back in the afternoon and I wanted to get everything straight. Let whoever it was come back again in the evening. I started to go out of the French windows when the knocking started again. I strode to the door and pulled it open.

'I'm very sorry, surgery's finished. I . . .'

'Hallo, Neville.'

For the moment I was quite disorientated. Then I got it. Exchange the neat brown trilby for a battered busman's cap, the check overcoat for a driver's navy blue jacket. The face was the same. Like a friendly prune.

'Walter! How are you? . . . HOW ARE YOU?' Walter smiled and grasped my hand. 'COME ROUND TO THE HOUSE. MEET BETH AND SARAH. PLEASE DO.'

He came through the surgery into the garden and stopped for a moment. There was the sweet sound of birdsong from the cherry tree.

'That's a robin, isn't it? . . . I've had the operation,' he added with a smile.

This was not the first time I had witnessed the result of a successful stapedectomy, but it was the most dramatic. The ossicles, the tiny bones in the middle ear, had been approached by the surgeon through an operating micro-scope. With the finest of instruments a tiny graft of vein had been put in place and a plastic strut inserted, enabling, once more, sound waves to be transmitted from the eardrum to the nerve of the inner ear. Walter could hear perfectly – at least, out of one ear.

He was enchanted by Beth and did not stop talking. He reached in the carrier bag he had brought with him and gave her a box of chocolates. Then he produced a toy for Sarah. A plastic double-decker bus. It had been carefully painted in the livery of the Westhaven Bus Company. He talked about his operation.

'I couldn't stand the noise at first,' he said. 'I had to put cotton wool in my ear – they've only done one so far. But, by God, the noise that bus makes. I suppose it was because I was deaf and couldn't hear the gearbox that they gave me the noisiest bugger – excuse me, Beth – in the whole depot.'

I didn't have the heart to tell him that all the buses he drove were quickly reduced to that level of agonized decrepitude.

'They say, in the hospital, that it might seize up again. But they've got all kinds of new operations coming along.'

He was right. The developments in middle-ear surgery would transform the lives of many people. Lonely people. Reluctantly, he stood to go. On the front doorstep he reached into the bag again.

'Just a little something for you, son. I know that I said they were tin cans but I suppose that they must have saved my life a time or two.' He handed me a flat parcel. 'God bless and a happy Christmas.'

He leant over, kissed Beth's cheek and was gone.

I opened the package. A framed print of a Crusader tank complete with all the markings of the Seventh Armoured Division, the Desert Rats. On the back, written in a large simple hand 'To my friend, Neville, with my ever greatfull thanks. Walter (Jessop)'. I quickly rubbed a hand across my eyes.

Harry returned home that afternoon. Mary, who preceded him by three days, had aired the house and got everything clean and tidy. In the event, Harry had decided not to dispose of the library.

'Obviously not the time to sell,' he had confided.

He was still on crutches with his right leg in a non-weight-bearing plaster. When the front door opened he was nearly flung to the ground as Albert leapt upon him.

'Albert! Albert!' The old dog slobbered all over his face. 'Albert! You great fat thing!' Harry was right. He was enormous. The Goddens had utterly spoiled him.

Beth, Sarah and I sat with Harry in the lounge as he luxuriated in front of the open fire. He took a pipe from the rack on the mantel and sucked it contentedly.

'Found out something in hospital. You don't need any tobacco at all. It's just as good without – and a damned sight less trouble. Like a dummy I suppose.'

Albert snored at his feet.

'Well, young man. I hope you've not left me too much work to do.'

He pulled himself to his feet. 'That six-month trial period, by the way. I think we've had long enough to decide. You will be my partner, won't you? ... Good. Of course you will. I'd better sort out the mess then. I expect the Formbys will want to see a proper doctor.' Harry clonked off on his crutches to start the evening surgery.

We decorated the house, our first real home together, with enthusiasm and excess. Beth had to cut two feet off the top of the Christmas tree I had bought before it could be wedged under the ceiling in the living room. Paper chains criss-crossed in a profusion of colour and tinsel cascaded from every shelf. The house was gaudy but glittering. Red, green, silver and gold. The crib on the fireplace I had made from pieces of log and the Hong Kong figures brought gifts to the Hong Kong Christ child.

Sarah stood transfixed with wonder as the tree lights were switched on, her eyes sparkling with the reflected colours. Every afternoon she had to be taken into the town to see the 'funny Father Christmas man'.

The window of the sweet shop near the picture house was a work of art. Every Christmassy thing was there; crackers, novelties, chocolate liqueurs from Switzerland in little wooden chests, orange and lemon slices, assortment boxes, tins of toffee, caramels, fruit drops, all against a background of coloured foils, cotton-wool snow, reindeer and snowmen. In the middle stood a figure that drew Sarah and the other children again and again. About eighteen inches high with fat rosy cheeks, a Father Christmas nodded his head from side to side giving little saucy winks. It was inevitable that Sarah should want to go into the shop, as colourful and as festive as the window.

'Hallo, Sarah,' said the nice lady in the sweet shop. 'I think I've found somebody who'd like to go home with you. Would you like that?'

'Yes please,' said Sarah. She knew a soft touch when she saw one. The nice lady reached under the counter.

'Here we are.'

'It's a pussy,' squealed Sarah and clutched the soft cuddly toy to her chest.

'Say "thank you", Sarah.'

'Thank you.' Sarah turned her face upwards and pursed her lips in anticipation. The nice lady gave her a kiss.

She said that her son was on duty over Christmas and hoped to be down sometime in the New Year. Success had its own particular pain. It was easy to tell that she was happy for him, but if he hadn't gone to medical school he could still have been living in Amblesham or a neighbouring town. Accessible at every Christmas.

'You must miss him,' I said.

'I do – and his wife – she's a lovely girl. But when you come to think about it . . .' She was right of course.

I went outside. They had started to play carols around the Christmas tree in the Market Square.

The ward sister phoned me up from the hospital about Quentin Goodfellow.

'We can't keep him in any longer. There just aren't enough beds. We'd like him to stay but two of our wards are being closed down.' Quentin was approaching the end of what sounded like a very full life. A tall, elderly gentleman, voice and manners the products of Eton and a period spent in the Brigade of Guards, seemed out of place in the sparsely furnished council bed-sitting room that was now his home.

He already had his colostomy when he moved into our area from one of the outlying villages. The discharge note from the hospital said that he had had a carcinoma of the rectum. At operation he was found to have secondary deposits in his liver. His time was limited. It was not his only disability. He was also crippled with arthritis.

'From my film days, Doctor. Always used to do my own stunts.'

A doctor becomes very used to confabulation, the stories of the old or the drunk which have been told so many times that to the teller they become the truth.

'In Hollywood. In the silent days, of course, before the talking pictures.'

'You were an actor?'

'Oh yes. Not a star. But, I suppose, what you'd call a supporting actor. The obligatory Englishman. But then,' he laughed, 'I could have been any nationality. Nobody could hear my voice!'

236

I decided that he'd been an extra.

'I have some old pictures if you'd be at all interested.'

'Of course.' Crowd scenes? He went to the small chest of drawers next to the sink.

'This was me then.'

A magnificent, archetypal Englishman. Dressed in tails. Slim, elegant, with a fine moustache.

'And this is me with Chaplin.' Charlie Chaplin's arm was around his shoulders. 'And with Douglas Fairbanks, senior, of course.' It was signed 'To Q. Grateful thanks. Douglas.' Another photograph, 'And with John Gilbert. Sad, of course, he never survived the talkies. And this one was taken at a little party at the Barrymores'. That's Lionel, Chaplin, Mary Pickford – they had founded United Artists of course with D. W. Griffiths and Douglas Fairbanks – and there, you can't see him properly, is Buster Keaton.'

Quentin was in the middle of the group. It was all true.

'I suppose I got tired of it in the end,' he said. 'That, and I also had a nasty attack of rheumatoid arthritis. That's how I got these.' He held up his twisted fingers. 'Lost most of my money in the Crash.' He gave me an ironic grin. 'Thought I'd be careful, put it all in shares.'

It was at the beginning of December that he had developed pneumonia and had been admitted to the medical ward at Westhaven General. Unfortunately, he had recovered too quickly. He would have enjoyed Christmas in hospital and it would have enjoyed him. I phoned up Griff Thomas and Ron Godden. I knew both were in the local Rotary Club. The Christmas tree in the Market Square was their main fund-raising event, money for the needy at Christmas.

Each day, at the surgery, little gifts arrived for Beth and me – and Sarah. And dozens of Christmas cards. 'Thank you for all your help. Mr and Mrs Bignell.' Bignell? I couldn't remember them at all. Vic Wheeler dropped in with a bottle of his homemade blackcurrant gin.

'Keep the cold out, that will, Doctor.' I took a sip. Ribena and aviation spirit.

From the Tarrington-Bagfords, a bottle of Albanian Chablis. 'Soames says that the local wine correspondent raved about it. So he bought two bottles,' Millie confided. 'He threw away half of his so it must be pretty awful, so I got you this as well.' She produced an old bottle thick with dust and cobwebs. 'A bottle of his best port. He won't miss it, and it will go quite beautifully with a slice of Stilton.'

Beth always bought me Stilton at Christmas, believing it to have strong aphrodisiac qualities. We bought Millie some new secateurs. Soames, a large cigar.

Mr Singh, an Indian gentleman who worked for a tea importer in Brighton, arrived at the surgery with a strangely shaped brown paper parcel. He had come back earlier than planned from a holiday in India because his children could not stand the heat.

'You are not, most certainly, to open this parcel until Christmas Day, Doctor.' I felt the package for clues. 'No. No. No. No. You mustn't cheat. But I will tell you one thing. When you press down the switch the Taj Mahal lights up!'

I thought I'd better not mention Goa to him. The Indian army had invaded the old Portuguese colony a few days before. A peace-loving man, I didn't think he'd appreciate it in this season of good will.

The world was still a dangerous place in 1961. The war had been over for sixteen years but Eichmann's trial had brought back terrible memories. Berlin was split by a wall. And Cuba. First the Bay of Pigs, and now there were rumblings of more direct confrontation. Surely America wouldn't be daft enough to invade Castro's infant socialist state? The Russians would be bound to intervene and then there wouldn't be a hole deep enough to hide in.

Reginald got a friend from the chapel to drive him to the

surgery. His knee was much better and he was happy to tell me he had fully recovered from his dreadful experience at Robson's stores. It had upset him so much, he said, that it had been necessary for him to go into hospital. But he had been allowed home for the Christmas period. To stay with the minister, 'a Christian man'. One rather hoped that he was. Could I accept a small gift?

As soon as he had gone I opened the parcel. A rather expensive aftershave, reputed, if one was to believe all the adverts, to make one totally irresistible to all women. There was a label on the back of the bottle. 'For demonstration purposes only. Not for sale.'

Two days before Christmas all hell broke loose. Panic time. We were faced with all the children who had been ill but weren't recovering quickly enough, those who had got something and all those who *might* be sickening for something. All to be treated with magical speed so that they would not be ill on Christmas Day. It was the busiest day of the year. Harry suggested that he do all the surgeries while I dealt with the day's calls.

Visiting elderly relatives were pitching over at all points of the compass. Aged aunts and uncles invited to share the celebrations, and shaken entirely out of their rather gentle lifestyles, were having coronaries or going into heart failure. Or both. A Christmas spent with the Queen's speech, a tin of chicken soup and a packet of shortbread would have been a good deal safer.

Diabetics became unstable. 'Go on. Just a little bit won't do you any harm.' Reformed alcoholics had just that one, then another, and another. Non-smokers became smokers again. Children were exhausted and irritable after sleepless nights. 'If you don't behave yourself, I'll tell Father Christmas not to come.' By the end of the afternoon, I had seen more than thirty people in their own, or somebody else's, home. Beth was waiting with another call.

'He says it's his wife. Strained her back lifting the new gas stove into the kitchen. He was afraid to do it himself.'

Mr Littlebone opened his front door with some difficulty. The hall was packed with boxes, bags, toys, clothes. Sacks of clothes! The living room was the same. I picked my way across the floor to where Mrs Littlebone lay on the sofa.

There was no doubt about her. She did have a bad back.

'That lazy sod,' she indicated her husband, 'won't do a bleeding thing. He might fool the Welfare but he don't fool me.'

'She's only joking, Doctor,' said Mr Littlebone, pushing a pile of unwrapped games off a high-backed chair and sitting down with great care.

'Can we have a home help, Doctor James?' he asked. 'What with the two of us being crippled. It's either that or . . .' a choking sob broke into his voice, 'the little ones will have to go into care.'

'I'm sure you'll manage for a day or two, Mr Littlebone.' The 'little ones' included two daughters, aged fourteen and fifteen, neither of whom worked nor went to school. I looked around me.

'My goodness! This looks like Santa's grotto!'

'We've been very lucky,' said Mrs Littlebone. 'We've had toys and clothes and things from the NSPCC and the Red Cross.'

'And the WVS,' said Mr Littlebone, 'and the church.'

'Three churches,' said Mrs Littlebone. 'The Congregational, the Protestant and the Catholic. I'm a Catholic,' she added.

'And the union were very good.' The secular was not to be outshone.

'The Salvation Army. And the Welfare, of course. We had six dozen eggs!'

Thank God! I thought. No more letters for a week or two. Out of the window I could see the dustbins at the back. Brimming over with discarded gifts.

I gave Mrs Littlebone a prescription for some painkillers. The head of the household accompanied me to the door. I was struck by the sudden change in him. He had already insisted that I accept a box of figs from a pile of a dozen or more.

'None of us eat them. Horrible.' But there was a kind of . . . benevolence in his manner. He took my hand and shook it.

'Doctor,' he said, his voice throbbing with sincerity, 'I have no intention, at present, of suing *you*.' I felt that I belonged to a small privileged minority.

Christmas Eve came wet and windy. The phone rang so infrequently I checked with the exchange that it was working properly. There was nothing wrong with it. Nobody had time to be ill. The first call was not a visit.

'Neville. Harry. How are you?'

He had phoned to remind us that we were invited to tea on Christmas Day – we would be having our own Christmas tea that coming afternoon – and to thank us for our present.

'I can never wait until the twenty-fifth. Had to have a look. Thank you very much. Quaint little chap, isn't he? Reminds me of my old commanding officer. Genuine Staffordshire, obviously. You shouldn't have gone to such expense.'

At 2 p.m. there was a knock on the door. Commander Dymock. He had recovered completely from his renal colic. Beth appeared beside me.

'A happy Christmas to you both.' He handed me an unwrapped bottle of Harveys Bristol Cream and doffed his hat to Beth. 'Mrs James – if I may be permitted to say so – you look . . . charming.' He smiled and stepped back. 'I have to go. Lots more calls to do. Once again, Merry Christmas.'

A message from the vicar. His eight-year-old daughter, Rebecca, was most unwell he said. She felt sick and seemed to be very feverish. She was even having difficulty standing up.

She did look very woebegone. The stocking already hung at the foot of her bed but it was unlikely that its owner had any thought about the night's impending visitor. She was more involved with the plastic bucket that stood beside her on the floor. I took her temperature. Normal.

I thought I'd better look at her throat.

'Say "Aaahhh", Rebecca.' As soon as her breath hit me the diagnosis became instantly apparent. She confirmed it immediately by vomiting up a quantity of brown liquid into the bucket. She was drunk. A somewhat depleted bottle of sweet sherry purloined from Mummy and Daddy's collection was found under her bed.

I had to stop a while to make sure she recovered properly. Alcoholic poisoning in children can be reached with quite small doses. She would probably remain teetotal for, at least, the next fifteen years.

I did one other visit that afternoon. I hadn't been asked. It was purely an act of self-indulgence.

The door was unlocked and I let myself in. Quentin Goodfellow sat back in his one comfortable chair watching the television that the Rotary Club had brought him earlier in the day. It wasn't new, the picture was snowy and slightly out of focus, but it was his.

Beside him on a small stool was a cardboard box full of tins and packets of food, also from the Rotary. Across his lap rested an open box of Eat Me dates. He was popping one, daintily, into his mouth.

'Quentin?'

He turned. A smile that defied the years.

'Doctor!' He opened his hands and with a theatrical sweep of the arm that encompassed the television and the little box of food, 'Were you responsible for this . . . largesse?'

'No. No. It was the Rotary club. They like to give parcels and things to people at this time of year. People who . . . live alone, or haven't been well.'

I had managed not to say 'down on their luck'. He knew it.

'I expect they had you on a list given to them by the hospital.'

He turned to the television again. 'You'll excuse me, but this is very exciting. I knew Stanley and Oliver before they started working together for Hal Roach. Oliver was very sensitive, amiable, very nimble for a large man. But Stanley, he was the brains, he had the ideas.'

I sat with him for a few minutes. I could have watched Laurel and Hardy all day. Quentin rummaged in his box and produced a packet of custard cream biscuits.

'Have one of these, Doctor. They're delicious.'

The film ended. The old man turned towards me. An old man with cancer, with severe arthritis of the hands which made every change of the colostomy bag a painful and prolonged operation, with crippled legs, a man who had lived at the centre of Hollywood society in its most splendid, exciting, riotous days.

'Do you know, Doctor,' he said. 'This is the nicest Christmas that I think I can ever remember.'

BANG went the crackers. The table was loaded with sausage rolls, mince pies, cold ham and pickles and a large Christmas cake with Santa Claus and Rudolph on the top. Beth unrolled her motto.

'Which horses have got their eyes closest together?'

'The smallest horses.'

'Oh, Neville!' She shrugged away. 'You looked!'

'No, I didn't. I've got the same one.'

We did some bartering. 'My magnifying glass for your Scorpio ring. After all I *am* a Scorpio.' I think she would have given it to me anyway.

I had eaten too much. No training for the culinary marathon of the next few days. I had bought the turkey. Beth had had to amputate both legs before it would fit in the oven. Mr Pearce at the butcher's had assured me that it was a bargain. Swore on his honour as a Red Cross officer.

The phone rang. Henri the cook had abdominal pain. Damn and blast! I should have guessed he wouldn't have taken my advice. I was glowering when I reached the door of his house. His wife let me in. Normally a rather serious lady, she gave me the broadest of grins. Drinking, I supposed.

'Where's the patient, then?'

Feeling somewhat nonplussed by his wife's jocularity, I was ushered into Henri's bedroom. He was lying on the bed, his face screwed up with pain. As soon as he saw me he sat up with a start and burst out laughing. My glare soon scared his mirth away.

I thought that, before I tore into him for disturbing my few hard-earned hours of festive relaxation, I would examine him to confirm the biliary colic, brought on no doubt by dietary indiscretion. I lifted his pyjama jacket.

'How long have you had those!' I asked in amazement.

'They came out two or three days after I saw you. I didn't want to bother you again. You're so busy. But I just couldn't stand the pain any more.'

The pain, as usual, had preceded the rash. The pain that I was sure had come from his gall bladder. Now it was all there to see. A great swathe of inflamed skin extending from the middle of his back, around the lower right ribs and on to the upper part of his abdomen – over the gall bladder area, indeed. Skin covered in angry red and blue blotches and the unmistakable blisters of herpes xoster. Shingles!

I gave him some stronger analgesics – there was no other treatment for the distressing complaint – and went into the living room to explain the situation to his wife. I was quite serious, but she continued to grin all over her face. I had made a diagnostic error. It wasn't that funny.

By the time I got home I had started to mellow. The commander's sherry was improving my mood. It was also stimulating my kidneys.

As soon as I got in through the front door I went straight to the loo. Relieved, I looked up to see my face in the mirror. I knew it so well. A face, though still young, suggesting judgement and clarity of thought. Dependability. The wise eyes, the striking eyebrows, the elegant nose, the mouth shaped into a knowing, sardonic grin.

But this time, the whole was surmounted by a large red and blue Noddy hat which had been pulled out of a cracker half an hour before.

EPILOGUE

Christmas Eve 1984

'What's the commonest cause of abdominal pain, high fever and vomiting in a small child, Jimmy?' I asked.

The trainee looked down at the little girl on the examination couch. Her mother watched, anxiously.

'Could be a virus infection.' He thought for a moment. 'Pyelitis. Appendicitis. Could be a hundred and one things. But the commonest? I've not thought of it that way. Not seen the epidemiological figures.'

Jimmy Race was very good. Bright, sensible, kind. For some years now we had been a training practice and our Health Centre had been enlivened by the presence of the trainees, young doctors who came to do a year with us before entering general practice as principals in their own right. They kept us on our mettle.

'Now, if we had a practice computer,' Jimmy was riding his hobby horse, 'I could tell you with the flick of a switch.'

I leant down towards the little girl. 'Open your mouth wide and say "aaah", darling.'

She obliged. I showed Jimmy. The tonsils were large, very red and covered in yellow spots.

'Acute tonsillitis. It is nearly every time.'

Jimmy frowned. 'She didn't say anything about a sore throat.'

'They very often don't.' I turned to the mother. 'She'll have to have them out, Lorraine.'

'Oh, Doctor!'

'Five you say? You were exactly the same when you were her age. I remember. Always getting tonsillitis. You were never out of the surgery.'

Lorraine had three children. Toyah was the eldest. She put her face down by the little girl.

'You've got to go into hospital and have your tonsils out, Toyah.' The child began to whimper. 'Not now, this afternoon! Not until after Christmas.'

Not for the next year or two, I thought, with our local ENT waiting list in its current situation.

'We are on BUPA,' she added, as if reading my thoughts. 'Ron's firm put all the workers on it, and their families.'

On the private scheme the little girl would have her tonsillectomy before the end of January. We were rapidly becoming a two-nation state as far as medical care was concerned.

'In that case, I'll give you a letter for Mr Nashton at his consulting rooms.' Lorraine turned to the little girl again.

'There you are, Toyah, you'll have your own little bedroom. A colour television even.'

'The letter will be ready,' I thought for a moment, Christmas Day tomorrow, Boxing Day . . . 'in four days' time.'

'Well. Thank you, Doctor. I'm sorry to have to disturb you today.' She got up to leave. 'Are your family going to be together for Christmas?'

'Yes – in instalments.' Sarah and her husband would be coming for lunch on Boxing Day, Andrew and his girlfriend on Christmas Day.

'A happy Christmas, Doctor.'

'And to you, Lorraine. And the family.'

Jimmy started to leave. 'You'll excuse me, Neville. Promised Jenny I'd get home early to help with the packing.'

I clicked my tongue. 'Kitzbuhl for Christmas, eh?' Not

quite, I knew, but times *had* changed.

He smiled and stopped at the door for a moment as our administrator came in. Caroline Harris. Personable and efficient.

'How are you, Caroline?'

She winced. 'Slightly fragile after last night's shindig!'

The Health Centre party. Our annual knees-up. The six doctors of our partnership, the trainee, the dozen or more receptionists and secretaries, the five health visitors, the seven district nurses. All with respective spouses.

'Just to let you know that Doctor Grastick and Doctor Kearson have done all the visits between them. Doctor Harris and Doctor Brown have finished the surgeries. You've only got one more patient.'

'OK.' I smiled. 'I'll be through in a minute.' Everybody was waiting to get cleared up and go home.

It was a particularly busy time of the year for all the staff, who, apart from their ordinary duties, were involved in helping the charities target their help to the needy. Gone were the days, hopefully, when the few Littlebones of the world received more than they could use whilst the many had nothing at all.

I tidied up my desk and picked up the Christmas cards that had come to me at the surgery. I liked to take them home to show Beth. A few years previously I had received one from a religious order in the USA, 'Christmas Blessings. Harold'. This year, as usual, there was a card for a charity involved in research into blood diseases. From the Farmers. The print on the card was a Christine Woods watercolour. In later years, following her death, the lives of many patients with aplastic anaemia were to be saved by bone marrow transplant.

The last patient poked his head around the door. He was wearing a large multi-coloured Rastafarian hat. Without being asked he slouched into the room and flopped into the chair opposite me. He flipped an envelope across the desk.

'That fo' you.'

I took out the card. 'GODDEN AND JENKINS. CHARTERED ACCOUNTANTS. Mr Ronald Godden and Mr Winston Jenkins have pleasure in announcing that from 1 January 1985 Mr Michael Richards BA will be joining their practice.'

'Congratulations, Michael.' He beamed and we shook hands across the desk.

'Thank you, Uncle Neville.'

He moved awkwardly in the chair and winced slightly. His back had never completely recovered from the spinal tuberculosis he had developed when he was nine. That had been a time of great pain, when it seemed that the sickle cell would take him.

'And Uncle Winston says that he might be a bit late getting to your party. He's got to go down to a small do at the police station first. For the magistrates . . . a Perrier party.' He smiled.

'Still, I must be off.' He eased himself out of the chair. 'Love to Auntie Beth. Tell Sarah and Andrew they're invited to the party at my flat. For the less elderly!'

Before going home I drove over to Alfriston to get the sausages to go with our Christmas dinner. Same sausages as ever, same butcher. A permanent fixture. Traditional. Boater tilted at a saucy angle over the round, rosy face.

But the rest of the village, like so much else in the Sussex Downs, had changed. Gone were the mud tracks and pastures. They were now replaced by tarmac roads and the immaculate houses of the middle class. Neatly coiffured hedges where there had been blackberry brambles, the accents of the farmyard replaced by those of the City office. Shops that had once sold bacon or cough medicines had now become gift boutiques. But when the tourist invasion abated and the village had time to get its breath, it was still a place of extraordinary beauty.

On the way back, I passed the site of old Charlie's bungalow. He had had his way and had seen out his days there, dying less than a month after old Jake. The wooden building had been knocked down and the new houses built, many years since.

Just outside Amblesham a police car overtook me then waved me down. A man in the uniform of a chief superintendent got out, came up to my side of the car and tapped on the window. I rolled it down.

'Have you been drinking, sir?'

'No.'

'Then perhaps,' said Griff, 'you'll pop over and have a little one with me and Megan when you finish work.'

He was due to retire soon as Chief of Westhaven Police, a job he had done for some years with warmth and distinction.

'Might not have time, Griff. See you at our party, anyway.'

'OK.' He drove off.

Beth and I had a quiet lunch. There would be one missing face this year – Commander Dymock. Ever since that first year in Amblesham he had arrived at 2 p.m. on every Christmas Eve. Always with a bottle of Harveys Bristol Cream. Always delighting Beth by doffing his hat, wishing her the compliments of the season and telling her that she looked younger than ever.

This year, it was not to be. He had been in bed for three weeks and his carcinoma of the pancreas had reached a terminal stage.

I was helping to get the living room ready for our evening party when, at 4 p.m., a car pulled up outside. Mrs Dymock got out of the driver's seat and opened the passenger door. The gaunt figure of the commander appeared, hacking jacket and cavalry twills hanging loose on his emaciated frame. Leaning heavily on a stick, he made his way painfully slowly towards our house, clutching a bottle.

I opened the front door and waited, Beth beside me.

'A little something for Christmas, Doctor. I'm sorry I'm a little later than usual.'

'Come in for a moment, Commander.'

'Afraid not, old chap. Too many things to do. More calls you know.' He smiled at Beth and doffed his hat.

'Ah, my dear. A very happy Christmas to you. I must say, you look younger than ever.'

We watched him totter back to the car, to be taken home. To his deathbed. I felt Beth clasp my hand.

'You are lucky,' she said, 'to see how special people can be.'

She didn't have to tell me. The nice lady in the sweet shop had said the same thing many years before.

Rhanna
Christine Marion Fraser

A rich, romantic, Scottish saga set
on the Hebridean island of Rhanna

Rhanna

The poignant story of life on the rugged and tranquil island of
Rhanna, and of the close-knit community for whom it is home.

Rhanna at War

Rhanna's lonely beauty is no protection against the horrors of
war. But Shona Mackenzie, home on leave, discovers that the
fiercest battles are those between lovers.

Children of Rhanna

The four island children, inseparable since childhood, find that
growing up also means growing apart.

Return to Rhanna

Shona and Niall Mackenzie come home to find Rhanna unspoilt
by the onslaught of tourism. But then tragedy strikes at the heart
of their marriage.

Song of Rhanna

Ruth is happily married to Lorn. But the return to Rhanna of her
now famous friend Rachel threatens Ruth's happiness.

Storm Over Rhanna

The 'islanders' popular minister, Mark James, mourns the tragic
loss of his family, and turns to Doctor Megan Jenkins for comfort.
But Megan has a post from which she cannot escape.

'Full-blooded romance, a strong, authentic setting'
Scotsman

FONTANA PAPERBACKS

Helen Forrester

Twopence to Cross the Mersey
Liverpool Miss
By the Waters of Liverpool

– the three volumes of her autobiography –

Helen Forrester tells the sad but never sentimental story of her childhood years, during which her family fell from genteel poverty to total destitution. In the depth of the Depression, mistakenly believing that work would be easier to find, they moved from the South of England to the slums of Liverpool. The family slowly win their fight for survival, but Helen's personal battle was to persuade her parents to allow her to earn her own living, and to lead her own life after the years of neglect and inadequate schooling while she cared for her six younger brothers and sisters. Illness, caused by severe malnutrition, dirt, and above all the selfish demands of her parents, make this a story of courage and perseverance. She writes without self-pity but rather with a rich sense of humour which makes her account of these grim days before the Welfare State funny as well as painful.

'Records of hardship during the Thirties are not rare; but this has features that make it stand apart' *Observer*

FONTANA PAPERBACKS

Teresa Crane

A Fragile Peace

It was a lovely summer's day – perfect for a garden party. Everything seemed at peace for the Jordan family. But by the time the party was over, the Jordans' tranquil, ordered existence had been shattered.

The year was 1936.

Molly

Molly is a fabulous saga set in London's East End at the turn of the century. It is about the struggles of Molly O'Dowd, a young Irish girl, who comes to London penniless and in search of a job, and who ends up running several companies. It is about the men in her life, about the family she raises. It is a marvellous picture of working-class life at that time, teeming with wonderful characters, and alive with the changes imposed by both industry and impending war.

The Rose Stone

When Josef Rosenburg, fleeing the Jewish pogroms of Imperial Russia, reached Amsterdam, he owned nothing but the clothes he stood up in. By the time he reached London, he had the price of prosperity in his pocket – a prosperity that had been bought at an appalling cost.

FONTANA PAPERBACKS

Richard Sharpe

bold, professional and ruthless
is the creation of

Bernard Cornwell

A series of high adventure stories told in the grand tradition of Hornblower and set in the time of the Napoleonic wars, Bernard Cornwell's stories are firmly based on the actual events.

Sharpe's Eagle
Richard Sharpe and the Talavera Campaign, July 1809

Sharpe's Gold
Richard Sharpe and the Destruction of Almeida, 1810

Sharpe's Company
Richard Sharpe and the Siege of Badajoz, 1812

Sharpe's Sword
Richard Sharpe and the Salamanca Campaign,
June and July 1812

Sharpe's Enemy
Richard Sharpe and the Defence of Portugal,
Christmas 1812

Sharpe's Honour
Richard Sharpe and the Battle of Vitoria, 1813

'The best thing to happen to military heroes since Hornblower.' *Daily Express*

FONTANA PAPERBACKS

Fontana Paperbacks: Fiction

Fontana is a leading paperback publisher of fiction. Below are some recent titles.

- ☐ THE GATES OF EXQUISITE VIEW John Trenhaile £3.95
- ☐ LOTUS LAND Monica Highland £3.95
- ☐ THE MOUSE GOD Susan Curran £3.95
- ☐ SHADOWLIGHT Mike Jefferies £3.95
- ☐ THE SILK VENDETTA Victoria Holt £3.50
- ☐ THE HEARTS AND LIVES OF MEN Fay Weldon £3.95
- ☐ EDDIE BLACK Walter Shapiro £2.95
- ☐ THE POOL OF ST. BRANOK Philippa Carr £3.50
- ☐ FORTUNE'S DAUGHTER Connie Monk £3.50
- ☐ AMAZING FAITH Leslie Waller £3.50
- ☐ THE CORNELIUS CHRONICLES BK 1 Michael Moorcock £4.95
- ☐ THE CORNELIUS CHRONICLES BK 2 Michael Moorcock £4.95

You can buy Fontana paperbacks at your local bookshop or newsagent. Or you can order them from Fontana Paperbacks, Cash Sales Department, Box 29, Douglas, Isle of Man. Please send a cheque, postal or money order (not currency) worth the purchase price plus 22p per book for postage (maximum postage required is £3.00 for orders within the UK).

NAME (Block letters) _____

ADDRESS _____

_____

While every effort is made to keep prices low, it is sometimes necessary to increase them at short notice. Fontana Paperbacks reserve the right to show new retail prices on covers which may differ from those previously advertised in the text or elsewhere.